WRECKED

WRECKED

MARIA PADIAN

Algonquin 2017

Published by
Algonquin Young Readers
an imprint of Algonquin Books of Chapel Hill
Post Office Box 2225
Chapel Hill, North Carolina 27515-2225

a division of
Workman Publishing
225 Varick Street
New York, New York 10014

First paperback edition, Algonquin Young Readers, September 2017.
Originally published in hardcover by Algonquin Young Readers in October 2016.
Printed in the United States of America.
Published simultaneously in Canada by Thomas Allen & Son Limited.
Design by Liz Casal.

LIBRARY OF CONGRESS CATALOGING-IN-PUBLICATION DATA
Names: Padian, Maria, author.
Title: Wrecked / by Maria Padian.
Description: First edition. | Chapel Hill, North Carolina : Algonquin Young Readers,
2016. | "Published simultaneously in Canada by Thomas Allen & Son Limited." | Summary:
"Offers a kaleidoscopic view of a sexual assault on a college campus that will leave readers thinking
about how memory and identity, what's at stake, and who sits in judgment shape what we all
decide to believe about the truth"—Provided by publisher.
Identifiers: LCCN 2016020315 | ISBN 9781616206246 (HC)
Subjects: LCSH: College students—Juvenile fiction. | Rape—Investigation—Juvenile fiction. |
Young adult fiction. | CYAC: Rape—Fiction. | Universities and colleges—Fiction.
Classification: LCC PZ7.P1325 Wr 2016 | DDC [Fic]—dc23
LC record available at https://lccn.loc.gov/2016020315

ISBN 978-1-61620-745-8 (PB)

10 9 8 7 6 5 4 3 2 1
First Paperback Edition

FOR MY SON AND MY DAUGHTER.

WRECKED

· · ·

Doors stand open down the long length of hall. Bright bulbs of conversation drift between them, sparked by bursts of laughter. Girls slip from one room to the next carrying armloads of whisper-weight dresses, lovely and soft.

They cluster in Jenny's; her roommate is away. They comb, unasking, through her closet. Toss the contents of their own on her bed. Try this. That color is so good on you. I have shoes for that; what size do you wear?

The air feels electric as they make each other beautiful.

· · ·

1

Haley

Haley wakes to pain. Actually, to clapping. "Happy" is this month's ringtone. It pulls her from a fitful nap. Glowing red knives pierce the space between her ears when she moves her eyeballs.

Sunlight peeks around the edges of the shades in the dark dorm room. The windows are closed, and it's hot. Why does Jenny always shut the windows?

From her iPhone, happiness rings.

She gropes at the top of the desk, locates the solid rectangle, squints at the screen. It's her mother. Again. She answers the call with her thumb.

"Hey."

"So I just got off with the people at the health center, and we're all agreed that this would be easier if you'd sign the release papers. They won't talk to me and they can't talk to your doctors at home until you do."

Haley doesn't answer. Her thoughts take shape in molasses. She hears her mother, she understands, but her tongue feels thick. She wades thigh-deep through something dark and sticky in search of words.

"Haley, are you there?"

"Yeah. What time is it?" she manages. She doesn't feel like opening her eyes again to check the phone and see for herself.

"Two o'clock. Were you sleeping?"

"Trying to." She doesn't attempt to hide the annoyance in her voice.

"I'm sorry. I don't know when is the right time to call. But this is important."

"I told you I would do it, okay? It'll happen."

"Haley." The patient tone. Which is not patient at all, but just short of anger. What a relief, if she'd just yell. "This is serious. Your treatment team at school can't—"

"Treatment team." Haley repeats the words like she's tasting them. Trying to decide if she likes or even recognizes the flavor.

"The doctors who are monitoring you," her mother says.

Haley mulls this over. Considers this disconnect between the image her mother must have of a state-of-the-art medical facility and the shabby reality of the MacCallum College health center. She'd managed to drag herself over there this morning: Coach's orders. Sat in an excruciatingly bright room and answered questions from a friendly nurse who took her temperature and wrapped a blood pressure cuff around her arm. Talked to a bald doc who confirmed—surprise, surprise— that she'd suffered a concussion when she and the middie from Jefferson College both went up for that header at Saturday's game.

Stars. A glorious explosion of fireworks as her brain banged against the side of her skull. She actually remembers the impact, unlike her two previous concussions, when she'd blacked out and had to be told afterward what had happened.

On the grass, a familiar helmet of pain encasing her head, she heard whistles, calls for a knee-down. *No no no. Still three weeks left of the regular season. No no no . . .*

Funny how that was her first thought. Not paralysis or permanent impairment, but play time. How long she'd sit the bench.

"You know, Mom, I sort of decided sleep was more important than hauling my ass back across campus so you can know what my blood pressure is."

"What sort of an answer is that? This isn't about me or what I do or I don't know! It's about the health center having access to your medical records back home and the doctors being allowed to speak to one another. I can't give them the go-ahead! You're eighteen and considered an adult, and *you* have to sign the release of records forms."

Her mother's voice, an irritant on a good day, is an instrument of pure torture at this moment. Haley suspects that if she doesn't end the call soon, her head will literally explode.

"Mom. It's my third concussion. We know the drill." No reading, no computers, no television. No soccer. Especially no soccer.

"Now, you see, that's the problem. Your third concussion—says who? The emergency room doc at that Podunk hospital where your coach dragged you? Haley, these people are trained to stitch up drunks on a Saturday night. Did anyone give you an impact test?"

Oh god oh god make it end. Haley considers turning off the phone. For days. Although that would most likely prompt an actual visit from her mother.

"She said . . . No. No, they didn't do an impact test. They didn't need to. She said I was pretty typical. And the guy at health services just asked a few questions, then told me to go to bed." Haley hears her mother sigh impatiently. This is not the answer she wants.

"Without an impact test, how can they possibly monitor your progress?"

Not a real question. Rhetorical. And not at all what her mother's really thinking. *How can they know when you'll be ready to play again?* Haley fills in for her.

From the slough of molasses in which her thoughts move, another emerges: *Don't tell her what Coach said.*

Coach, who had ordered Haley into her car after they returned to campus and the rest of the team unloaded from the bus. Coach, who drove her straight to the local hospital and sat with her until the young woman doc on duty checked her out. Who returned her to the dorm, where Saturday night was in full swing. When they pulled up to the curb outside Haley's building, they could hear the pulse of music through the closed windows of the car. A steady stream of laughing students poured in and out the front doors. Every light in every room was on.

"Maybe this wasn't such a good idea," Coach remarked. "They would have let you stay overnight at the hospital."

"I'll be fine," Haley replied. "You get used to dorm noise."

"Well, sleep is your most important medicine right now. Rest, water, and lots of sleep."

Haley began to nod, then thought better of it. Her head felt like it rested atop a pike. She was about to get out, but Coach kept speaking.

"You know, since I was sitting with you when the nurse did the intake, I couldn't help but overhear you tell them that this is your third concussion."

Haley stilled. *Here it comes.*

Coach sighed. "I wish I'd known. Not only today, when I played you so aggressively, but last year, when I was recruiting at Hastings." She didn't sound mad as much as she sounded . . . sorry.

Haley didn't speak. The soccer-powerhouse Hastings School, where she'd repeated junior year and ultimately graduated, seemed like a lifetime ago.

"You've made a great contribution this season, Haley, especially considering that you're only a freshman," Coach said. "But for now you need to focus on your health, so you'll be contributing from the bench."

The bench. Followed by the door. As in, *Don't let it hit you on the way out, girl.*

"The health center is closed on Sundays, but I'm going to see if the doc will come in to check on you. I'll let you know."

She was dismissed. That much was clear. Haley swung the door open to the night air, the sounds of the party under way. She turned to face Coach.

"Thanks for helping me out this afternoon. I really appreciate it. I . . . I'm sorry I've let you down."

Coach didn't look at her. She glanced in her rearview mirror. Flipped the directional, signaling left. She was done.

"I'll call you tomorrow," Coach said. "Try to get some sleep."

Some part of Haley—the angry part, the *why-me?*-head-throbbing part—wants to tell her mother right now that no impact test on the planet can help her. She's cooked. Stick a fork in the girl—she's done. Benched for the rest of this season, and next year? Probably won't even make the roster.

Some part of her resents carrying this alone. Some part of her wants her mother to feel bad, too. Another part feels sick that she screwed up. What was she thinking, talking about a third concussion in front of Coach?

Before she can say another word to her mother, the door to the room swings open. It's Jenny. Weighed down, as usual, by a massively overstuffed backpack. She glances at Haley lying in bed with the phone to her ear and flashes her an apologetic look. As if she's interrupting. She always acts like she's interrupting. Like it isn't her room, too.

"I need to go," Haley says into the phone. "I promise, I will deal with the forms today." She ends the call before her mother can speak again. She turns off the ringer, closes her eyes, and lays the phone on her chest. It takes too much energy to reach up and replace it on the desk.

She hears the hushed sounds of Jenny moving around.

"She's like a mouse," her teammate Madison had once commented. "I mean, you turn around and she's *there*. Like, when did she slip in? It's almost creepy." Madison, who does everything at full speed and full volume. "She even looks like a mouse. Kind of little and brown-haired."

"You just don't get the charms of 'petite.' She's actually really pretty," Haley countered. It was a kick-your-own-dog reaction: she gets annoyed with her roommate, but no one else can. She understands Madison's impatience with Jenny.

7

Jenny is überstudious and soft-spoken, while Madison is . . . not. Which, in Haley's case, is a good thing. She loves being Madison's teammate; appreciates being Jenny's roommate. Randomly paired in a sprawling freshman dorm, their paths rarely cross. Haley is either at practice or hanging with her teammates or cramming in the library. Jenny, premed, practically lives in the lab. They navigate their separate lives efficiently and politely.

They are perfect living companions.

Nevertheless, Madison's observation stuck, and before long the whole team referred to her as Jenny-Mouse. Not to her face, luckily. Haley lived in dread that Jenny would overhear one of them.

"Hey," Haley says from the bed, eyes still closed.

"I'm sorry; you didn't have to hang up," Jenny says.

"Actually, you did me a solid."

"Your mom?"

"Yup."

Jenny doesn't reply. Six weeks of overheard conversations is all Jenny needs to completely get Haley's mom thing. She doesn't comment. But she doesn't judge, either.

"How are you?" Jenny asks. "I heard you got hurt at yesterday's game."

"Bashed heads with a Jeffersonian," Haley says. "Concussion."

"Ouch."

"Serious ouch. Third-time serious ouch." Haley hears a creak. Jenny sits on the opposite bed. "Which is why I've been so out of it," she continues. "You've probably been wondering why I've been lying here in the dark."

"No, your friend Madison told me. Listen, I'm really sorry about last night." The bed creaks again. And again. Little jouncy squeaks.

Haley scrolls back to last night: Coach dropping her off. The screaming lights, warm bodies packed in the halls as she pushed her way up to her room and closed the door to the rager that persisted until dawn. She remembers turning the dead bolt, crawling into bed.

"What happened?"

Jenny doesn't answer. Jenny doesn't answer for so long that Haley actually turns to face her. The cell phone slides off her chest and hits the floor. When she reaches down to pick it up, she glances at her roommate.

Jenny has drawn her knees up to her chest and wrapped her arms tightly around them. She rocks slightly, forward and back. Her gaze is fixed ahead, at nothing in particular, and her eyes brim with tears.

"Jenny?"

"I got in . . . really late," she says. "And I turned on the overhead light. Anyway, I think I woke you up. You kind of . . . yelled. *What the hell, turn that thing off.* I'm sorry; I didn't know you'd been hurt, or that you were even in here."

Haley tries to place this. It's disorienting to hear someone describe something you did that you absolutely cannot recall. At least, not the same way. She tries to remember details from Saturday night besides crawling into bed. The furor of the partying going on right outside her door.

A few bits come back. The door did open. A giant maw of white light and thrumming, sound made tangible, unleashed at her. She remembers thinking: *Jenny*. Being surprised it was Jenny. Because Jenny never stayed out late.

She doesn't remember yelling. She doesn't remember saying anything.

"I'm really sorry," Haley says. "I don't remember that at all, but I was pretty out of it. Light and noise are killer right now. I probably just . . . reacted."

Jenny continues to rock. "It's okay. You felt terrible and I woke you up. I was pretty out of it, too. I drank some stuff at a party and it really hit me."

Haley sits up. Her eyeballs threaten to pop from her skull, but this warrants her attention. Jenny-Mouse at a party?

"Seriously? You partied? *My* roommate? Jenny, I'm so proud of you!" Haley manages what she hopes is an enthusiastic smile but suspects is more like a grimace.

"Yeah, well, don't be." Jenny presses her face into her knees, blotting her eyes against her jeans.

"Hey," Haley says. "It's okay, I'm not mad. God knows I've come crashing in here late plenty of times."

Jenny doesn't answer. But she does unlock her knees, rise from the bed. She moves to her desk, begins fussing with some papers.

Haley tries again. "So where was this party?"

"Conundrum," Jenny says.

Haley's eyes widen. Conundrum is one of the houses on campus. Some are "interest" houses and named appropriately: Green House for the environmental activists, Light House for students into religion. Others are just named after famous alums, and you could apply as a block and get to live with a pack of your friends.

10

Conundrum is supposedly an interest house for people from different clubs. An institutional effort to combat the social silo effect of people hanging out only with their teammates or fellow choir members or rock wall buddies. Officially, it's meant to be an eclectic blend of students who wouldn't normally hang out together.

Unofficially, it's people who like to rage. Whenever, for whatever.

"Wow. Go hard, girl."

It's the wrong thing to say. Jenny whirls around.

"Yeah, well, you know what? It *sucked*. The party sucked! I don't know why I went. This guy I hardly know invited me. And it was a big, huge, stupid mistake." Jenny moves to the closet. She yanks out her towel and grabs her toiletries bag. She really does remind Haley of a frightened mouse.

"Jenny. What's wrong?"

The girl shakes her head hard, her long brown hair obscuring her face. "Nothing. I really don't want to talk about Saturday night. I'm going to take a shower." Jenny bolts from the room. The door slams.

What the hell? Fine. Be psycho. Next time I won't ask.

A fresh wave of pain crashes behind Haley's eyes. She needs to lie down again. But first: water. Haley steps over to the mini-fridge where she's stashed bottles of Poland Spring.

Jenny's backpack rests against the fridge door. Haley grabs the top loop to pull it out of the way . . . and it won't budge. She pulls again, and fresh daggers shoot up her neck into the bottom of her skull.

What is in there? Haley can't help herself: she unzips the bag. It's stuffed with science and math textbooks, the type made with the ultrathin, photograph-rich paper that results in boulder-heavy books. Haley rezips and push-drags the thing out of the way, then retrieves a water. She takes a long, deep swig from the bottle before returning to her bed.

As she settles her head gently on the pillows and closes her eyes, she's struck by how many times she's seen Jenny heft that pack over her shoulders. She's almost never without it; it's like a fifty-pound growth she scurries beneath, from dorm to library to lab.

That girl is way stronger than she looks.

．．．

The walls of Conundrum throb, a testament to the power of stereo speakers. The windows rattle slightly, but no one hears that over the music. Doors slam, water streams in the showers. Deep male laughter erupts in short bursts.

The dusky air outside the house is deceptively still. It is the silence before the starting gun. The final breath before the plunge.

Looming night trembles with possibility.

．．．

2

RICHARD

Her hair, like milkweed spilling across Richard's chest, smells of wood smoke. A few strands cling to his lips.

Downstairs something clatters in the kitchen. The shower, on the other side of the wall behind their heads, thrums with the uneven staccato of water hitting a plastic tub. The scents of bacon and coffee seep into the room.

"You're like a dog," Carrie always teases him. "I've never met anyone more sensitive to smell."

"Rrrruff," he'd replied the first time she compared him to a dog. He'd buried his face in her neck and taken a good long draw, as if to prove her point. Goat milk soap. The laundry detergent she liked from the natural foods co-op rising from the sheets as he pressed her back into the bed. They were in bed the first time she'd said it.

They were usually in bed.

"Dude," Jordan had said with an exaggerated wink to Richard shortly after their first public appearance as a couple. Jordan had spotted them in the dining hall, seated across the table from each other, silently concentrating on the chocolate chip pancakes stacked on their plates. Carrie didn't usually come to the dining hall. She preferred cooking for herself in the big communal kitchen at Out House, the building where she and all the other students into hiking and camping lived. But that morning there were no eggs in the fridge and she wanted pancakes, so they made the long walk across campus for brunch.

It was a Sunday. Richard remembers this because even though he wasn't particularly hungover that morning, he was dreading the long afternoon ahead: a boatload of number theory to get through and a paper due by noon Monday that he hadn't started. He was thinking he'd need to get back to his room to collect his stuff before heading to the library. He was also thinking, *More coffee*, and he was about to ask Carrie if she wanted a refill when she reached across for his free hand. Didn't break stride on those pancakes, didn't look up from her plate, but laced her fingers through his and held them there while she ate.

That's pretty much how and when Richard—and everyone, including Jordan, who saw them that morning—knew: they were a thing.

Richard wants to pull the hair off his mouth, but he's afraid Carrie will wake, and he's not ready for that yet. The room is bright—she refuses to draw blinds at night, claiming she likes to rise with the sun—but he's the one always woken up at dawn while she's impervious to the light. Once up, though, she springs to action. She doesn't exactly bolt from bed, but extricates herself from the tangled sheets and heads for the shower before his eyes fully focus.

"Good morning . . . I guess?" he'd said the first time he stayed the whole night and witnessed this routine. She was sifting through her closet, quick-clicking the hangers as she parsed her clothes. She had her back to him, and he was treated to a view of her naked butt. "Whatever happened to pillow talk?"

Carrie pulled out a kimono and slid her slim arms through the sleeves. It had a red, yellow, and black dragon festooned across the back. She turned, smiled at him. Grabbed a mesh bag from the top of her dresser.

"I told Gail I'd meet her for breakfast downtown," Carrie said. She was at the door, hand on knob, when she reconsidered. She returned to the bed. Bent to plant a barely-there kiss on the side of his face. "Plus I'm not really the pillow-talk type," she said. "See you later?"

Before he could answer, she was gone. He listened to her footsteps, heard the bathroom door open and close, and only when he could make out the unmistakable sounds of water gushing through faucet did he get up, retrieve his clothes from the floor, and leave.

Here's what Richard's never told her: sometimes, after they've spent the night together, he doesn't shower. He carries her with him throughout the day, lifting the back of his hand to his face and breathing in her lingering scent. The shampoo she uses. Her skin. He can't get enough of it. As opposed to her, jumping in the shower as soon as she's awake, staying in there too long, and, according to her housemates, using up all the hot water and making them late.

She's right. He must be part dog.

The racket from downstairs increases as voices are added to the mix, and Carrie stirs. Instinctively he tightens his arm around her. Her head, which has been tucked warmly between his chin and shoulder, lifts. The veil of blond hair lifts as well, detaches from his lips.

"Hey," he says.

Carrie squints, wrinkles her nose. Shifts slightly away from him and buries her face in the pillow. "Who the hell is banging the drums?" she moans. She moves as if to rise, but he holds her.

"Just because your housemates are frying tempeh sausage instead of sleeping in doesn't mean you have to get up," he says.

He feels her relax slightly. She widens her eyes. They're burnished brown, flecked with gold.

"It's not tempeh," she mumbles. "It's tofu."

"Same thing," he replies. He waits for her to argue with him, but she closes her eyes.

"How much did we drink last night?" she says instead.

Richard blinks: no pain. He runs his tongue over his teeth: no cotton mouth. His eyes sting a little, but that's probably from the smoke. A bunch of them had been sitting around a campfire they'd made in one of those metal dishes. A very Out-House-y way to pass a Saturday night. As opposed to the usual weekend "activities" in his house.

"Not much," he says. "But I can't speak for you."

She rolls over, stares at the ceiling. "My skull feels like eggshells."

"Want me to get you a glass of water?"

"Oh god. Would you?"

He pulls his arm out from underneath her and flips back the comforter. The cold air in the bedroom hits him like a slap; the students in Out House thrive on keeping the thermostat at igloo levels. It's only October, but nights and mornings are cold. He searches quickly for his boxers. He's already gotten an earful from the Hippie Witch, who shares the floor with Carrie, about seeing him slip into the bathroom without them.

"Nobody needs to see your naked ass first thing in the morning," she cawed, like some crow, the morning he'd just needed to take a piss and mistakenly thought the coast was clear. He doesn't get why Carrie lives with these people. It's not like the house is that great.

"Hippie Witch caught me," he'd reported the morning it happened. Carrie had gotten up and the dragon kimono was on.

"You know I hate when you call her that," she'd said. "She has a name: Mona." She'd brushed past him with the mesh bag, exiting.

"Exactly. Mona the Hippie Witch," he'd directed at her retreating back, but she didn't laugh. She also didn't seek out his company for the next thirty-six hours; not even a text. Then, around eleven o'clock at night, while Richard was studying alone in his bedroom, Carrie knocked. He opened the door. She stepped in and her mouth was on his and she was unbuckling his belt before the latch fully clicked shut.

He figured she'd gotten over the Hippie Witch comment. But he'd learned his lesson.

Words, which Richard batted carelessly among his friends, were powerful things to Carrie. With the guys, he slipped easily into some shorthand that didn't mean much beyond what was just said in the moment, possibly less, since their word choices were reflexive, unconsidered. For Carrie, words were volatile, intentional, Molotov cocktails of meaning.

Deep down, Richard knows she's got a point. He should respect accuracy in language. But choosing words carefully was one thing; navigating minefields of political correctness was another, far more exhausting, thing.

Sometimes he wonders why he's with her. Then Jordan reminds him.

"Older women have . . . knowledge," Jordan had commented the Sunday of the chocolate chip pancakes. He'd tracked Richard down after brunch, discovered him in the library, and dropped his laden backpack on the long table where Richard had just started on his problem sets. Jordan sat. Waited.

"They do," Richard agreed. That was it. He wasn't sure he was ready to talk about Carrie. He wasn't sure he knew what to say.

"So, this is a thing now?" Jordan continued. "You, the lowly sophomore, and Eco Carrie? Who just happens to be a senior?"

Richard laughed. "People call her that? Seriously?"

"Uh . . . everyone calls her that. Maybe not to her face. I mean, she pretty much is, right? Lives in the nuts and berries house, protests fracking, wears hemp . . . or does she eat it? Can you eat hemp?"

"No, but you can smoke it."

"Oh. Does she?"

"She wears flannel, eats local, and would never smoke," Richard said, immediately sorry he'd taken the bait. He wasn't superstitious, but for some reason he hadn't wanted to jinx

19

their relationship, or whatever it was. Hadn't wanted to expose it to the brutality of his friends' conversations. The whole thing felt as fragile and random as a bubble to him: one wrong move and it'd pop.

She was the one you always noticed who never noticed back. The type who couldn't quite disguise her curves inside oversize clothes—overalls and plaid shirts, soft dresses brushing the tops of scuffed Carhartts—this girl-woman-goddess with untamed hair, half held in place with a fist-size clip.

He still couldn't get over that she'd chosen *him*. Neither could Jordan.

"Way above your pay grade, don't you think?" Jordan had teased.

Richard forgave the dig. Jealousy was the highest compliment. He'd rewarded Jordan with a wink and no comment. *Let him imagine.*

The bathroom, where he goes to fill a glass of water for Carrie, is shrouded in mist. Hot air from the shower mingles with frosty air from the wide-open window, creating a mini meteorological event. Moisture drips from the ceiling, like it's raining indoors. *How is this environmental?*

He slips out before the someone who has created their own personal rain forest emerges from behind the plastic curtain. *Gotta be the Witch.* Hypocrite of the highest order. Her dad, a VP for some oil company, pays her tuition so she can stick it to him by growing her red-blond hair into white-girl dreadlocks and organizing protests against the college's portfolio of investments in climate change–related industries.

Hell, what's *not* a climate change–related industry? If the Hippie Witch had her way, exhaling would be outlawed.

Carrie has shifted to a half-sitting position, a pillow rolled behind her neck, cradling her head. While he was in the rain forest, she had retrieved the dragon robe. She lies atop the covers now, arms folded across her chest, robe wound tight across her body. He holds the glass out to her and slides beneath the comforter.

"Thanks," she says. She drains the glass, hands it back to him.

"More?" he asks.

She closes her eyes and presses her head back into the pillows. "I'll get the next one myself." It's an effort for her to remain inert like this. She is seriously hungover. "Wow," she says. "Why did we drink so much?"

"I had no idea *you* were drinking so much," he replies. He'd pregamed with Jordan and the guys at their place, Taylor House, before arriving late to the bonfire at Out House. The guys had given him a hard time about leaving for Carrie's.

Earlier in the semester they'd been cited for damage at Taylor. Their parents were all sent fairly hefty bills covering a broken window, a smashed couch, and a hole-punched wall. In addition to the fine, they were also banned from hosting parties. So Jordan and Co. had come up with the brilliant solution of getting the house next door, Conundrum, to host for them. With them. Whatever. Taylor supplied the booze, Conundrum the location.

Richard had wanted no part of this plan. For one thing, his parents couldn't afford the fines. *He* couldn't afford the fines. His mother was in tears when the bill from the college arrived; his father furious.

"How bad is it?" he'd asked his kid sister, Ellen, over the

phone. A junior in high school, Ellen got to witness the parental reaction firsthand.

The hesitance in her voice as she carefully chose her words with him was more upsetting than his dad's anger. "They keep saying, 'What's gotten into him? This is so out of character,'" Ellen said. A pause. "I mean, you never drank when you lived at home, Richard."

"That's because I was always in training for cross country," he said. "Not anymore." When he'd arrived at MacCallum, he quickly learned his high school times weren't good enough for the team.

"Still." That was all she said. All she needed to say.

Jordan had been pissed when Richard said he was heading to Carrie's instead of the party at Conundrum.

"Seriously? You're blowing off the best party of the fall to sit around singing 'Kum Ba Yah' with a bunch of eco freaks?"

Richard laughed. "I plan to spend very little time with the inhabitants. Except for one."

By the time he arrived at Out House, the campfire was already dying down. Couples were peeling off and small groups were moving on to the next party at another location. Carrie, seated in an Adirondack chair at the edge of the fire ring, jumped up when she saw him. In front of everyone there she planted an enthusiastic kiss on Richard's mouth.

She was always more aggressively affectionate after a few drinks.

"I kind of got the sense that you'd been drinking more than usual," Richard says. "Then, when we came to bed, it was obvious."

"I don't remember walking up the stairs," she says. A small line forms between her eyes as she attempts to recall the night before. "No, wait. I do."

He leans in. He kisses behind her ear, breathing in softly. His favorite place to kiss her. "I hope you remember more than just walking up the stairs." His lips migrate to her shoulder.

She sits up straighter. "What?" she says. "What should I remember?"

He slides closer. "Woman, you pretty much raped me last night. I've never seen you so . . . energetic."

His words have a Taser-like effect. Despite the pain that he knows blooms behind her eyes, she sits bolt upright with surprising speed.

"Don't say that. Don't say 'rape' like it's some sort of recreation. Jesus, Richard."

He exhales audibly. *Great, here we go again.*

"I'm sorry," he says instantly. "That was wrong. You know I didn't mean anything by it, Carrie."

"Actually, I have no idea what you meant by it. What did you mean?"

He scootches up to a sitting position. "You were just really into it last night. Not that you aren't always into it. But last night you were really . . . assertive. And it was good, okay? I liked it." He says the last part softly. "You liked it, too."

She swings her legs over the side of the bed and stands.

"Don't presume to tell me what I like, Richard. Or maybe I should start calling you Dick? I wouldn't *mean* anything by it." She begins her march to the door.

"Carrie. C'mon, don't be like this."

She grabs the mesh bag.

He slips from the bed and stands, barring her passage at the door.

"Move," she says.

He folds his arms across his chest. "Not until we talk."

She tries to push past him, reaching for the knob, but he blocks her.

"Richard, *move*."

He doesn't budge.

Shocked surprise spreads across her face. Carrie is not used to being thwarted.

"You are not going to stomp off in a huff," he says calmly. "We are going to talk like civilized people. Can you be civilized?"

"Are you threatening me?" Incredulity in her voice.

"See, that's what I don't get. You see talking as a threat. That's not good, Carrie. It suggests you have problems with basic communication."

"I'm not talking about talking. I'm talking about you, standing there, not letting me out of my own room!" Her voice rises. The shower sounds from next door have stopped. If she starts yelling, the Hippie Witch might decide to involve herself.

Richard leans back against the door. "What I said about last night? That was stupid. I'm sorry. I was being . . . what do you call it? . . . glib."

She doesn't respond.

"This is the part where you say, 'I accept your apology,'" he continues.

"I don't know if I can be with such an insensitive dumbass," she says instead.

"Sure you can," he says. "Because you know I don't mean anything by it. You're just so damn indoctrinated by the PC police that you have to hate on anything that isn't überenviro-feminist. It's killing your sense of humor, Carrie. Do you even have one left? Seriously, what makes you *laugh*?"

Carrie's eyes narrow. "A lot of things make me laugh. Here's what doesn't: hate speech. Words that promote violence against women. It doesn't take a genius to understand that."

He nods. "Even a dumbass like me gets that." He thinks he detects a flicker of light in her eyes when he refers to himself as a dumbass.

"You know what?" she says. "When you apologize for the stupid things you say? It's not because you *get* what you've said or you're even sorry for saying it. You're just sorry I'm annoyed."

"Well, of course I'm sorry you're annoyed! What's wrong with that? Would you rather I enjoyed annoying you? Wow, pissing off Carrie is great! That's one hell of a good time!"

"I *so* wish you weren't such a Neanderthal."

"Yeah, until you *want* a Neanderthal," he mutters.

"What was that?"

"Nothing." Richard steps away from the door. He's tired. He glances around the room for his clothes. He'll leave while she's showering. She never invites him to stay for breakfast.

He expects her to move to the unblocked door. But Carrie has more to say.

"Richard, do you not get what I do on Tuesday nights?"

He sighs. Of course. Her shift. Her all-important, saving-the-world-one-hysterical-girl-at-a-time shift, answering the phone at the college's just-created helpline. Which is supposed to be a rape crisis line, but has turned out to be where freshmen females call when their underage roommates barf uncontrollably after drinking too many vodka shots. They call the helpline instead of campus security. Or an ambulance.

At least, that's how Carrie described her first two weeks answering the line. She almost seemed disappointed that nobody was sexually assaulted on her watch.

His jeans are draped over the back of her desk chair. He pulls them on.

"I asked you a question," Carrie says.

"I apologized," Richard says evenly.

She stares at him. "Wow."

He pulls his T-shirt over his head. "And yes, I'm perfectly aware of how you spend your Tuesday nights. Trust me: I've heard it." He glances around the room for his sneakers. They were tossed near the dresser. As he yanks on his socks and shoves his feet into the sneakers, Carrie moves to the door. Hand on knob, she turns.

"So, this is the part," she says carefully, "where I say 'See you later.'"

He looks up at her. It's a far cry from accepting his apology, but probably as good as he'll get.

Then Carrie surprises him.

"But instead I think I'm going to say 'See you never.' 'Cos I'm done trying to explain basic shit to you."

"You're blowing this way out of proportion."

She laughs. A short half laugh. "Am I? Richard, we're always fighting."

"Always? See, that's an exaggeration. Right there."

"Fine. Usually. We're usually fighting. Whatever. I'm tired of being mad. And it's not like this was ever going anywhere."

Richard stops midlace. He straightens up and stares at her. "So that's it? We're breaking up? Just like that, over a stupid comment I apologized for?"

Carrie flashes him one of her vintage are-you-kidding-me? expressions. She turns the knob. "Breaking up? That assumes we were ever together."

Richard has no words for this. If she had slapped him across the face, he wouldn't be more surprised.

The door is open now, and he can see into the hallway. Mona walks briskly past, toward her bedroom. He wonders if she's been listening. As she leaves the room, Carrie glances over her shoulder at him one last time.

Then the door closes with a soft click.

．．．

"Are you sure we can come?"

"Yes! He said to bring friends."

"How do you know him, Jenny?"

"He's in my economics class."

"Brandon, right?"

"Brandon Exley."

"Oh. Jenny. Wow."

It's not her dress. She doesn't own anything like this. Black, with thick shoulder straps studded with rhinestones and sequins, a scoop neck. An airy fabric falls straight down in crumpled folds, floats around her body. Ends mid-thigh.

"Do you think I'll be cold?"

"You look amazing!"

"Shoot, girl. I may have to let you keep it. Looks way better on you than on me."

．．．

3

Haley

Haley's seen these women before. Just not in her room.

The black woman with the super-short-pretty-much-shaved hair and the blonde. The pretty white-blonde she passes on Tuesday and Thursday mornings on her way to the gym. It's a scheduling thing. You get into patterns, pass the same people who are retracing their patterns. Dining hall, class, library, dining hall. They tread invisible paths into the side-walks, only to shake it all out and start afresh each semester when the schedules change.

Haley and the blonde have become smiling strangers. That's how she refers, in her mind, to people she doesn't know but sees every day. It would be unfriendly not to smile, but weird to actually speak. Haley assumes the blonde lives in one of the interest houses near the athletic center and she's heading to a class on the days she passes Haley on her way to the gym.

Now she sits on Haley's bed. The woman with the short hair sits on the other bed. With Jenny. With her arm around Jenny's shoulders. As Jenny cries.

"Oh. Hey," is Haley's startled response. She's not supposed to be here. She's supposed to be on her way to history, but got hung up at the dining hall. Then forgot her notebook. And her phone. Haley keeps forgetting things. It's her first day back at classes, almost a week after the concussion, and while the pain has been mostly replaced by pressure, the fuzzy-headedness persists.

The blonde, who recognizes her instantly, is equally surprised. "Hey," she says back.

Awkward silence follows.

"Is everything okay?" Haley asks, which is ridiculous because it's clearly not.

The two visitors look at Jenny, who blows her nose into a tissue.

"It's my roommate," Jenny tells them. They look Haley up and down.

"Do you need to get in here?" the short-haired woman asks.

"Just have to grab my notebook," Haley says. She walks between them to her desk and picks up the notebook and phone. The only sound is Jenny sniffling. As she turns to leave, Haley exchanges glances with the blonde. Her wide, copper-colored eyes communicate nothing. Her mouth forms a thin half smile. She nods good-bye, dismissing Haley from her own room.

What the hell? Haley thinks as she power walks to the class she's already late for. They haven't been speaking, her and Jenny. Not beyond the automatic "Hey how's it going." Frankly, Haley's pissed. She'd apologized for supposedly yelling the other night; wasn't that enough? And you'd think, given how awful she's felt this week, lying in their room with her head throbbing, Jenny would've been maybe a little thoughtful? Offered to bring her a sandwich, or at least *ask* how she was doing, especially after Haley's parents showed up? You know things are not going well when the 'rents show up and it's not Parents Weekend.

Instead, Jenny-Mouse was more furtive than ever, bordering on unfriendly. Avoiding eye contact. Huddling on her bed with her back to Haley, whispering into her phone. And that's if she thought Haley was asleep. If Haley was awake and Jenny's phone went off, she'd tell whomever on the other end, "I can't talk now. I'll call you later."

As if I give a damn about her little dramas. Haley pushes open the doors to the lecture hall. It's a big survey class, American history from the colonial period to the Civil War, and she slips unnoticed into an empty seat in the back.

She's had her fill of drama lately. This morning at breakfast, for example. When she broke the news to Madison that she was off the team.

Madison stared at her across the dining hall table. "That so. Utterly. Sucks."

The crowded room was a riot of light and noise. Haley felt far from great, but the docs told her she could give the big dining scene a try.

Madison was the first one she'd told.

"There's still two weeks left of the regular season," Madison persisted. "Can't you get back for postseason?"

"It's not about the postseason, or any season," Haley said.

"It's about *ever*. Coach won't play me. She's afraid if I bang my head again and permanently damage my brain, we'll sue the college. I'm a liability."

Madison waved one hand dismissively. "Sign a waiver or something."

"Not an option."

"Why?"

"Because Coach said no! Trust me: it came up. If she doesn't *want* to put me out on the field, she doesn't have to. Play time isn't a right. It's a privilege."

Not Haley's words. Repeated words. From yesterday's meeting. With her mom and dad. Coach. The college medical director, who reviewed the results of Haley's impact test (they finally did one) and pronounced her soccer career officially over.

The look on her mother's face was priceless. Her mouth popped open in this little O as the doctor explained the risks she faced if she concussed again. Haley's first thought was: *That's what they mean, in novels, when they describe someone's jaw dropping in surprise.* And she was surprised by her own detached observation. As if this weren't happening to her. As if the defining activity of her life hadn't just come to an abrupt end.

She was surprised that she felt nothing beyond mild curiosity, while her mother appeared tearful and her father grim.

Actually, that's not true. She felt awful about Coach.

It hurt, the way she shook their hands, businesslike, and hurried off to some other appointment when they were done. Hurt, the way she responded when her mother brought up signing something. A waiver.

"You may be willing to put your daughter at risk, but I'm under no obligation to do so," she'd said. Steel in her voice. "Participation on my team is not a right. It's a privilege. And Haley revoked that privilege when I recruited her and she neglected to tell me she'd had multiple head injuries."

There was a long silence following that. Broken by Haley's mom.

"Your kicking her off the team would appear to support our decision to withhold that information. The fact is if she'd *volunteered* her *private* medical records, you wouldn't have recruited her. And if she hadn't bumped heads with someone last weekend, she'd still be your starting striker."

"And still be at risk for permanent brain injury," Coach shot back. "May I ask, what's the goal here? No pun intended."

Haley's father rose. "The goal," he said quietly, "is good health and an education." He extended his hand toward Coach, who stood as well. "Thank you. *We* wish you and the team every success." He looked pointedly at Haley's mother. "Let's go."

That was when Coach spoke directly to Haley.

"By the way, you haven't been 'kicked off.' You are benched due to injury and expected to attend every game. Your teammates will want you there, and I want you there, right on through to the end of the season."

Haley could feel her own grateful smile. "Thanks."

Then Coach hurried off without another word. Her mother had no choice but to do the same.

Madison seemed exasperated after Haley repeated this story. "Haley—duh!" she had exclaimed. "Listen to the woman. Benched is not kicked off! Give yourself time."

Haley wondered what part of this Madison wasn't getting.

Madison leaned close, her eyes inches from Haley's. "You *will* be back on that field," she insisted. "Cocaptain."

That's when Haley's sturdy walls of detachment came tumbling down.

"Cocaptain" had been their private thing since preseason.

MacCallum had a strict no-hazing policy for all sports teams, but that didn't prevent the "bonding" that involved new members drinking to excess and behaving ridiculously. A week after arriving for practice, the soccer captains held a team-only party at an off-campus apartment. Mini red cups, each with a shot and a half capacity, were handed out upon arrival.

"Hang on to your cups," they were commanded.

The game was charades, and you were timed. Frosh on one team, upperclassmen on the other. If your team didn't get the clue within two minutes, you all drank a cup. A senior made up the clues. So naturally, the frosh got stuff like *"Cymbeline"* (which turned out to be a play by Shakespeare) while upperclassmen got *"Friends."*

An hour into it, the frosh were wrecked.

"This isn't going to end well," Madison wheezed into her ear at some point. "We need help."

Just then, it was Haley's turn. She somehow got to her feet and staggered across the circle to where one of the older girls handed her a slip of paper. She stared at the scribbled writing: "Backstreet Boys."

"Can I sing?" Haley asked.

The older girl scoffed. "It's *charades*."

"C'mon. We're dyin' here," Haley pleaded.

"Oh, let her," another girl said. "They were still in diapers when that group was popular."

Haley turned to her. The whole room swayed when she shifted her focus. Damn. "If we get it, you have to do what I say." Whatever was in those red cups had made her bold.

The other girl smiled. She wasn't worried. "We'll see."

Haley dropped the paper, and someone with a stopwatch began counting down: "Three, two . . ." Just as she reached "one," Haley's eyes fixed on the snack table. Someone had brought a sheet cake in the shape of a playing field, with shaved coconut dyed green for grass. There were two plastic toy goals at each end.

She knew what to do.

Tripping over a couple of girls, Haley grabbed a goal off the cake, pulled Madison to her feet, and dragged her to the middle of the circle. Frosting and coconut clung to the edge, but that didn't stop her: she shoved the thing over Madison's head like a hat. Before her friend could react, Haley got down on one knee, as if she were proposing.

"You are," Haley crooned, "my fire. My one. Desire. Believe. When I say." She turned to the other frosh. Rolled her hand, eyes wide. *What next?*

"I want it that way!" they all sang.

Haley jumped up, her head bobbing in encouragement.

"Backstreet Boys!" someone yelled.

"Yes!" Haley screamed. Fist pump. She pointed to the upperclassmen. "Drink on the chorus!" The frosh cheered; the others moaned.

"But we. Are two worlds apart," she continued, amazed at how well she sang after a few shots. All the frosh joined in for the rest of the song, yelling "Drink!" to the upperclassmen after each increasingly hysterical repeat of "I want it that way."

Even Madison, who kept the goal on her head for the rest of the party, belted it.

Both sides surrendered after that, retreating to the snacks. As Haley used a napkin to help Madison wipe traces of buttercream from her ears, one of the seniors approached them.

"Well done," she said, grinning.

"Thanks," she and Madison said in unison.

"You know," the senior said, ducking her head and drawing them close, as if she didn't want to be overheard, "you two have been playing great. Everyone thinks you'll be the only freshmen to start."

Haley could feel Madison dig one finger excitedly into her back.

"Cool," Haley said, hoping she wasn't slurring the word. The room felt like a slow carousel ride.

"And if I had to guess," the girl continued, "I'm looking at two future captains. Right here."

As she walked away, Madison stage-whispered, "Oh. My. God!" into Haley's ear. "Cocaptains!"

It became their thing after that. They knew it was smug and completely inappropriate, because who knew what would happen over the course of four years, four seasons?

Like this. A career-ending injury. It takes a while to absorb what that means. Which is why she can forgive Madison for not getting it straight off.

But it was still fresh enough that the word threatened to bring on the tears she'd avoided until this morning's breakfast. She hustled straight out of the dining hall following that, and would have made it to class on time if she hadn't forgotten the notebook.

The history lecture hall is wonderfully dim and this prof is big into PowerPoint, so the potential for dozing off is great. Haley does her best to concentrate, but the low lights and the images only further lull her cloudy thoughts. Her head jerks up at the herdlike sound of shuffling feet moving toward the door. Class over.

Once outside, Haley blinks in the sun. A slight ache in her neck foretells pain to come. She has one more class, then she's done for the day. She pulls out her water bottle and unscrews the cap. She's about to take a long swig when she hears her name.

"Haley, right?" The blonde from earlier stands at the foot of the wide staircase. She takes a few steps up toward Haley. "I'm Carrie," she says. "Sorry about before. Back at your room. You must have thought we were totally rude."

"A little," Haley admits.

"Do you have a minute?"

Haley gestures around them with her hand. The sea of migrating students. "I've got class."

"Which way? I'll walk with you."

Haley hesitates. "I'm sorry, this is totally weird. What's up?"

Carrie looks around. The entrance to the lecture hall is crowded with students. She steps closer to Haley. "I'd like to speak to you privately. About Jenny. She asked me to talk to you."

Haley's eyes narrow. "Jenny can't tell me whatever it is herself?"

Carrie purses her lips.

That's when Haley sees him. Over Carrie's shoulder, at the foot of the stairs: Cute Guy, from math tutoring. Her class doesn't have an assigned teaching assistant, so if you have questions you can go to the math lounge where some upperclassman genius is usually on duty. She went once for help with a tough problem and spotted Cute Guy across the room. This sandy-haired sophomore who seemed to know everyone taking multivariable calculus. Cute Guy wasn't asking questions; he was answering them.

Haley had started going to the lounge on a regular basis after that. It turned out to be a great study spot, whether you were doing math or not.

But now Cute Guy is staring at them. Actually, not "them." He seems rooted to a spot on the sidewalk, aiming his X-ray vision at Carrie. Like he's waiting for her. Willing her to turn.

"It's complicated," Carrie says, turning to see what Haley is looking at. A flicker of impatience crosses her face. "Let's just walk, okay?" Carrie says abruptly. "I can explain everything."

· · ·

They don't hear him over the percussive, insistent thump. He steps into the room, turns down the volume.

"A little help?"

They follow him down the stairs, their feet thunderous on old wood. Outside to the small paved area behind the house. A station wagon is parked near the door, its back end low. He raises the hatch to reveal cases of beer. A brand-new plastic green garbage can. Cartons filled with bottles of clear liquid.

"Let the games begin, gentlemen," Exley says.

· · ·

4

RICHARD

He's been following her.

This doesn't make him proud. But Richard can't help it. He wants to see who she's with. Where she goes. The tilt of her head as she speaks to people he doesn't know.

He wants to see if she exhibits signs of the ache that's been twisting his gut. So he trails, at a distance, while she saunters to class. Lingers over chai at the library café. Marches purposefully downtown with her string bag to the food co-op, where she'll load up on organic produce, farro, local cheese. He used to remark, amazed, at the prices she was willing to pay for these items.

Her face is smooth as she moves through her days. She looks more beautiful and self-contained than ever.

When he can't stand the silence anymore (she responds to none of his texts or phone messages), he decides to make sure she sees him. He will force a response, something, a glance even, that acknowledges his existence on the same campus, the same planet.

Normally, he'd be nowhere near the history building at this time of day. Neither would she, so it strikes him as odd. Her whole morning has been out of joint. She and Gail had breakfast at the dining hall (which they almost never did), then set off across campus to one of the freshman dorms. He didn't have class, so he waited on a bench, a comfortable viewing distance from the entrance.

I've become a stalker. This is bad. He's got it bad.

"Have a little pride, man," Jordan said when he confessed that he'd been following Carrie. They were drinking beers in the Taylor common room. Jordan had been unsympathetic. "It shouldn't be that much work," he said. "Constantly watching every word you say? Putting up with her ridiculous friends? There are more fish in the sea, and they are way easier to hook."

Richard regretted telling him. Not that Jordan was wrong. It *had* been too much work. But Jordan didn't get that he felt bad anyway. It was like some little piece of him had been surgically removed, and he was looking around for it. In a dark tunnel without a flashlight. Making an idiot of himself in the process.

Richard knew it wasn't good.

"See, you made the wrong choice," Jordan continued. "Not just about Eco Carrie. That was the big wrong choice. About the weekend in general. Shouldn't have blown off our party."

Richard smiled. "Seriously? If you had a choice between sleeping with a gorgeous woman or raging with the guys? Give me a break."

Jordan tilted back his head and drained his beer. "I didn't have to choose."

Richard looked at him skeptically. Jordan was usually a lot of talk when it came to women. Whether there was any action connected to that talk was debatable. More than a few guys at the house had a running bet that he was *all* talk.

"Seriously?" Richard repeated.

"Freshman." Jordan winked. He reminded Richard of a raccoon, with his cunning point of a face. Those cute animals that cock their little heads then tip your trash.

"Hmm," Richard responded. Which Jordan interpreted as encouragement.

"Exley invited her. And she brought others. So you would not have been lonely, my friend."

"Hitting on freshmen is sort of like shooting fish in a barrel, don't you think?" Richard said. "I mean, as long as we're sticking to your fish metaphor."

Jordan laughed. "And that's a problem . . . why? If the whole point is catching a fish?"

Richard shook his head. "Whatever. Just not my style. At least one of us had a good weekend."

Jordan popped another beer.

"So are you going to see her again?" Richard asked.

"Who?"

"The freshman."

Jordan snorted. "See, this is what I'm talking about. This is why you are moping around with your tail between your legs. News flash: no one's trying to get married. Except maybe you."

"I'll take that as a no."

"Hell no," Jordan replied, laughing. "I mean, don't get me wrong. She was great. But this is college. It's a freakin' buffet!

When else in our lives are we going to be surrounded by so many females our age? Besides, it's not like we exchanged numbers or anything."

"Or could find your phone the next day," Richard added.

"True. God, we were wrecked. Exley mixed an entire trash can of Skippy."

"Skippy?"

"Beer, ice, vodka, and Country Time lemonade," Jordan ticked off. "Has to be Country Time. Something about the sugar."

Richard wrinkled his nose. "Since when did our man Exley become such a bartender?"

"Dr. Exley," Jordan corrected. "He's got a PhD. *People Hafta Drink.*"

Richard laughed in spite of himself. As he drained the rest of his beer, he thought about what Carrie would make of this conversation. He could picture her disgusted expression. Which was why, in the weeks they'd been together, he'd never introduced her to any of his housemates. That had been easy: except for the one time she'd surprised him in his room, they'd always gone to Out House. And he'd said nothing to the guys about her. Until Jordan spotted them the morning of the pancakes.

Richard had been the last man chosen for Taylor. His freshman year roommate and running buddy, Joe, wanted Richard to live with him at the party house, Conundrum, but Richard decided to pass. It was looking like he'd end up living in a basement single in one of the old dorms (his room draw number sucked) when Jordan, whom he also knew from their frosh hall, said they needed one more guy to fill out the application for a house block. Richard jumped at it. He was pumped when they got it. He'd be part of a pack of twenty guys, most of whom he knew, living in his own (closet-size) bedroom in a three-story house.

Then Richard met Jordan's friend Brandon Exley.

Richard was no stranger to partying, but nothing prepared him for Exley. A boarding school veteran, word was the guy basically stopped living with his parents at age fourteen. It wasn't simply that he drank a lot, and drank harder stuff than anyone—he did. It wasn't that he did drugs, and not just pot—he did. It was the grim purposefulness to Exley's partying that set him apart. The closed look in his eyes as he stood in the dim corner of a room, draining one red cup after another, watching. Laughing without smiling. You didn't see him talk to girls, but when he was ready, he'd move from his place on the wall to the dance floor in the center of the room and begin grinding with whomever he'd decided to target that evening. At some point, you'd see them leave together, his arm around her waist as they stumbled upstairs.

Exley disliked Richard instantly, stiffening like a restrained animal that senses a threat the moment they met. Richard didn't really get it, but the more he got to know Exley, the more it made sense. It was like the guy needed someone to provoke, to target, and fixated on Richard. Exley was always pushing Richard to drink more than he wanted, goading him if he slowed down. Mocking him for tutoring math instead of joining the rest of the guys for beer pong or pool shots at the house. When they got cited for damage and banned from hosting parties, Richard was actually relieved.

As Richard stands just behind a tree near the entrance to

the history building, watching Carrie, who seems to be waiting for someone, a wave of urgency breaks over him. He can
fix this. He *needs* to fix this. He takes a deep breath, relaxes
his shoulders, and observes. It occurs to him that this is how
he attacks tough math problems: avoid panic, take one step at
a time. There is always a solution. It always, ultimately, reveals
itself.

Richard steps out from behind the cover of the tree and
plants himself behind her. At the same moment, the doors
to the building yield, letting loose a stream of bodies. They
break around Carrie as she remains in place, her gaze fixed on
a point at the top of the stairs. She doesn't turn. He takes one
step closer.

She speaks to someone. A girl who has just come out.

Richard knows her. Recognizes her, anyway. She comes to
tutoring, although he's never worked with her. Soccer Girl (the
sweatshirt she always wears gave that away), who sometimes
doesn't ask for help at all but simply studies in the math lounge.

He notices Soccer Girl's hesitancy as she answers Carrie.
She wrinkles her forehead, looks beyond Carrie as if she's impatient to move on. That's when Soccer Girl sees him, and
their eyes lock. Surprise unfolds across her face.

Carrie turns to see what's so interesting over her shoulder.
When she picks out Richard, she flashes him a furious look,
then whips her head back toward the girl. More words are
exchanged between the two of them, then the matter is set-
tled and they begin walking together. They pass him on the
sidewalk, Carrie's eyes fixed ahead at something, anything
except him.

It's not turning out the way he intended.

45

* * *

Music seeps from someone's room, not clear which. The volume is turned up, and several doors down someone else sings along. A few more join in from another room, then the whole thing goes hall-viral.

Girls who never thought they could carry a tune are belting it. Girls who never thought they could dance are shaking it, down the hall, in dresses and jeans and gym shorts and sweatpants. They hold hairbrushes like microphones, they whip out their cell phones and blind themselves with repeated flashes from their cameras.

From the bathroom, one girl emerges, shower-fresh, wrapped in a towel. She stands in the center of the hall and, diva-like, sings.

They laugh so hard they gasp for breath, falling against each other for support.

* * *

5

Haley

Haley's not a hugger.

Never has been. Not even when Haley was little and girl-hood was defined by sleepovers and whispered secrets, giggles and body-rocking laughter over practically nothing. And hugs.

Spontaneous, random hugs. On the playground. At the swim club. Before school, after school. In the hallways as they changed classes. On the couch in someone's den, the big TV room, group-hug pileup with a bowl of popcorn knocked over in the crush. Body language that declared, emphatically: *We Are Friends. Best Friends. Forever.* And when they got older? Instagram-Snapchat-Facebook-posted documentation of girl-love, those hugs. The imprimatur of success: *Me and my besties. #HavingSoMuchFun*

It wasn't instinctive for Haley. She could feel herself tighten awkwardly when friends threw their arms around her. Her return hugs were swift; she always let go first. It wasn't that she wasn't physical—just the opposite. Haley was the first to rush the goal and hurl herself at their keeper when they won a game; the first to slap your hand in encouragement after a tough point; the first urging everyone together in a midfield huddle, heads bumping, arms laced over hunched shoulders.

That felt genuine to her. The rest . . . not. So when she opens the door to their room and finds Jenny waiting, as Carrie promised, she is startled by her own response.

Haley drops her pack and walks straight to where Jenny sits on her bed, open laptop resting on her knees, a box of tissues at the ready. She ignores all that, even the stray used tissues. She ignores the polite, respectful distance that has made them such good roommates and slides herself onto the thin wedge of bedside next to Jenny, the computer tilting dangerously. She feels her own eyes fill as she throws her arms around the girl's shoulders and, wordlessly, squeezes tight.

Oh, Jen. I'm so, so sorry, she doesn't say out loud.

Her roommate shakes with silent sobs. Haley just holds on. She doesn't know how long.

When they finally move apart, Haley stays on the bed. Jenny's face is creased and red-streaked. Her eyelids look raw.

"I feel terrible. I had absolutely no idea," Haley says quietly.

"How could you? I didn't tell you. I could barely admit it to myself."

"That's what Carrie said. But she said you've been really brave."

Jenny angles her head away. "I don't know. If I'm so brave, how come I didn't fight him off? How come I let this happen to me?" Fresh tears begin to form in her eyes. "I don't feel brave. I feel stupid."

Haley covers Jenny's hand with her own and squeezes. "It takes bravery to speak up. It takes super bravery to report . . ." Haley stops short of saying the word. For some reason, she feels like that would upset Jenny even more. She doesn't know why. It's just a gut feeling. She's relying on her gut for all of this. Plus, Carrie's advice.

The older girl got right to it. Once she whisked Haley away from the history building, she revealed that she was a volunteer for the sexual assault response team at the college.

"Your roommate, Jenny, was raped last weekend," Carrie said. "My friend Gail and I are both volunteers. We've been helping Jenny get the support she needs. After you walked in on us this morning, she told us you didn't know. She asked me to tell you."

That scene in the room. The tears, the air smog-thick with tension. Haley finally got it. "Oh my god! What happened? Is she okay?"

Carrie shook her head. "I can't discuss any of the details with you. Privacy, you know? Physically she's fine. But mentally, not so good. She's shaken. Classic trauma, really. Just like they described in our training sessions."

Classic trauma. Haley had no idea what that meant.

"She'll need lots of support," Carrie said.

"Of course. What about her family? Do they know?"

"Yes. They're flying in tonight. From Ohio," Carrie added.

Haley felt a prick, the slightest twinge, of annoyance. *Uh, she's my roommate. I know where she's from.*

49

"She's going to need to process. A lot," Carrie continued. "Be prepared to listen. Sometimes at inconvenient times, if you know what I mean."

"No. What do you mean?"

"Late at night. In the dark, in bed, when there's nothing to distract her from the thoughts. When she keeps replaying the attack, over and over, in her mind." Carrie's voice was steely, the words delivered like short, swift blows. "Or maybe unexpectedly, middle of the day, while you're doing homework together in your room? Suddenly she'll start to cry. Maybe she won't speak at all, but just need someone to be with her. Don't ask questions. Just be present."

Haley stopped walking. She faced Carrie. "You seem to know an awful lot about this."

The older girl held Haley's gaze for a long moment before answering.

"I'm not a survivor, if that's what you're wondering," she said. "Although, in a sense, we all are. Survivors of the rape culture." She was speaking loudly. They had stopped beneath a cluster of trees, a quiet intersection of sidewalks, but students walking yards away on a parallel path shot them curious looks. Even Carrie noticed. They continued walking.

"I know you've been dealing with your own issues lately," Carrie said, her tone a bit more hushed. "Jenny told us you were hurt playing soccer. But she needs you right now. I don't get the impression she has a lot of friends."

"She works a lot. She's got two labs *plus* multivariable. It's killer."

"It would absolutely suck if she withdrew over this." Carrie grimaced. "Victims do that. The trauma, plus the academic pressure, is just too much. We can't let that happen. We have to let her know that she is not alone. Especially as the complaint process moves forward to a hearing and her stress increases."

"Hearing?"

"She's going to file a formal complaint with the college against her rapist," Carrie declared. "She's not letting him get away with this."

"Wow."

"She's so brave," Carrie continued. "This has been really hard for her, but she's doing the right thing. Not only for herself, but for all of us. Listen." Carrie pulled out her cell phone. "Give me your number. We should talk for real, not like this. I can get you up to speed on what to expect and how you can support Jenny." She looked at Haley, finger poised over her phone.

They come back to her now as she sits with Jenny, Carrie's startling eyes. Metallic brown. Coppery. She pushes the stray thought away. The invading, distracting, nonrelevant thought. *Focus on Jenny.* A Herculean task, given the post-concussion landscape of her bruised, barely-able-to-concentrate brain. She glances at her watch. It's not quite time to reload the Tylenol, but the ache behind her eyes has been steadily increasing all morning. She rises from the bed and heads toward the mini-fridge.

"Want a water?" Haley asks. Jenny shakes her head. Haley pulls out a bottle for herself, then sits on her own bed. She fishes through her backpack for the gelcaps. "When are your folks getting here?"

Jenny takes a deep breath. "Tonight. After dinner." She looks like she might start crying again.

"But that's good, right?" Haley says gently.

"I guess." Jenny begins playing with the tissue she holds. Twisting it tightly around her fingers. "Telling them was . . . really hard. Awful, actually." She looks at Haley with brimming eyes. "I've seen my mother cry before—tearjerker movies, sad stories. But never heard her sob. Until the other night, when I called them." Jenny's eyes drop to her lap. She's pretty much twisted the tissue into a tourniquet at this point, and her fingertips are bright red. "I think half the reason I waited to report it was because I dreaded that call. And tonight? It'll be the first time I've seen them. Since . . ."

"Yeah," Haley says. *This* she gets: that "first time" meeting with your parents. When they tell you they love you, but you no longer *feel* like the girl they thought you were or want you to be. The soccer star and perfect student, happy and "killing it" at college. Now past tense, and the new you reflected in their voices, in their eyes. Their disappointment and pain like gasoline poured on your personal pyre.

If it was hard for her, what must this be like for Jenny?

"Then there's my father," Jenny continues. "He's beyond angry. He called the dean's office and wanted to know why they hadn't expelled him already, 'what are you doing to protect my daughter,' blah, blah, blah. They told him they've got a process and they have to stick to the procedures they have in place and . . . well. He can get pretty worked up."

"It's his daughter. Of course he's worked up," Haley says.

"Yeah." Jenny sounds unconvinced.

Haley pops four Tylenol into her mouth at once and washes them down with a single gulp. She stretches out on her own bed and closes her eyes. "Expel him," Haley repeats. "He's another student." This realization blossoms in her head. She'd assumed otherwise. She had no reason to assume anything, of course, except . . . she had. She'd assumed darkness. A burly stranger, some man reeking of alcohol and unwashed clothing. Surprising Jenny as she walked back to her dorm alone late Saturday night. After she drank too much at a Conundrum House party. One of those houses on the fringes of campus, where it was thickly wooded and quiet.

Jenny doesn't reply. Which is when Haley remembers she's not supposed to ask questions.

"I'm sorry," she says immediately. "You don't have to talk about it."

"You don't have to apologize. It's fine."

"No, seriously, I'm sorry. I mean, I'm here if you do want to talk about it. But I'm also here if you . . . don't."

"Thanks."

They're quiet for a while. Haley attempts to relax the muscles in her neck, will the little soldiers of advancing pain to retreat. The room is hot. God, Jenny *always* closes the windows. Haley can't handle getting up again, straining to lift the heavy-paned thing.

"What did you think of her?" she hears Jenny ask.

Haley frowns. "Her?"

"Carrie."

"Oh." Haley considers. There's a lot one could say. "Intense. Beautiful. In a Viking sort of way, but without the horned helmet." Jenny makes a sound that could be a soft laugh. "What do you think of her?"

"Same. Especially the beautiful part. It surprised me, actually, when I finally met her. I didn't picture her like that. We'd been talking on the phone on and off for a couple of days, and she had this . . . voice. I want to say strong, but that's not really the word."

"Emphatic?" Haley supplies. "Convincing?" *Bossy,* she doesn't add.

"Yes, exactly. But then, when I finally met her and Gail? I didn't expect her to be so pretty. Weird, right?"

"I don't know. Do we match our voices? What if you talked to someone behind a screen, then they had to describe what you look like based on your voice. Would they get it right?"

"Good question." Jenny is quiet again.

"How did you picture her?" Haley continues. It's an effort, to keep talking. The warm room, the headache. She wants to sleep. But Carrie said Jenny needed to talk.

"Zits."

Haley startles. "Zits?"

"Her voice felt like a bad complexion to me," Jenny explains.

Haley can't help it: she laughs out loud. Who knew Jenny-Mouse had a sense of humor? "She's got the most amazing eyes, doesn't she? I kept wondering what color they were."

"Amber," Jenny says without hesitation. "It's from lipo-chrome. A yellow-colored pigment. I noticed, too."

"Pardon my French, but how the *hell* do you know that?"

"I'm a biology major," Jenny says, as if that explains it.

"You're a biology genius, more like."

"Yeah. Real genius," Jenny says quietly. The tears return to her voice.

"I thought only snakes had yellow eyes," Haley says quickly.

"Yellowish," Jenny replies, sniffling. "But also some cats. Owls. A certain penguin, found in New Zealand."

"Cool," Haley says. "And good to know. I was feeling the reptilian in Carrie, but maybe she's more feline."

It's the wrong thing to say.

"There's nothing reptilian about her," Jenny says sharply. "She's kind. And smart. She's been helping me *so* much. Do you know, she actually went with me to the health clinic so I could get an STD test? I really don't know what I'd have done without her. I've been so . . . alone. So totally alone in this. She and Gail have helped so much."

"I know," Haley says quickly. "She's nice. I wasn't hating on her. I just don't know her." She hears the quick whoosh sounds of tissues pulled from the box.

"Nothing is what it looks like. Or sounds like," Jenny says, almost viciously. "Think a rapist is some tats-covered dude with a knife? Try a friendly guy with a great smile."

"I'm sorry, Jenny," Haley says. "I wasn't judging. Not you, not Carrie, no one." But Jenny doesn't seem to hear.

"Here's one thing I've learned: the real snakes in the world? Don't look anything like you'd expect them to."

. . .

He conducts this symphony.

The dissonance of laughter and grunts as they grapple with the keg and stagger-stumble up the steps, the foaming liquid swaying side to side. The diminuendo of an empty trunk as strong arms heft cases of beer, bottles of vodka. The crescendo of assembly: hauling, dragging, piling, stacking.

The tune-up complete, Exley surveys.

The evening's ingredients. Fuel for all their expectations.

. . .

6

RICHARD

It's not Richard's day to be on duty at the math lounge, but he goes anyway. And sure enough, she's there: at the long table, textbook and papers spread out.

You get to know the regulars. The Frantic Freshmen from Calc II, who wave their C-minus midterms in your face and insist they scored in the high seven hundreds on the math portion of the SAT. You have to talk them down. Then there are the Multivariable Geeks, who were feeling pretty good about themselves . . . until they started Multivariable. They spend a good portion of their time—and his—agonizing, out loud, about whether they should switch their majors to economics.

Luckily, there are a few reasonable students who have a question or two about their problem sets. They get the answers, then move on. Finally, you've got the folks who just like to study here, who might not even take math. The lounge is comfy.

Soccer Girl is a hybrid of the latter two, although most days, she'll camp out in the cushiony seats and do work. Once, she fell asleep, her mouth slightly open, the history book she was reading in midslide off her lap. Without waking her, Richard had removed the book before it fell, marking her spot with a slip of paper and placing the closed volume on the floor next to her chair.

She smelled like honey and vanilla. The dryer sheets his mom uses.

When Richard enters, she's deep in conversation with Useless Brent, their heads bent over her paper. He takes a seat at the end of their table. And waits. Like Richard, Brent earns work-study dollars as a tutor, but unlike Richard, Brent doesn't do much to explain math concepts to anyone. More times than he can remember, Richard has had to bail him out.

"I really think it's an inverse tangent we want here," he hears Brent say.

Soccer Girl doesn't look convinced. "I'm thinking inverse cosine."

Brent takes her pencil. Literally grabs it out of her hand and begins marking up her paper. Her shoulders rise and fall noticeably as she takes a deep breath.

"Hey," Richard says. They both look up. "Want me to take a crack at it?"

"We're good," Brent says grumpily, ducking his head back to the paper.

Richard looks at Soccer Girl.

Yes! she mouths silently at him.

He grins and moves to the chair across from them.

"I've got this," Brent repeats.

Richard ignores him, reaches across the table, and flips her homework sheet around. They're working on the chain rule. "What don't you get?"

"We're trying to resolve this integral, and I think we're dealing with an inverse cosine, but Brent says inverse tangent," she explains.

"You're not even scheduled today," Brent protests.

"Hey, I'll take all the help I can get," Soccer Girl says pleasantly.

Richard scans the page, thinking. "Totally an inverse cosine," he says, flipping the page back toward her.

"Yes!" she exclaims. She fist-pumps. Heads turn in their direction.

Brent gets up. He walks to another table where a group of freshmen are arguing about a proof.

"No need to get huffy," Richard says under his breath.

"Guess that was rude of me," she says, laughing. "I should apologize."

"Nah. He should apologize for being a dweeb. Anything else?"

"No. That was it. Thanks." But she doesn't move.

"Are you a math major?"

"I've been here all of seven weeks. I have no clue what my major is. You?"

"Pretty much." He shrugs. "I keep taking math courses."

"And clearly rock at it," she adds. Trace of a smile. "I'm Haley, by the way."

"Richard," he replies. "Nice to meet you. Now that I know your name, I won't have to think of you as Girl with the Soccer Sweatshirt anymore." He thinks this is an okay thing to say. But her expression clouds. "Team sweatshirt, right?" he asks.

"Used to be on the team. I mean, I'm still 'officially' on the roster. But I got hurt, and . . . well, let's just say it was a career-ending injury." She tries to smile when she says this, but her eyes aren't laughing.

"I'm sorry. What happened?"

"Can you two take it somewhere else? I've got a test tomorrow." This from someone at the table next to theirs.

"Sorry," Richard mutters at him. He looks at Haley. "Whoops."

"Actually, I was just heading down to the café."

"That sounds good," he says, and waits.

Haley smiles, this time with her eyes. They walk out together.

"Anyhow, you were saying?" he asks as they descend the stairs to the Hard Math Café. She walks alongside him. Richard considers himself average tall. This girl is eye level.

"Uh . . . what?"

"About your injury."

"Oh. Right. Concussion. I've been pretty out of it, dealing with pain, missed almost a week of classes. Still pretty out of it, actually. I mean, that one problem you helped me with was taking *hours*."

"Calc II homework used to take me hours, even without a brain injury."

"Thanks. Still." She sighs. "It's frustrating." They reach the door to the café. Richard pulls it open, and she walks in ahead of him.

"Must suck to not be able to play anymore," he comments. "Are you sure you're done for good?"

"It's my third concussion. No one in their right mind would

put me on the field again. And it's not like this is the World Cup or we're playing for money, you know? I'm expendable."

"Hey. No one's expendable." He says this mock-severely.

"Turns out I am." She's looking with great interest at the board listing the day's specials. "I may just have to get a big fat chocolate brownie to go with the java. Eat my feelings *and* get an extra caffeine boost. It's a win-win."

"Well, we can't let you face that brownie all by yourself," he says. "That's not how we do it at the Hard Math Café."

"I'm not sharing," she says seriously. "You'll have to get your own, Math Dude."

A hesitant grin takes shape on his face.

Haley breaks out a full-fledged smile. She presses her shoulder against his, a little shove. He staggers slightly. "Ha. Fine." Her eyes return to the board. "I'll give you a piece. Small piece."

They take their coffee and her brownie to an empty table. Along the way she stops at the filling station and pours milk and Sugar In The Raw into her mug. Once seated, she leans back, breaks off a corner of the brownie, and holds it out to him. Richard holds up a hand and shakes his head, so Haley pops it in her mouth.

"Good, because I'm actually not one of those splitting types," she says.

"Splitting types?"

"You know the way women always split meals at restaurants? Like they don't want to admit that they can finish an entire entrée?"

"That's a thing?"

"Go out to dinner with a bunch of women your mom's

age and I guarantee they will *all* share. 'Oh, who wants to split the ravioli with me?' 'Anybody want to share the free-range chicken?'" Haley slips into this dead-on imitation of a middle-aged woman. Adds a sort of cackle. He laughs. "This girl eats the whole brownie," she says. "And the whole entrée. By herself."

"I'll remember that."

"Unless dinner seriously sucks," she adds.

"Hmm. Define 'sucks.' "

She looks thoughtful. "Tofu steaks," she decides. "I do salad bar on those nights." Richard laughs again.

They're both quiet for a minute. It occurs to him that Haley's comment makes an excellent segue.

"Speaking of tofu," he asks nonchalantly, "how do you know Carrie Mason?" He thinks he notices her eyes widen ever so slightly. "I saw you talking to her last week."

"I don't," she says. "She knows my roommate. But now you have to tell me how you jump from tofu to Carrie."

"Is your roommate a militant vegetarian?"

Haley smiles. "I don't think she's a militant anything."

"Well, Carrie is. A militant everything, actually."

She laughs. "How do *you* know her?"

"We dated," he replies. Her eyes definitely widen now. "What?" he says. "Is that such a shock?"

"Uh . . . yes."

"Okay, I want to ask why, but . . . maybe I don't?"

Her gaze, which has been locked on his pretty much throughout this whole conversation, breaks off now. She purses her lips, glances over his shoulder toward the counter, the espresso machine. The exit.

"Listen, I don't know you *at all*, so I shouldn't judge," she begins.

"Now you *have* to tell me."

She shrugs. An okay-you-asked-for-it gesture. "You seem sort of easygoing. Carrie seems really intense." She polishes off the rest of her brownie. Sits back and regards him.

"That's it?"

"Isn't that enough? I mean, from the outside I'd say you aren't one bit compatible. If you guys were an analogy, I'd say you are to preppy as she is to . . . earthy. You are to bacon cheeseburger as she is to . . .'"

"Tofu steaks?"

"Lentil loaf."

"Tempeh hot dogs."

Haley screws up her face. "Ugh, that stuff is nasty. Tempeh. What exactly *is* textured protein product? Brrr!" She shudders.

"Isn't it made from soybeans?"

"That's tofu."

"I think they're both made from soybeans, but I'm not sure."

She wags one finger at him. "You should be proud of that ignorance. You should wear your lack of soy knowledge as a badge of honor."

"Okay, so now you're sounding like a militant carnivore."

"Nah. I just like to eat real food that tastes good."

Richard raises his mug, laughing. "Here's to that." They clink. "You sound like my sister, Ellen."

Haley sips her coffee. "You have a sister who's into food?"

"She's not some foodie, but she is . . . enthusiastic about food," he explains. "Can't get enough of it, actually. She's a swimmer."

Haley smiles, lips closed. "I don't have siblings."

"I'm sorry."

One corner of her mouth turns up. "Most people who hear that tell me I'm lucky."

"That's because their siblings probably suck," he explains. "My little sister is definitely the coolest member of our family."

Haley tilts her head. "How so?"

Richard pauses. It suddenly feels strange to be telling this girl he doesn't know about Ellen. He's not sure he even mentioned to Carrie that he had a sister. Did it ever come up?

"Well, she puts up with me," he finally says. "And I'm a handful."

Haley laughs. Then they're both quiet for a minute.

"For someone who doesn't know Carrie, you seem to . . . know Carrie," Richard tries again.

Haley wraps her hands tightly around her mug before answering. "She just gives a strong first impression. I mean, what do I know? Maybe she's a closet math genius and you're an Earth First! commando. You must have something in common."

Richard smiles. He decides not to mention the one interest he and Carrie shared.

"So are you?" she asks.

"What?"

"An Earth First! commando."

"I can't even recycle," he confesses. "You know how the college puts those two bins in our rooms? One for trash, one for recycling?"

"I know, right?" she interjects. "So confusing! Like . . .

Fritos bags? Not really plastic, not really paper. What do you do with them?"

"I end up putting most of it in the trash," he says.

"I put most of it in the recycling," she says. "I guess that makes us trash-neutral. We cancel each other out."

"I don't know," he says. "I mean . . . Fritos? There's some serious carbon footprint there."

"Not okay?"

"Okay by me. I'm a big fan of dorm vending machines. But in the enviro-kid Olympics, those Fritos slow you way down."

Haley laughs. She laughs with her mouth open and her head back. Like someone who laughs easily and often. This conversation is not going at all as he'd intended, but he doesn't mind.

"Anyway," he continues, "I think Carrie would agree with you. That we weren't a fit."

"But you don't agree?"

"No, you're right. We weren't compatible. I'm just not the sort of person who gives up easily. Especially on relationships."

She drains her coffee. Rolls her paper napkin into a ball and stuffs it into the empty cup. "Sounds like you're not over it."

"Oh, it's over. Totally," he says. "It's just . . . recent."

Haley glances over his shoulder, breaking eye contact. Is it his imagination or has her expression clouded again?

She stands, looking around for the trash can. "That's too bad."

He's not quite sure what she means by that.

"I should go," she continues. "I have an appointment at the health clinic. One of those really useful half hours where they tell me I have a headache and eventually it will go away."

He rises. He's barely touched his coffee. "Let me guess: you think health services is useless?"

"It is what it is. But hey, thanks again. For the help."

"Any time," he says. "See you around."

Haley slouches into her backpack and heads for the exit. Before she walks out, she turns, sees that he's still watching, and waves. This little waist-level wave, sort of a half wave. It's totally goofy. And cute. Seriously cute.

She disappears through the door. Only then does it occur to him that he never got around to asking her what she and Carrie were talking about the other day.

・ ・ ・

It's almost enough. Almost.

"Want to just stay in tonight? And dance?"

"Dance party!" someone yells. Speakers blare. A window is opened. It's already hot inside.

They bear so little resemblance to their weekday selves. Their book-toting, note-taking selves. Gray-hoodie, no-makeup, coffee-chugging selves. Restrained, focused, deliberate selves.

Something within them wants to break apart.

Wants to melt into music.

・ ・ ・

7

Haley

Fritos. Did she *really* tell him she eats Fritos?

Better yet: *Get your own, Math Dude.*

There's a reason she's never had a real boyfriend. For the longest time she's been blaming it on soccer. All those weekends during high school when she was either resting up the night before a big game or traveling for tournaments? She'd never had time for boys. Never had time for those big high school parties, the illicit drink-and-make-out fests in houses where the parents were away. That's why she had to cajole one of her teammates' brothers into taking her to prom. Not because she was a complete idiot about guys—she'd just never had time to meet any.

But now it's apparent: she *is* a complete idiot about guys.

Her phone chimes. Text message.

Location change. We r @ dean of students office.

She quickly types back "*k*" and picks up the pace. Jenny asked her to come to a meeting. Didn't say what it was about, exactly. And it starts in . . . three minutes. She'd spent too much time with Cute Guy. Correction: lost track of time talking to Cute Guy.

Further correction: lost track of time embarrassing herself in front of Cute Guy. Whose name is actually Richard. Who she's already lied to. Because she didn't know how to tell him she has a rendezvous with her recently raped roommate and god knows who else from the college.

She hopes it's not Carrie. She can't look at her right now.

Because she totally, completely *gets* what Richard has (correction: had) in common with Carrie. Honestly, what straight guy wouldn't? The woman is crazy gorgeous.

Maybe she should consider switching from Fritos to tofu. How long would it take for the beautifying powers of all that health food to sink in? Could she gag it down?

When she enters the Dean of Students Office, Jenny is already there, sitting on a bench in the lobby, the ginormous backpack parked at her feet. She smiles when she sees Haley.

"Sorry I'm late," Haley begins.

"It's fine. We can go right up." Jenny stands, lifting the pack and swinging it over her shoulder with one smooth motion.

Their feet creak up the stairs. About half the buildings on campus have been remodeled to some approximation of shining, smooth efficiency. Not this one. The wooden steps are worn in the center from generations of students making the climb. The moldings around the doorjambs are thick with paint. "*Love* this building," Haley says.

"I know, right?" Jenny says. "It reminds me of my grand-mother's living room."

Haley decides not to point out that she was joking. Instead, she pauses when they come to a landing.

"So, before we go up. Why are we here?"

Jenny glances up the stairs, then back down. She looks like she's trying to decide something. Like a mouse caught, frozen, when you flick on the overhead lights.

"We're meeting with Carole Patterson," she says slowly. "There's something I want to ask you, and I thought she'd be a good person to explain it."

"Wait, who's Carole Patterson?"

"She's the person in charge whenever there's a judicial thing on campus," Jenny explains. "She coordinates every-thing." She starts walking up the stairs again.

Haley doesn't budge. "Why can't you ask me yourself?"

Jenny stops, but doesn't turn. "Can we just go up?"

"Jen. You don't always have to go through a third party with me. I don't bite."

Jenny finally turns. "I know. I'm sorry. This is just . . . a lot. Okay? It helps to have someone else explain."

"Is it just this Patterson person?"

"Yeah, I think." Jenny continues her trek up the stairs.

Haley follows.

Carole Patterson's door is ajar, her voice a friendly "Come in!" when Jenny knocks. The first thing Haley notices is a big window and a massive, flaming maple just outside. Through the fluttering leaves she glimpses a row of campus buildings, a sloping lawn, dots of students lounging on grass or throwing Frisbee.

A woman wearing khakis and black clogs crosses the room, hand extended, as they enter.

"You must be Haley," she says. As she smiles, spider-web creases fan the corners of her eyes. Her grip feels cool and powder-dusted. Like a gymnast's, preparing for a routine on the bars. "I'm Carole Patterson. Please call me Carole." She motions them to a trio of wooden college armchairs arranged in front of a bookcase.

"Great view," Haley comments as they sit.

"I think it's safe to say that's the most magnificent tree on campus," Carole agrees, her eyes wandering to the maple. "Especially this time of year."

"It looks like a migration of monarchs," Jenny says.

"I'll bet you know a lot about that," Carole says. She looks at Haley. "Your friend never ceases to amaze me with what she knows about biology."

"Me too," Haley says. "Amaze, that is."

Carole has a manila folder on her lap. She opens it, glancing quickly at the paper on top. Haley can't read what it says, but it looks like bullet points.

"How are you doing?" Carole asks Jenny. Not unkindly.

Jenny's jawline tightens. She doesn't answer.

"Have you given any more thought to taking some time off?"

"I can't take time off. I'll fall too far behind."

"Your professors would accommodate you," Carole says.

"You've spoken to my professors?"

Haley detects panic in Jenny's swift question.

"No, we would not violate your privacy that way. But the college has a policy of accommodation in cases of illness or mental distress. You could keep up with your assignments from home and—"

"I have labs; I can't do them from home." Jenny cuts her off quickly, ending the topic.

Carole's eyes return to her lap, the folder. Her face is a mask. Haley imagines that if you Googled "expressionless" and searched for images, this face would pop up. "Let me update you on where we are," Carole continues. "The respondent in your case was notified this morning. As of today, he knows that you have filed a complaint against him. He has a copy of your statement." Sharp breath from Jenny. There are tissues on an end table near Carole. She holds the box out. Jenny pulls one, dabs her eyes.

"What did he say?" she asks, voice shaky.

"I'm sorry, but I can't discuss that," Carole says. "He has three days to respond to this office, in writing, to your complaint. At that point you can read his statement."

Jenny blows her nose. Carole sits quietly.

"And then?"

"If he decides not to contest, then the college will decide what sort of sanction is in order. If he decides to challenge your complaint, then we'll proceed with an investigation and hearing."

"So what do I do until then?"

"There's nothing to do until he responds."

Jenny blinks. As if Carole has suddenly spoken to her in a foreign language. "So he's just . . . walking around," Jenny says. Asks. Haley can't tell which.

"We've discussed this," Carole returns mildly. "There's a process."

72

"I know," Jenny says quickly. "I just . . . don't want to see him."

Carole clasps her hands neatly atop the folder. "You have every reason to feel safe. Your classes don't overlap, and as of today he's restricted from entering your dorm as well as the library and dining hall you designated. You can go about your normal business."

Normal business. Process. The words jar Haley. Not only because there has been nothing "normal" or "businesslike" about her roommate lately, but also because she's gotten an earful about "process."

Just the other day she'd walked into their room moments after Jenny concluded a shout fest on the phone with her father.

"He's mad at the college, so he's yelling at me," she said before Haley had even put down her pack. Her face was red, eyes raw. Haley didn't need to ask who "he" was.

"Now Daddy Dearest wants me to file a report with the police," Jenny continued. "At least that's what his lawyer is telling him I should do. He says the college won't expel my rapist until their hearing is finished, but they *could* kick him out if a criminal investigation is underway. In other words, if I go to the cops, he's off campus. At least for a while."

Haley sat on her bed and wondered what to say. Within days of reporting the rape to the college, the pixie-cute Jenny of early September had devolved into an unkempt mess. The constant, frenetic showering following the Conundrum party had been replaced by a hygiene strike: no laundry, stringy hair, questionable tooth brushing. Formerly a library-and-lab rat, Jenny had taken to studying exclusively in their room. Eating there, too, which hadn't blended well with the sour laundry odors.

"Cops?" Haley asked.

Jenny laughed. "*Not* happening," she replied. "Do you know what they make you do? Something called a rape kit. It's . . . beyond awful. Carrie explained it. They examine you, naked, on a table. Take photos. Comb and swab every inch of you." Jenny shuddered. "Like getting raped all over again. I know it's how they collect evidence, but I can't. I just. Can't."

Haley nodded sympathetically. "No one blames you, Jenny."

Jenny snorted. "Except my dad. He thinks I'm being ridiculous. 'File a report!' he says." Jenny dropped her voice to this deep, guttural imitation. "'Get the cops to shake a confession out of this guy. None of this namby-pamby college shit!'"

"Could they?" Haley asked. "Get him to confess?"

Jenny shot her this give-me-a-break expression. "Doubtful," she said. "Meanwhile, I'd be dealing with hearings, lawyers, juries. For months. Years, even. But if I only report it to the college? A lot quicker. Carrie says it could be over by Christmas."

"Well. There's your answer," Haley said.

"Not my father's answer. Meanwhile, all my mom does is cry and beg me to go home. Like I want to come home so everyone can pressure me to go to the police?"

"Parents find ways to put the pressure on even if you're not home."

It was curious, the way her relationship with Jenny had shifted so much since the beginning of the year. Maybe it was because Haley was around more, now that she didn't have practice. Maybe because Jenny was around more. Maybe because they had something to talk about. Still, there were things Jenny wouldn't say. There was still a little bit of the scaredy-mouse in her.

Like, why did she need to ask her something in front of Carole Patterson?

As if she can read her mind, Carole turns to Haley now. "Has Jenny discussed with you what your role will be if indeed this goes to the hearing phase?"

"I have a role?" Haley asks.

A flicker of irritation crosses Carole's face. "Jenny?"

"We haven't talked about it yet," Jenny says. "I was hoping you could explain."

Glancing down at the manila folder again, Carole purses her lips to a thin line, like a pale pink slash from cheek to cheek. She produces two handouts, each stapled neatly in the upper left-hand corner. She hands one to each of them.

"Both the complainant and the respondent in a sexual assault case have the right to an advisor throughout the entirety of the process," she begins. "This is someone who may be present with them at every step along the way. Every step," she repeats, looking at Haley. "They can offer advice and support outside hearings and meetings, but not during. The advisor can be an attorney. It can also be a dean or trusted faculty member. However, Jenny wants you to be her advisor."

"Me?" Haley blurts.

"I want a friend in there with me," Jenny says. "I'm already getting lots of advice." She directs these words at Carole. As if this has already been discussed.

Carole turns to Haley. "This will be quite a commitment,"

she says. "Of time and energy. Most importantly, you must be discreet. You must not discuss these proceedings with anyone. That's harder than you think."

"Jen." Haley looks at her roommate. "I want to help. Really, I do. But wouldn't you be better off with someone who has experience with this sort of thing?"

"I want a friend," Jenny repeats. "I want someone I trust. Who *gets* what's going on around here." She stares pointedly at Carole.

"What about your chem prof?" Haley persists. "You like her. Or Carrie? Or—"

"I like my chem prof fine," Jenny interrupts, "but I barely know her. And Carrie's not allowed because she's a SART person."

Haley turns to Carole. "SART?"

"Sexual Assault Response Team," Carole explains. Her eyes betray nothing.

No one speaks for a minute. Haley can't say no. Only a total jerk would say no. And this annoys her. Because she's being asked, but she doesn't really have a choice.

"I think you should reconsider, but if not, then . . . okay," Haley says.

Relief spreads across Jenny's face.

Without another word, Carole produces one more sheet from the folder, handing it to Haley. She also glances at her wristwatch.

"This is a confidentiality agreement that you must sign in order to be Jenny's advisor. Please read it thoroughly before you sign. Any discussion of this case outside the proceedings is a code of conduct violation.

"The sections of the handbook I've printed out for you detail every step of the sexual assault hearing process," she continues. "Until the respondent answers the claim there's no action pending, but in the interim please take a look at these pages and familiarize yourselves with what lies ahead in the event of a hearing. Haley, I've highlighted the sections in your packet defining the role of the advisor." She looks at them expectantly. "Do you have any questions you'd like to ask me?"

Haley suppresses the urge to laugh. Is she kidding? Several zillion questions flood her brain, all elbowing each other out of the way so she can't focus on a single one. "Can I call you if I think of something?"

"Certainly," Carole answers.

"Actually, I have a question," Jenny says. Carole turns to her. "About the confidentiality. I can talk to Haley, right?"

"Well, yes. Since she's your advisor. But Jenny, we have excellent counseling services here at the college if you need someone to talk to."

"What about the SART leaders? The ones who took my call? Do they count as counselors?"

Carole looks uncomfortable for the first time. "Think of the Sexual Assault Response Team as the ambulance. They are first responders. Now it's time for the doctors to take over. Your best resources are trained counselors, Jenny. Not other students."

Jenny doesn't look happy with this answer.

Carole stands, so they do, too.

"I'll be in touch as soon as we have the response." She turns to Haley. "You may return the signed confidentiality form to my assistant. Thanks for coming in."

In the hall outside Carole Patterson's closed door, Jenny drops her pack and throws her arms around Haley.

"Thank you!" Jenny whispers fiercely in Haley's ear. "Thank you so much!"

Haley's head swims as they descend the stairs. The groaning wood is practically verbal. *Stu-pid! Stu-pid!* each step seems to say. What has she just agreed to? She'd been totally caught off guard.

And scaredy-mouse managed to get what she wanted.

． ． ．

Boxes, bottles, cases, hauled inside: he begins.

The lemonade hisses softly as he pours it into the plastic garbage can. A cloud of yellow dust rises: four containers. Then, water: six gallon jugs. The air in the room smells sweet.

When he unscrews the vodka and begins draining whole bottles into the can, they take notice. Low whistles, laughter. The can slowly fills. He calls for someone to bring in the first case of beer.

He pops a can, pours.

"Stand back and watch the doctor at work, boys," Exley says.

． ． ．

8

RICHARD

When Richard hears the soft knock on his door late that night, he doesn't move. Seated at his desk, his hands freeze above the keyboard of his laptop where he's been tapping out a paper. The handle turns, and his door opens a crack.

Seriously, though?

It's Jordan. Who looks awful.

"Can I come in?" Jordan asks. As he walks in. Space is tight, pretty much just a rectangle with enough square footage for a bed, chair, desk, and dresser. Jordan sits on the bed.

"What's up?" Richard asks. This is not Jordan's usual Wednesday night face. For one thing, he's sober. Wednesday is pool shots at Taylor: full shot glasses positioned at each of the six holes of their basement pool table, and your opponent had to drink whenever you pocketed a ball. You had to drink two shots if you scratched.

Richard hardly plays anymore. At the beginning of the semester he'd made a point of heading down to the basement on Wednesday nights after he returned from tutoring. A treat, he told himself, following hours helping frosh with their problem sets. But a month into it, with Thursday morning classes a hungover torture, it didn't feel like much of a treat. Felt more like an expectation. Especially since if he decided to pass he had to endure rude comments the following day about his absence. Especially from "the Doctor."

He'd used Carrie and Wednesday nights at her place as his excuse. "I know you want me, Exley, but she's hotter than you," Richard fired back one morning when Exley's smack talk was too much to handle. A bunch of the other guys were around and they laughed. The Doctor backed off after that, but they both knew: lines had been drawn.

Jordan had never joined in with Exley's goading, but he'd never defended Richard, either. Jordan was a Wednesday night regular, scheduling no class on Thursday before ten a.m. Richard suspected he chose his major based on which ones offered the most afternoon classes.

"Shots canceled tonight?" Richard asks.

"Shots?" Jordan looks puzzled. "I didn't go. My parents are in town."

Parents Weekend is still a ways off. "Is everything okay?"

Jordan runs his hand through his hair. "Listen, I have to ask you something. Do you remember last week, when you and I were talking about the Conundrum party?"

"And finishing off that Blue Moon we found in the fridge," Richard says.

"I told you about that girl I met? The freshman?"

Richard nods.

"Did you repeat that to anyone?"

Richard tries to remember what Jordan said. Something about fish. Something about Country Time lemonade. He definitely remembers Jordan bragging about getting laid that night.

"I don't think so." Richard doesn't tell him he's been too preoccupied licking his wounds over Carrie to get around to publicizing Jordan's sexual exploits.

"Well, did you or didn't you?" Jordan demands. "I need you to be sure."

"Whoa." Richard puts his hands up. "I'm *sure* I did not repeat what you said."

Relief spreads over Jordan's face.

"Mind telling me what's up with you tonight?"

"I just need to know, okay? Something's going on."

A boulder of dread thuds in Richard's gut. More damage, this time at Conundrum? His parents can't handle another fat bill arriving in their mailbox. Or maybe the college heard about the party and decided to kick them all out of housing. Would it help that he wasn't there, or would they not care?

Then Jordan surprises him.

"So that girl," Jordan says, "the one I told you about? She's telling people I raped her."

Richard's shock feels cold. His brain goes numb, processes in slow motion. Responding, in words, is not an option.

"Late last night, I'm checking my e-mail," Jordan continues, "and I see a message from the Dean of Students Office, telling me I need to be at a meeting there at eight o'clock this morning. Didn't say why exactly, just that I had to be there to talk about violating community standards or something. I assumed it was more stuff about dorm damage. But I asked a few of the other guys and none of them got the e-mail. Just me.

"So I go there and they send me in to see this woman named Carole Patterson. She tells me I've been reported for sexual misconduct. She says I have three days to respond to the charges, and then the college is going to investigate." Jordan tosses his hands up. "I was like, what? I mean, it took a minute for this to sink in. The woman's, like, blah blahing at me, talking about process or something, I don't know, I just keep hearing the word 'process,' and finally I say to her, 'Hold on. Somebody is accusing me of *rape*? I thought this was more about the dorm damage!' And she basically says yeah, and I'm scrolling back in my mind to what I've been doing and who I've been with the last few weeks, because you'd think if you *raped* somebody, you'd kind of know it. But I'm drawing a complete blank, so I ask her, 'Who the hell is saying this?' And she tells me it's that girl who came to our party last weekend. She's telling them I forced her to have sex, and now the college is doing this whole investigation."

It occurs to Richard that this is the moment when hidden cameras are revealed and people jump out from behind closed doors shouting about how it's all a joke. Because this can't be real. Jordan and the guys are messing with him not only for ditching the party last week, but also for blowing off shots tonight.

But Jordan's teasing drawl is absent. In the close room, he smells like fear. It's metallic and blue-edge sharp.

"That's messed up, man." Richard doesn't know what else to say.

Jordan laughs. A short, cutting sound. His face, in the desk lamp light, contains shadows. He looks exhausted. "No shit." He shakes his head from side to side, as if he can't believe his own words.

"What are you going to do?"

"Just spent the last three hours in a hotel room with my parents discussing that. They pretty much flew up the highway with my lawyer uncle right after I called them."

"They brought a lawyer?"

"Uncle Bruce," Jordan says, "who's a real hard-ass. Until you need a hard-ass. I wasn't a big fan of his advice."

"Which was . . . ?"

"He wants me to fold," Jordan says, spitting out the words. "Can you believe it? He says colleges hate this sort of thing and just want to make the problem go away. He says all a girl has to do these days is point her little finger and *bam!* Dude's expelled. He says I should withdraw. 'Don't argue with them!' he says. 'Get while the going's good, start fresh somewhere else. Withdraw before they even begin their investigation and your record is clean.' "

"Do your parents want you to withdraw?"

Jordan makes this sound, like a snort. "My dad's all over the map. He keeps saying stuff like, 'But Jordan's a legacy! A double legacy!' Like MacCallum cares that he and Mom are alums? Like his crappy thousand-dollar-a-year donation makes a difference? Give me a break. My mother just keeps boo-hooing."

Richard tries not to react to this. Even with financial aid, his parents struggle to pay his tuition. And forget about donations. "So what are you going to do?" he repeats.

"Here's what I'm *not* going to do: act like I did it and withdraw," Jordan says. "I didn't rape that girl, and I'm sure as hell not slinking out of here like I did. I mean, think about it. If I quit and don't defend myself? I don't just look guilty, I look like some chickenshit, running away!"

"Can't argue with that," Richard says.

"Hell no."

They sit quietly for a moment. Then Jordan clears his throat.

"So I'm going to fight it. I'll tell Carole Patterson, in writing, that I didn't rape Jenny James."

Jenny. It's the first time Richard's heard Jordan give the girl a name.

"Thing is . . ." Jordan pauses.

Richard feels his chest tighten. Here it comes. Jordan wants something.

"My uncle," Jordan begins.

"The hard-ass."

"Yes, him. Uncle Hard-ass." Jordan attempts to smile, but it doesn't stick. "He says if I decide to fight the charge, I can't say that I had sex with her."

"How are you going to manage that? Since you did."

"See, that's what I need you to forget."

Richard is not sure he's heard correctly. "I'm sorry?"

Jordan sits forward on the edge of the bed.

"Listen, Richard. Just do me a favor, okay? Don't tell

anybody I was with Jenny. If you're asked, tell them you didn't go to the party and don't know anything about what went down that night."

He hears roaring. Distant, like something loud very far away. It reminds him of when he was a child at the beach and held a conch shell to his ear. "Wait a minute. Are you telling me you plan to *lie* about this? And what, you want me to cover for you? What the hell, Jordan?"

Richard stands. He's no crusader. Unlike Carrie and the people she hangs with, he's never stood on a street corner and held up a banner, or signed some pointless online petition. In Carrie's eyes, that indifference was a big strike against him. He can live with that.

But he's not a liar. And he can't live with becoming one for Jordan Bockus, no matter how innocent he might be.

Jordan waves him off. "Is it a lie to say you skipped out on the party to be with your girlfriend? Sounds like the truth to me."

"What if I'm asked what you said?"

"No one will ask you what I said."

"And what about when they ask you?"

"I'll say 'I did not rape Jenny James.' Because I didn't." Jordan sits back, arms folded across his chest, and waits for Richard's reaction.

"You're kidding, right?"

"Not kidding. Uncle Hard-ass's advice."

"That's it? You go in front of some, I don't know, tribunal? And they ask you questions and all you say is 'I didn't rape Jenny'?"

"Pretty much."

"Your uncle's an idiot, man. You'll look guilty as hell."

"That's what I told him. But he changed my mind."

"Oh? How'd he do that?"

"It's a long story and I'm sick of talking about it. All I need to know is: can I count on you?"

Richard pauses. None of this feels right to him. He's sorry they ever cracked open those Blue Moons. Or talked about any of this.

"You can count on me to tell the truth. Totally," Richard says. "Anybody asks, I'll tell them I didn't go to the party, I was with my girlfriend that night, and I've never laid eyes on this Jenny person. But if I'm asked what you *told me* . . ."

"No one's going to ask you that, Richard," Jordan says quietly.

"If I'm asked what you told me," Richard repeats, "I'm not going to lie. I will answer the direct question."

He fully expects to see anger on Jordan's face, but instead Jordan seems to be weighing what Richard says. As if this is not as bad, nor as good, as he'd hoped to get out of him.

Then Jordan stands. He puts his hand out. It's an oddly formal gesture. Richard, surprised, extends his, and they shake.

"That's all anybody's asking. Thanks, man." Jordan steps to the door, hand on knob.

"So what now?" Richard can't resist asking.

"She wrote out this whole description of what happened— talk about fantasy, I don't know *what* planet that girl is from— and I have to respond, in writing, in a few days. My uncle says keep it simple. Just say: not guilty. But man, there's a part of me that wants to set the record straight. Seriously, she is out of her mind."

Something occurs to Richard. He should probably edit what follows, but it slips out.

"Was Exley messing with the drinks that night?"

Jordan looks confused for a moment. When it dawns on him what Richard is implying, a brief flicker of anger passes over his face. He replaces it, quickly, with a familiar mocking smile.

"No. And for the record, I don't need to roofie some girl to get a little action." Jordan opens the door, but before he steps into the hall he turns to Richard. "Of course, you didn't just hear that," he says, winking.

Jordan leaves, the door clicking quietly behind him.

· · ·

Tamra, one of the girls from the hall, motions them into her room. The beds are lofted high, bunked at angles to create more space. The walls are papered with bright posters, a state flag, photographs. They hide the old tack holes and tape traces of girls who came before.

Jenny hasn't been in this room. Until now.

Tamra closes the door. She holds a long paper bag. From it she pulls a clear bottle with a silver-and-red label.

"Pregame, ladies," she says.

· · ·

9

Haley

Part of Haley is totally psyched to find Carrie sprawled on her bed when she opens the door. She knows it's voyeuristic, semistalking, in a way. But she's crazy curious about her and Richard, and has been wondering if she'll get a chance to squeeze some info out of her.

Another part of Haley just wants to cry. She'd come back in order to sleep. She gets so tired in the afternoons. Jen's usually at the lab this time of day; their room should be empty. Instead, Carrie the Viking is here. With her friend. Gail. Who's stretched out on Jenny's bed.

Jenny's nowhere in sight.

"Hey," Carrie says, smiling brightly at Haley. Her teeth are miraculously aligned pearls. She's reading, propped up on one elbow, long legs crossed, shoes off. Colorful socks Haley recognizes from the organic cotton rack at the food co-op.

"Hi." Haley drops her pack. "How'd you get in here?" Jenny's gotten fanatical about locking their door.

"Jenny let us in. She had to run out to drop off a paper, but she'll be back," Gail says.

Great. Haley concentrates on not looking pissed off. She opens the mini-fridge and pulls out a bottle of water, careful not to slam it shut. *Another meeting of the Victim's Support Club. When did my room become headquarters?*

She knows this isn't fair. But no one around here seems to get how crummy *she* feels.

It's gotten bad enough that the other day she called her mother.

"What's going on?" Mom said when she answered. She didn't bother to mask her surprise. Or say hello. It wasn't often that Haley's number came up on caller ID.

"Hey," Haley began, then stopped. *Oh my god. I'm going to cry.*

She couldn't remember the last time she'd cried to her mother. That behavior belonged to a different era. She remembered it. Being a little girl, believing her mother was the most amazing person in the world. Telling her everything. When you're little, if you don't tell your mother, it's like it never happened.

She can't remember when, or why, this changed. There was no big scene, no single issue. Just a feeling that something no longer fit, like a cotton T-shirt that spent too much time in the dryer. A disagreement over something small that became a gradual hardening of positions. A tone that became habit. One morning you just woke up and realized no way in hell would you tell your mother anything. At least, not anything that mattered.

So the call surprised them both.

"Is something wrong?" Haley heard, which brought on a gush of tears.

She still wasn't right, she explained. She felt . . . third person-ish. Detached. Like she was an observer rather than a participant in her own life. She had tons of work: reading, papers, math she should be knocking out but instead took her hours. She'd read a sentence only to realize she couldn't repeat back to you what it meant. Worse yet, reading gave her headaches. She kept falling asleep in the library, falling asleep in lectures. And even though her deans had given her plenty of accommodations, she was more and more stressed over the growing mountain of missed deadlines.

And then there was Jenny. She told her about Jenny. She had no idea whether that was forbidden or not, but she didn't care. It wasn't as if her mother were going to spread the word around campus. So she spilled: from the night it happened to Carrie and Gail and right on down to Carole Patterson. She told her about the advisor thing. She told her about Jenny always being in the room now. Needing to talk.

For once, her mother didn't interrupt. When she finished, there was silence. Haley wondered if they'd been disconnected. But then her mother spoke.

"I'm going to say something and I don't want you to take it the wrong way. But I'm your mother, and my primary concern is *you*.

"First: you need a room change. A single. I'm going to call your dean and get the ball rolling on that. You need sleep and rest, and while I'm terribly sorry about what's happened to Jenny, the last thing you need right now is a roommate in crisis."

Haley sniffled. "Mom, no—"

"Second," her mother continued, oblivious to the interruption, "you need to contact that Carole person and tell her under no circumstances can you be involved in this case. You are not well and cannot make this commitment. Besides, it's ridiculous. That girl needs an adult from the college to help her!"

"Mom, it's not like that. She already has adults involved. Plus her parents, which is a whole other issue. I think she just needs a friend. She doesn't know a lot of people."

"Well, can't that rape crisis person be her friend? What'd you say her name was? Casey?"

"Carrie. I don't know. Frankly, I think Jenny could use a break from Carrie."

"Sounds like you need a break from Jenny."

"Mom. She's been raped."

"I know this sounds cold, but that's simply not your problem. Your health needs to be your focus right now. Promise me you will extricate yourself from this."

She had called for conversation and support, and instead got directives. Typical.

Why did she think talking to her mother was a good idea? When it came to their relationship, Haley felt like a dog that eats its own vomit. She knows it will be awful, but she keeps returning for more.

"Fine," Haley said. "I'll talk to Carole as long as you promise not to contact housing. I want to handle that myself." They ended the call soon after that.

She never called housing. And her only contact with

Carole Patterson was to sign the confidentiality forms and leave them at her office. She doesn't know what to do about her growing mountain of work, lingering pain, and lack of privacy, but ditching Jenny is not the solution.

Of course, finding Carrie Mason in her room when her head is pounding sure makes her think twice about a single.

Gail sits up. The tiniest pinhead of a diamond pierces her nose, and her lips are glossed Ripe Raspberry. Her kohl-lined eyes, Cleopatra-esque, are a dramatic yin to Carrie's makeup-free yang. "Hey, Jenny told us you're going to be her advisor at the hearing. Good for you!"

"Have we heard there's definitely going to be a hearing?" Haley drinks from her bottle. "I didn't know he'd responded yet."

"No, not yet, but we're kind of assuming." Gail looks at Carrie.

"God, I hope so!" Carrie says. She bounces up. "It'd be anticlimactic if the creep just ran away."

"Got away, more like," Gail says. "If he withdraws voluntarily, he can enroll in another college and prey on other victims. He needs to get taken down."

"But isn't it better for Jenny if he leaves? She wouldn't have to go through some trial," Haley says. *I wouldn't have to go through some trial.*

"It might be easier for her in the short term, but is that closure?" Carrie asks. "Is that justice? Months or even years from now, will she regret that her attacker never had to own up to what he did? That he might have even gone on to rape again?"

"See, that's why she really needs to go to the police," Gail says. "I'm with her father there. If he slips through the college process, they can go after him another way."

"That train has left the station," Carrie says, not bothering to hide the disappointment in her voice. "Without a rape kit there's not much the cops can do. And it's too late for that."

Buzz saw. That's how this feels. Haley's been in her room less than two minutes and the whirl of words sounds—and feels—like a saw in her head.

She really can't handle it right now.

"You know, guys, I'm sorry to interrupt this little strategy session, but I was hoping to get some shut-eye." *Boundaries*, she thinks. *You're not being a bitch; you're setting boundaries.*

That had been her father's suggestion. He'd called her. The night after her failed conversation with Mom.

"I understand you feel responsible for this girl," he'd said. "But you need to look out for yourself as well. Set boundaries. Say what *you* need. Even if it feels awkward, you're better off. You'll avoid doing things you resent."

Dad has always been big into boundaries. He claims most of the dysfunction in their family is the result of poor boundary-setting.

"I'm sorry," Gail says immediately. "We'll get out of your hair." She and Carrie begin to pick up their stuff and make for the door.

"You don't have to wait in the hall. I just don't need some therapy session going on in here right now is all." She sees Gail flash Carrie a look. But they don't comment. Instead, they re-settle on Jenny's bed.

Her bed now vacant, Haley stretches out. She'll shut the blinds once they leave. Sleep as long as she needs to. Right through dinner, if necessary.

Someone's phone pings. Text. Not hers; she turned the sound off.

It's Carrie's. She hears her make this annoyed sound, a semigroan, when she reads it.

"Let me guess: lover boy? Still whining?" Gail asks.

Carrie laughs. "No. It's Mona. They've rescheduled the house meeting *again*."

Gail tsk-tsks in disappointment. "Too bad. I've missed those heartrending pleas for your forgiveness."

"Yeah, you're the only one." Carrie snorts. "I was *this close* to reporting him for stalking."

Gail winks at Haley. "Some women call them 'admirers.' Carrie calls them 'stalkers.'" Carrie fake-punches her. "Give him a break," Gail says. "You broke his heart."

"Misogynists don't have hearts."

"Okay, if you two are going to keep me up, you at least have to tell me who you're talking about," Haley says. But she knows.

"This absolutely *adorable* young thang Carrie was sleeping with," Gail says, barely able to conceal the glee in her voice.

"Please," Carrie says. "I'm really not proud of this."

"Two years younger and, ooh, hot," Gail continues. "For a white boy, that is." This makes Carrie laugh.

"I didn't take you for a cougar, Carrie," Haley says.

"Carrie the Coug!" Gail exclaims. "Oh, I like that!"

"Thanks, Haley," Carrie mutters. "The last thing she needed was more ammunition."

"Spill," Haley persists.

"What can I tell you?" Gail says. "He was the latest on the Carrie Mason love-'em-and-leave-'em list. Seriously, Carrie, you will leave a trail of tears behind when you graduate."

"Trail of mistakes, you mean."

"I should have made your mistakes," Gail says, sighing.

"I still don't know what happened," Haley says.

"I led with my libido is what happened," Carrie says matter-of-factly. "Which usually isn't a problem, unless the guy in question gets serious and wants a relationship. Which this guy did. Turns out he's a complete Neanderthal. *And* a stalker. When I told him it was over, he started following me! Seriously, I saw him pop up in places I know were not part of his schedule. Plus he was texting me nonstop. Wanting to talk. I was one text away from going to campus security about him, but then he quit. Just bam, nothing. Finally got the message, I guess."

"You are harsh, girl," Gail says. "She doesn't realize the effect she has on men, so she's all surprised when they can't let her go."

Carrie sits up when Gail says this. The teasing expression has left her face, and she suddenly seems serious.

"Truth? An unwanted 'admirer' is like an unwanted pregnancy. I haven't been busting my butt in college to get all entangled with some guy—I'm here for an education. If I were a man, people would call me career-focused. But instead, I'm, what? A tease? A heartbreaker?"

Before Gail can comment, the door opens. Jenny. Her face brightens when she finds them all in the room.

"Hey, sorry that took a while. The professor was there and we started talking. Hi, Haley."

Carrie and Gail are already off the bed.

"Why don't we head out? Give your roommate some privacy," Carrie says.

Jenny nods, and the three of them walk out the door.

"See you, Haley," Gail says.

Haley waves to them, closing her eyes in relief.

Although now, sleep isn't really a possibility.

．　．　．

When his masterpiece nears the lip of the can, Exley tops it with a bag of ice. Then, he tests.

He dips a red cup, the ladle of the evening. He drinks. They watch, but he is unreadable as ever. He drinks again, a quenching pull that drains the cup. He looks at them.

"We're in business," he announces.

They fall upon it.

Cups brimming, cool and sweet. They drink, long and deep. It courses down their throats and spreads warmly: up their spines and across their shoulders, their necks, the backs of their heads. Behind their eyes. The room changes. Everything moves to a new rhythm.

．　．　．

10

RICHARD

The man leaning against the Audi parked outside Taylor House doesn't need to introduce himself. Jordan's resemblance to his uncle is uncanny.

"Excuse me, are you Richard Brandt?" He wears khakis and a black Polo shirt. The mallet-wielding horseback rider on the left side of the chest is purple.

Richard has finished classes for the day. This is when he usually returns to the house, changes, and goes for a run.

Uncle Hard-ass was the last thing he expected to find waiting for him.

"Uh, yeah," Richard says.

The man extends his hand. "Bruce Bockus," he says. "I'm Jordan's uncle. I hope you don't mind my dropping by unexpectedly. I wonder if we could talk? Somewhere private?" Uncle Bruce's grip is firm. A little too firm.

"Where's Jordan?"

"He's in class. He won't be joining us."

Richard shifts his weight from one foot to another. "Does Jordan know you're here?"

"He told me where I could find you."

"Yeah. Well." Richard glances at his watch. "I don't have a lot of time. I was about to go running, then I have to grab some dinner before math tutoring."

Uncle Bruce puts up both hands, palms facing out. "I just need a few minutes."

Richard breathes out heavily. "I guess we can talk in the common room. Usually no one's around this time of day."

"As long as it's private," Uncle Bruce says.

Richard presses his lips in a thin line. "It's as private as we're going to get." He has no intention of inviting this guy up to his room.

The first floor common area is empty. Richard leads Uncle Bruce to a couple of armchairs in a back corner. It's sunny, and in full view of the entrance. They sit.

"I understand Jordan has told you about what's going on," Uncle Bruce begins.

Richard nods but doesn't say anything.

"Jordan tells me you might have some concerns. In case you're asked any questions."

Richard decides to cut through the bullshit. "Mind telling me why you're here?" He knows how this sounds. He doesn't care. He's annoyed.

He's been annoyed all day, actually. Most of last night, too. After Jordan left, he had trouble sleeping. He had trouble thinking about anything but their conversation, turning it over and over in his mind, imagining things he'd rather not.

It had been a hookup, right? That's how Jordan described it. He could picture it: dark, loud, crowded, everybody wasted on whatever Exley had mixed that night. It's how these parties rolled, every weekend. The expectations were clear, the music predictable, the outcomes mutually satisfying. For guys and girls alike.

What went wrong? Because happy hookups don't end with someone crying rape.

He's sorry Jordan ever mentioned it. He feels lucky that he was at Carrie's that night and never stepped foot in the Conundrum party.

So why does he feel like he's getting sucked into the black hole of Jordan's mess?

Uncle Bruce laughs. "Fair enough," he says, but his expression has changed. Politeness has been replaced by something hard-edged.

"Because I'm not involved," Richard says. "I wasn't around the night this happened. I just live in the same house as Jordan. Along with twenty other guys. So what's up?"

Uncle Bruce sits forward in his chair. His knees practically touch Richard's. "You're not involved. Except you are one of only two people my nephew confided in about having sexual intercourse with someone that night."

"Listen, Jordan and I talked. I get that you don't want me to go around blabbing what he said. I didn't, and I won't. As far as I'm concerned, the less I say and the less I know, the better."

"That's good, Richard. I just want to make sure you understand why this is so important."

"I understand."

"Jordan seems to think you were concerned that he wanted you to lie for him. I'm here to assure you that no one wants you to lie."

"Like I told Jordan last night: I don't blab. But I don't lie. I'll keep my mouth shut, but if someone puts me on the witness stand and asks me what I know, I'll repeat what Jordan told me."

"Then we have to ensure that you never make it to the so-called witness stand," Uncle Bruce says.

Something about this doesn't sound comforting. "Excuse me?"

"We think we've figured out how to keep you off the list of witnesses. You'd never have to testify about anything."

"Oh? What's that?"

"Against my advice," Uncle Bruce explains, "Jordan is going to challenge this charge. Which is going to be a real shit-show. I don't want to tell you how poorly prepared colleges are to deal with this sort of thing. Plagiarism, dorm damage, public drunkenness—easy enough. But it's ridiculous to expect a kangaroo court of deans and dining services staff to adjudicate violent crime.

"But Jordan wants to fight. And according to the college handbook, both he and his accuser are entitled to have an advisor with them throughout the process. Hearings, interviews, anything related to the investigation, the student can have his or her advisor right there, on hand. Now, this advisor can't be a parent, but it can be a lawyer, faculty member, or dean. Or friend. So we thought of you."

Uncle Bruce has been blathering for so long that when

he suddenly stops speaking, the room is eerily quiet. Which makes what he's said feel even more like a gut punch.

"Me . . . What?" Richard asks.

"You for Jordan's advisor."

"Yeah, right," Richard says without hesitation. "Give me a break."

"I'm not joking."

"Sure you are." Richard stands. "This whole conversation's a joke. What part of 'I wasn't there, I'm not involved' do you not get?"

"Richard, please sit and hear me out."

"I think we're done."

"All you'd have to do is attend a few meetings with Jordan."

"I don't have time to go to meetings with Jordan."

"You'd just sit there."

"I don't have time to sit. I'm a busy guy."

"Richard, this is a good solution for you. If you're Jordan's advisor, the investigator would probably never question you."

"Why would he question me? I wasn't there!"

"You never know."

"And for the record: you all seem super worried about what I might say."

"You bet I am. I'm trying to make sure orange jumpsuits don't become a permanent fixture in my nephew's wardrobe."

It takes a second for his meaning to sink in, but when it does . . . Richard sits. Uncle Bruce runs one hand over his face, rubbing his eyes. He suddenly looks very tired.

"You think Jordan's guilty." The words slip past Richard's lips unintentionally.

"No. But I do think he stands a very good chance of being expelled. In a court of law, you have to find someone guilty 'beyond a reasonable doubt.' At a college hearing? You're guilty if 'the preponderance of the evidence' suggests it's more likely than not that you did it. That's a low bar. Guys like Jordan are getting thrown out every day. I'm sure some are guilty as hell. I'm also sure some are not."

"Is that why you told him to withdraw?" Richard asks.

"If he withdraws, he starts fresh, with nothing on his record. If he's kicked out for sexual assault, I can't think of another school that'd take him."

"Jordan says he didn't do it, and if he withdraws he looks guilty."

Uncle Bruce makes an impatient noise. "Listen, Richard, I'm going to be brutally honest with you. If he were my son, his room would be packed up and we'd be halfway down the highway by now. He thinks he has a chance of winning this, and since nobody ever says no to him, his parents are letting him try. Jordan is unfamiliar with consequences. He has no clue what's waiting for him.

"So at this point, I just want to keep him out of jail. You see, we don't know if this woman plans to go to the police and pursue criminal charges. Maybe she's already started that process, maybe not. But she could, at any time. Even months from now. And if she did, all the testimony from the college hearing could be used against him in a criminal court."

Uncle Bruce looks at him meaningfully. But Richard is slow to understand why any of this has anything to do with him.

"Richard," he finally says, "she needs physical evidence or a confession to prove rape. Let's not hand her a confession."

It's as if a light flicks on and he finally gets why Jordan's uncle is here.

"Listen, Mr. Bockus—"

"Call me Bruce."

"Yeah . . . To be brutally honest with *you*: I don't want to be Jordan's advisor. It makes it look like I'm on his side. And I'm not on any side, you know? I don't know what went down, and I don't want any part of it."

"Believe it or not, Richard, I know exactly how you feel," Uncle Bruce says. "But here's the fact: you are involved. You got involved the second Jordan confided in you."

Richard sighs. He doesn't like this guy. But he's right. The stink of this is all over him, whether he wants it or not. Damn Jordan. Damn this whole freakin' house. What a complete and utter fail. He wishes he had sucked it up with a random basement single somewhere. "How much of a time commitment are we looking at?"

"Not much. You don't even have to go to every meeting or hearing. Just a few, show the flag a bit. It'll all be over before the semester ends."

Richard glances out the window. The afternoon sun slants low; he'll have to skip either his run or dinner if he's going to make it to tutoring on time. Damn.

"All right. I'll do it," he says.

"Thank you," Uncle Bruce says. The relief is evident on his face. He stands. "I'm meeting Jordan for dinner before I head out tonight. He'll be pleased." He shakes Richard's hand.

He also reaches into his pocket and produces a card, which he thrusts at Richard. "I'll be in touch. But in case you have any concerns or questions, you can reach me at these numbers."

Uncle Bruce turns to leave. Richard thinks of something.

"You said I'm one of two. Who's the other person Jordan told?"

Uncle Bruce smiles. "I thought you said the less you know the better." He turns on his heel and walks out of the building.

• • •

Tamra measures a shot from the bottle and pours it into a plastic cup. She tops it with Gatorade.

"Here." She hands it to Jenny. Green liquid. Jenny sips. It tastes like lime with something else. It's sweet.

In the long mirror adhered to the back of the door, Jenny glimpses a girl. She wears eye makeup. Her hair is loose.

For a moment, she doesn't recognize herself in someone else's dress.

• • •

11

Haley

It's Haley's favorite time of day. Always has been, but especially now, with the light soft, the sky streaked salmon, purple, and blue. The chapel carillon chimes late afternoon.

She decides to go for a walk along the river path. She hasn't been cleared to exercise yet and imagines a new softness around the waistband of her jeans. She also needs a break. From her room. Her roommate.

Because he responded today. Jordan. He finally has a name, although her learning that was an accident. Jenny was so upset, she actually thrust the paper with his response and his name on it into Haley's hands the moment she walked into their room.

"In response to the claim of sexual assault made against me by Jennifer Louise James, I, Jordan Joseph Bockus, attest that I am innocent of the charge," Haley read aloud while Jenny paced. She placed the sheet on the desk.

Jordan Bockus. Haley didn't know him.

"Uh . . . okay," Haley said quietly. "What did you expect? That he'd fold and say, 'Yup. Guilty as charged'?"

"I didn't expect *nothing*!" Jenny exclaimed. "I wrote two full pages, single-spaced, explaining exactly what happened that night, and he basically responded, 'She's lying.' As if what I claim doesn't even deserve an answer!"

"Jen. He'll answer. He has to. There are going to be plenty of people asking him tons of questions."

"You should have seen the look on Carole's face when she gave this to me! I could tell she was pretty pissed."

"Carole Patterson expresses emotion? What's that like?"

Jenny was not in the mood to pick up on humor cues. "I asked, 'Is this unusual?' and she just said the respondent can say as much or as little as he wants, as long as he answers the charge. But I could tell she was surprised. And not in a good way." Jenny paced faster, which was no small thing in their tiny double.

Then her phone rang. Jenny grabbed it off the windowsill where she'd left it. She glanced at the caller ID, then slid her thumb across the screen to answer.

"Hey. So, he responded. You're not going to believe it." Jenny's eyes darted, searching. "I'll read it to you. Trust me, it won't take long."

Haley pointed to the desk.

Jenny snatched up the paper. "Carrie? Here, I've got it."

Haley didn't stay to listen. The perfect sunset beckoned. She grabbed her Windbreaker and headed out.

The river path is far from the athletic fields. At this time of day that part of campus is a hive: field hockey, football, men's and women's soccer. She walks along the road in the opposite direction for a few hundred yards, then turns onto a well-trodden grassy lane. Prime NARP territory: Nonathlete Regular People. Those who run for the hell of it, who enjoy the scenery out here. The other day she saw a fox. At first she thought it was a cat, but the plush red tail gave it away.

I'm a NARP now. Or not. She still "supports from the bench," so to speak, although she's begged off that for a while. The bright, slanting sun in the afternoon kills her, making it agony to watch the action on the field. So she's excused from practices, skips games . . . How is she on the team? She doesn't go out with the other girls at night anymore. Mostly because she needs to sleep, but also because she's not around when they make their plans—not to mention that she shouldn't drink. They eat as a team, late, practically as the dining hall is shutting down; she's been going earlier. Dinners have been a drag, actually. She can usually put her plate down with some of the other girls from the hall, but it's not like they're close. She barely knows them. From day one, when she arrived on campus two weeks early for preseason, it's been all about the team.

And it's not like Jenny's company. She haunts their room, skittering out for classes, grabbing food to bring back. Occasionally, like tonight, she'll agree to eat with Carrie and Gail in Main dining hall. The college has ordered this Jordan to only eat at the Grille or the small dining hall near the library.

Jordan. Isn't that a girl's name? At any rate, now she won't just think of him as the Guy Who Raped Jenny.

Less than a mile along the path, she hears fast steps approaching from behind. Haley moves to one side to make way for the runner. He doesn't turn as he trots by, but she recognizes the hair.

"Math Dude!"

Instantly horrified. Did she really just say that? She must have a subconscious death wish when it comes to guys. Or him.

He pivots, continues backward a few steps, surprise on his face.

She expects a quick wave, that's it. That's what you do when you're running: acknowledge people you know, but never stop. You don't interrupt the daily run; she gets that.

So when he comes to a full stop and jogs toward her, she's unprepared.

"Soccer Girl," he says, grinning. "Fancy meeting you out here."

"Former Soccer Girl," she corrects him.

"Right," he says. "Haley."

"Richard."

That's it. Neither of them speaks for a moment. Richard breathes hard.

"So. Going for a run?" she says. *Wow. You're a genius, Haley. Let's see: he's sweating, wearing running shoes, running . . . Obviously he's out here doing crossword puzzles.*

Luckily, if Richard Brandt—yes, she Facebook-stalked him and figured out his last name—thinks she is a complete idiot, he disguises it well. He glances at the trail ahead.

"I'm headed to the water tower. Want to join me?"

"I can't. Still not cleared to run."

"Catch you on the way back?"

The water tower is about a mile away.

"Sure," she says.

He takes off. Pretty brisk pace. Pretty cute butt.

"Dare to dream, girl." She actually says it out loud to Richard's retreating back. Never. Never in twenty zillion years would one of Carrie Mason's leftovers give her a second thought. Guys like that are used to . . . more. Experience. Beauty. Know-how. Of which she has absolutely none.

She'd be better off with a freshman like herself. Some eighteen-year-old who'd be oh-so-grateful for even the least bit of action. Not some hot sophomore used to sleeping with the most desirable woman on campus. Different set of expectations there. And there's no way in hell she can meet them.

She decides to turn back, get off the path, and head to the dining hall before he has a chance to catch up with her and she has a chance to further embarrass herself. But before she's fully retraced her route, she hears his returning steps. He slows alongside her, panting.

"Did you decide not to go all the way?" she asks.

"No, I did." The hair near the nape of his neck stands up in little soaked spikes. His gray T-shirt is dark beneath his arms, around his neck. "Double-timed it. How are you?"

"Good," she says.

"I run here all the time, but I've never seen you before."

"Well, I usually . . . used to be . . . at practice this time of day. But I'm trying to ease back into it, you know. Long walks. Hopefully I can run again soon."

"I pretty much need to run every day," he says. "I'm either

113

hooked on endorphins or just hyper. I don't know. Must suck to be inactive."

She sighs. "I hate it." They walk along in silence for a little while. It's surprisingly not awkward.

"So," he finally says, "when you're not playing soccer or doing calculus, what do you do for fun?"

She smiles. "People do other things for fun?"

"A few."

"Such as?"

"Hiking," he says. "Lot of great hikes around here."

"Haven't done any," Haley says. "I had games on the weekends, practice every day, then I'd catch up on work."

"Music," Richard continues. "Lot of good campus bands."

"Haven't checked them out yet."

"Okay . . . film? Do you like to go to the movies?"

"Love films, but I tend to just watch them with friends in our rooms. Usually on somebody's laptop. But one of my teammates showed up here with an awesome TV and DVD player."

"That's actually very antisocial."

"How's it antisocial to get together with a bunch of friends to watch a DVD? I'm not watching it alone!"

"Yeah, but you're just hanging out with the same people. You're not meeting anyone."

"I've got news for you: I don't meet people in dark theaters."

Richard laughs. "Point taken."

They walk along in silence a little longer. They've left the river path and are walking up the main drag leading to campus.

"You must think I'm pretty lame," she says. It just pops out of her mouth. More honesty than she'd intended. Why does this happen to her around this guy?

But Richard smiles easily. "I don't think you're lame at all. Sounds like you just don't get out enough."

"Hmm. Can't argue there. So what would you suggest?" She pauses. They're at the intersection. This is where she breaks off and heads to the dining hall. See you in math lab, Cute Guy.

"Well." He squints, looking up the hill and into the slanting sunset. "For starters, you could join me for dinner. That would be something new."

She struggles to look nonchalant. Business as usual. Yeah. She's cool.

"Sure."

Is it her imagination or does he look relieved? Like, did he think she'd say *no*?

"Okay. Uh, I need to shower, but that'll just take a minute. Want to walk to my house, then we can head to dinner from there? I live in Taylor."

Haley cocks her head, considering. She still hasn't figured out where all the different houses are.

"It's the one next to Conundrum," he adds. "Not far."

"Uh . . . sure," she repeats. She begins following him in the direction of the house.

Now the silence is awkward. She doesn't know whether that's because this suddenly feels like . . . something . . . or because he's mentioned Conundrum.

He lives in the house, sleeps in the house, right next door to where Jenny was raped.

She doesn't want to act weird. She hopes she's not acting weird.

"So," she says, "I hear Conundrum is the campus Animal House."

Richard looks straight ahead. "I wouldn't know. I'm having enough trouble keeping up with the animals in my own house."

"Oh?"

"We got a little carried away earlier this semester and are pretty much on social probation right now. No parties, and spot checks to make sure no one underage is drinking."

"Hmm. I wouldn't have pegged you for a hard-partying sort of guy."

He laughs, but he's not smiling. "There's hard and there's *hard*. I mean, I like to party. But when stuff is getting broken, people are getting hurt, and the place is ruined, it's time to back off."

"Are the people in the house backing off?"

"Most of them are. It's not a big deal, just have to lie low until the sanction is over. I'm actually a little relieved we can't host. My GPA needs to recover."

They approach Taylor. At this point the sun has set and lights are on. It's actually a nice house, one of the newer ones on campus. They go inside. There's a big common room on the first floor, with a huge fieldstone fireplace. Couches.

"You want to wait for me here? I'll just be a minute," Richard says. She nods, and he dashes off. There isn't anyone else around, and she finds a seat for herself in a big armchair in the back of the room. She sinks low into it; the springs beneath the cushions are broken.

The floors are sticky and smell sour from spilled beer. All of the furniture seems askew, as if it had been moved to the side then hastily shoved back with no particular layout in mind. The walls are dull white, but one large spot is whiter than the rest, as if it's been patched. The fireplace contains ash and burnt log remnants. Sheets of newspaper and a box of matches on the hearth.

Haley gets up, moves to a window. The house is set on a leafy lot. This whole part of campus seems tucked away.

From down the hall she hears voices. A group of guys heading for the front door. Their words carry.

"How about the Grille?"

"Why should we pay for the Grille when we can get free food in the dining hall?"

"Okay, fine. Let's go to Lower hall."

"Bockus, what part of this don't you get? They've got Philly cheesesteaks in Main hall, and some stir-fry vegan crap in Lower. We're going to Main."

"Seriously, man, what's up? Are you, like, allergic to Main hall all of a sudden?" The front door opens, closes, and their voices disappear.

Haley peers out the window again, but can't see much in the waning light.

Bockus. Where has she heard that?

"There you are. Ready to go?"

Haley startles. Richard has reappeared. His hair is wet. He's changed into a flannel shirt and jeans.

"Whoa," he says, laughing. He steps closer, touches her. This little gesture, his hand cupping the crook of her elbow. "I think I just scared you."

"You did. Lost in my thoughts."

"Sorry." His hair drips slightly onto the soft collar of his shirt. Like he hadn't taken the time to dry off properly. "Where do you want to go? I hear there's decent meat at Main tonight."

She tries to imagine the expression on Carrie's face as she walks into the dining hall with Richard. Haley realizes she'd rather endure tempeh at Lower hall than witness that face.

"Let's go somewhere quiet," she says. "I'm still avoiding light and noise."

"Tell you what," Richard says. "I've got a gift card for the Grille. Let's use it." The Grille has cozy, dim booths and great burgers. Jalapeño fries. This is good.

"Are you sure?" she asks. "I don't want you to have to use up your card . . ."

Richard steers her toward the door. "It's fine," he says, "as long as you know: I'm not splitting. This boy eats the whole entrée."

. . .

She floats. The dress floats. Their words, laughter, like bubbles, float.
Jenny twirls.
"Whoa, girl." Laughter. The room sways. More laughter. Music.
"Oh, I love this song!" Jenny knows the words. She sings. She's
surprised by her own voice, how it carries, brightly, even the high
notes. Soaring song, one of those that connects with a hidden place
in your chest. The others join in, girl chorus, singing this one song.
Their blended voices sound unnaturally good in their own
ears. They sound like, feel like, stars.

. . .

12

RICHARD

She has no idea how attractive she is.

This isn't a word Richard would usually apply to a woman verging on his height, who, if she weren't injured, could most likely outrun him and bench-press more than he weighs. Who wears no makeup, restrains her reddish-brownish hair in a permanent ponytail, and seems constantly clad in a revolving assortment of hoodies.

But Haley's got this freckle-sprinkled nose that turns up at the end. And it's positioned between these round blue eyes that laugh easily at his attempts at humor. And this warm flush that sweeps across her cheeks whenever she says something spontaneous and revealing. Which is often.

Sitting across the booth from her, fake-fighting over the last of the spicy fries, feels like being with an old friend.

Haley picks up one of the last, and biggest, fries.

"What's it worth to you?" she says, waving it before his face.

"I'll do your problem sets this week," he says.

She tilts her head, considering. "Nah. Tempting, but that's cheating. Plus I need to learn the stuff. Try again."

He picks up the limp pickle spear on his plate. "I'll give you my pickle."

She makes this choking sound, like barely contained laughter. "That is just wrong," she manages. "Sorry. You've got to do better or it's mine. They're all mine."

"Okay," he says. An idea comes to mind. What the hell. Just ask. "I'll trade you for an apple. A whole bag of apples. And what might possibly be the best apple pie on the planet. Range Orchards, just a few miles from campus, has pick-your-own and they sell all sorts of stuff: cider donuts, pies. I'll borrow a car from a friend and we can go this weekend. If you give me the last big fry *plus* the rest."

Richard holds his breath. He has no idea why he suggested this. Completely unplanned. He hadn't even thought of the local orchard where he went with his family last fall during Parents Weekend until just now. Ellen had loved it. "Stop me before I eat another cider donut!" she'd wailed after her third. He'd preferred the pie.

But he realizes that this is something he'd like to do. With Haley.

She doesn't answer. Instead she gets this . . . look . . . in those eyes, reaches across the table, and next thing he knows she's feeding him the jalapeño fry in question. She holds it until the last possible second, and is it his imagination or does she brush her fingers against his lips? She pushes the rest of the plate toward him.

"Well," she says with a sigh, "you drive a hard bargain, Math Dude. I would have fought you for these, but I love apple picking."

"Somehow I knew that."

"So we'll go this weekend?"

"Saturday. It's supposed to rain Sunday. Can you go Saturday?"

"It's a date."

The word hangs in the air between them. He knows it sounds like something she probably didn't mean . . . but in a way, it is. A date.

He has never gone on a "date" before. Unless you count prom. The one time ever in his young life that he formally asked a girl to accompany him to something.

He has absolutely no idea how this has happened.

"You want anything?" Haley says, holding out her cup. "I'm going to get a refill."

Richard shakes his head, and she slides out of the booth. They've positioned themselves in the corner of the Grille farthest from the drinks machines. As she crosses the room, winding between tables, Richard notices one lone diner, a guy, checking her out. Haley seems oblivious to his gawking, and after she passes him, the guy redirects his gaze toward Richard. Rises and walks toward their booth.

Jordan.

He slips into Haley's seat. "You're just a one-man move-on-dot-whatever, aren't you?"

Richard forces a smile. "I tutor her in math."

Jordan laughs. "Didn't look to me like any homework was going on."

"You wouldn't know what homework looks like. Anyway, what are you doing here? I thought everyone went to Main."

Jordan's expression clouds. "Yeah," he says, drawing the word out slowly. "I can't go there right now. Long story. We need to talk."

Over Jordan's shoulder, Richard watches Haley. She's ordering something at the counter. "I'll catch you later tonight," he says. A little too quickly.

Jordan looks at him curiously, then turns, glances in Haley's direction. "Okay, I see what's going on here," he says, twisting back and grinning at Richard. "Afraid I'll interrupt whatever you've got going with your new little lady friend?"

Richard resists the urge to shove him from the booth. "You can imagine whatever you like," he says easily. "But we've got a ton of calc to get through, so . . . beat it. I'll catch you later."

Jordan rises. Haley walks toward them now. She carries a tall water glass in one hand and two of those really good cellophane-wrapped M&M's Rice Krispies Treats in another. Jordan has to pass her as he heads back to his table. When he does, he says something. Brief, just a few words. Doesn't wait for a response, saunters on. Grabs his pack, shoulders it, and leaves the Grille.

When Haley sits, she passes Richard one of the treats.

"Friend of yours?" she asks, tilting her head toward Jordan.

"Housemate," he replies. "What's this?"

"Rice Krispies," she says. "My favorite. Which means you get your very own."

"The benefits of eating with a woman who doesn't share."

"You know it," she says, unwrapping hers. She breaks off a chunk, pops it in her mouth.

"So, what did Jordan say to you?" Richard plucks at the thin plastic covering the treat.

Haley's head snaps up. She looks startled. "What?"

. . .

The house begins to fill.

"Hey, you started without us!"

"Catch up, man."

"Exley, you're a genius."

It's the party before the party. The rev-your-engines part. The bring-it part. The part where they prepare themselves for whatever and anything and everything the night offers.

It's almost enough. Almost.

. . .

13

Haley

"What?" Haley exclaims. Jordan? It's like Richard's Tasered her with the name.

Richard is having trouble with the cellophane on his Rice Krispies Treat. They pretty much shrink-wrap them for freshness.

"My housemate," he says. "His name's Jordan. I thought he said something to you just now." He tries pulling, but the plastic won't rip.

She reaches across the table and grabs it from his hands. She slides a finger beneath the folds of plastic wrap, plucks the treat free, and holds it out to him.

"Thanks," he says, accepting it from her. He takes a bite.

"Jordan," she repeats. "I always thought that was a girl's name."

"Could be both," he says. "I like names that cut both ways. You know, non–gender specific? Taylor. Ryan. Francis. Although with Francis, you have to change the spelling."

"I've never met a guy named Francis."

"Frank," he tells her. "Every Frank's a Francis." He takes another bite. "You're right: these are good."

"What's Jordan's last name?" she asks. Casually, she hopes. There could be more than one Jordan on a campus, right?

"Bockus," he says. "Why?"

Shit. This isn't happening. Never, in all Haley's sort-of dealings with guys, has it been this easy. Like she's known him forever. Once she'd gotten over the nerve-racking attractiveness of Richard Brandt (usually these sorts of crazy good looks mess with her, making her say even more stupid things), being with him is so comfortable. Like pulling on a pair of favorite, stretched-out jeans.

Except these jeans live in the same house as Jenny's rapist.

Hang out with Jenny's rapist.

"No reason," she says. "I just ask random questions. Can't you tell?" She smiles at him.

Richard isn't buying it. "Did he say something rude to you?"

"Not at all. He just surprised me. As I passed him, he sort of leaned in and said, 'Watch out for that guy, he's a smart one.' "

Richard glances away from her. Drums his fingers on the table.

"Why? Is he the rude comment sort?"

"He thinks he's funny."

"But you don't?"

"Let's just say I'm not a fan," he says. He breaks off another piece of treat but doesn't put it in his mouth.

"Must be a drag to share a house with someone you don't like."

Don't say you like him. Please please don't say you like him.

Richard hesitates before answering her. When he does, he looks into her eyes. "He's mostly just annoying. He was on my freshman hall, and when he and some guys applied to live in Taylor, they needed one more person and asked me. I figured, great house, I'll have a single. I just wasn't prepared for the level of partying, and when we got sanctioned, my parents were really upset about the fines."

"Was it a lot?"

"A lot for us. I mean, I don't tutor math because it's fun; it's my work-study job. But some of these other guys? Like Jordan? His parents just toss cash his way. I don't think he even works during the summers."

Haley is quiet. She's only had one sort-of summer job herself. Part-time, scooping ice cream at the local stand in her town. She's always been too busy attending soccer camps to commit to a real job. Her parents pretty much cover everything, including her books and spending money.

"Well. I'm glad you tutor math," she says. This brightens the expression on his face.

"I don't mean to be negative," he says. "There's just . . . a lot of money at this school. It surprised me. Not only because I'd never known people with *this much* money, like, parents who run hedge funds sort of thing, but because it sets a bar for what you do. It affects who you hang out with. Like, you don't drink craft beer if you can only afford Natty Lite."

"And Taylor is full of craft beer guys?"

"With the occasional barrel of Everclear thrown in for fun."

I drank some stuff at a party and it really hit me.

Haley can't help it. She not only hears Jenny, she *sees* her. Jenny-Mouse, toddling off to some crowded house party in the woods. Older guys ladling red cups with god-knows-what from a barrel.

Was Richard there that night?

She has to go. She needs to think.

She's barely touched her Rice Krispies Treat. She rewraps it and tucks it in her pack for later.

"I'm chasing you away," he says. "Sorry; don't mean to be a downer."

"No, not at all. I'm just tired. And I'd love to sleep, but I have to at least attempt some reading tonight."

Richard nods, like he understands, but she can see he's not buying this, either.

"So give me your number and I'll text you about apples," he says, pulling out his phone.

"Great," she says, searching through her pack. "I'm pretty sure I can do that. Coach has let me off the hook for away games, so I think I'm free." She hears the conditional in her own voice. Setting up excuses already. They clang. Lame. So lame.

They exchange numbers, and she gets up. He remains seated in the booth. He smiles as she slides away, his mouth closed. Like he's determined to not seem like a guy who has just opened up to a girl who then decides to blow him off.

"See you," she says.

"Right," he answers.

Haley turns and walks toward the exit. *Could this possibly suck more?*

．．．

Jenny knows they call her Mouse. She knows she is invisible. And who can blame them? Hidden beneath the weight of her own books, still locked in the role of some parents' good daughter, she barely knows herself.

Until now. She has this: a party invitation. From an older boy. Bring friends, he said. And suddenly, like some brilliant ignition, some curtain rising accompanied by drumroll, she appears. In a thigh-grazing dress with capital to expend.

She's a girl worth knowing.

Tonight, anyway.

．．．

14

RICHARD

Haley's text on Saturday morning surprises Richard.

When she'd left the Grille so suddenly, Richard figured it was the last he'd see of her. *What the hell?* he'd thought as she walked away.

He hadn't pegged her for a snob. One of the rich-girl-beautiful-people. They usually can sniff you out early on, realize you're *not* going to be going along on the gang's spring break trip to so-and-so's parents' house in Aruba, or you *don't* have a car on campus, or you *don't* have a season pass to the nearest ski resort—so sorry, gotta run, end this conversation fast. *Because you, buddy, are not a wise investment of my time.*

He's met those girls before. Figured out how to spot them first and avoid wasting *his* time.

He'd thought Haley was different. But she's a soccer girl. And probably a super jock. You don't just show up and start as a freshman unless you're pretty damn good.

So the sudden flip, when he mentioned work-study? All of a sudden she "thinks" she's free for the apple picking she supposedly loves?

Then, she texts.

Apples?

It wakes him. Nine a.m. on Saturday morning. Taylor House is still. Most of his housemates won't be up for hours. A few might be lucky to make it to lunch before the dining hall closes. Then again, they might get up and stumble across campus to the home football game. Cruise an assortment of tailgate parties for a one-p.m. breakfast of champions: guacamole and chips with some cold beer to wash it down.

He peers again at his phone.

Apples?

He presses his head back into the pillows, focuses on the ceiling. Can he focus on the ceiling? The place behind his eyes aches with that Death Valley crack, where the earth splits from too long without rain. His tongue is made of sandpaper.

He'd succumbed to beer pong in the basement last night. His team didn't win.

The problem was the crap beer.

The problem was too much crap beer.

The problem was . . . too much.

But it's not like he'd had anything else planned for Friday night.

It was him, Rob, and Justin against three guys who had wandered in from Conundrum. He should've known better: Rob and Justin usually just watched from the sidelines. Guys from Conundrum pretty much majored in beer pong.

At one point they were taking a break while someone went upstairs to take a piss. He'd crashed onto the couch against the wall. The room was spinning, slowly, clockwise. He remembers thinking that wasn't too bad. End to end spins, where you rotate head over heels? Those were the spins to watch out for.

He remembers a piece of one conversation.

"So, did you all meet with Bockus tonight?" This from Todd, a Conundrum guy.

Rob and Justin looked blank.

"Meeting?" Justin asked.

Short laugh from Todd. "Guess he's in trouble," he said. "Some girl reported him after that party we hosted with you all a couple weeks ago. He's being investigated and had to give the college a list of people who were there."

"Damn," said Rob. "I didn't hear anything about this."

"Were you at the party?" asked Todd.

"What party?" said Justin.

"Exactly," Todd said, laughing. "People are conveniently forgetting about that party, let me tell you. I, for one, have no idea what Bockus was up to that night, and I sure as hell don't want to get nailed for serving alcohol to underage freshmen because he was being a dick."

"Wait, some freshman girl is upset because Bockus gave her a drink?" said Rob.

"Dude, you're stupid. A girl is accusing Bockus of *rape*."

They all turned when Richard said that. He hadn't meant to comment. But the beer loosened his tongue. He stared up at them and their revolving carousel of faces.

"Seriously?" Rob said.

"Trust me; I know," Richard said. He also knew about the "house meeting" Todd was referring to. He'd bumped into Jordan shortly afterward.

133

Jordan had to give the college a list of witnesses, for the investigator, and he'd gone to Conundrum to give people a heads-up. It hadn't gone well. They were furious he'd submitted their names. *What the hell, Bockus?* pretty much summed up their reaction.

Not about the rape charges, he told Richard. They knew he was innocent. About the booze. Everyone was worried the investigation was going to lead to *their* house getting cited.

"I haven't even told the Taylor guys yet," Jordan said. "Not looking forward to that."

"Yeah, the Doctor is going to *love* it," commented Richard.

Jordan had shrugged. "Exley's all set."

Richard's phone pings again.

No apples? This message includes a sad emoticon. The round yellow face sheds tears.

He can rally. Shower. Touch base with Justin to see if he can borrow his car. Drink water. Many glasses of water.

Give me an hour, he texts back. *Pick u up outside the union?*

Maybe he was wrong about being wrong about her. Which would be good. A double negative equals a positive, right? As he waits for her to reply, he realizes something.

Exley is all set.

He's the other guy. The one other person Jordan told about the night with Jenny.

And he's all set. What exactly does *that* mean?

His phone again.

Haley replies with another emoticon. This time, the yellow face smiles.

134

● ● ●

Pressed up against the wall in the darkest corner of the dark, packed room, Exley watches.

The bodies set in motion blur into one another, a fury of shadowed arms, grinding hips, faceless expressions masked in loose hair. An undercurrent of voices drowning just below the surface of the music, the sound a steady, rising tide as more arrive.

Jordan finds him.

"Best party yet," he half shouts into Exley's ear.

The Doctor nods, unspeaking. His eyes remain focused forward, at the center of the writhing room.

"Where are the girls you said were coming?" Jordan asks.

Exley tilts his head back, drains his cup. "They'll be here."

● ● ●

15

Haley

After hours of soul searching, Haley makes up her mind.

She likes Richard Brandt. A lot. Her gut tells her he's a nice guy.

So she will go apple picking with him.

And she will tell him about Jordan and Jenny.

It will be awkward. Possibly awful. It's an honor code violation, since she's sworn to privacy. But the other options suck.

One would be avoiding him. Blow off apple picking, stop going to math lab, pretend she doesn't see him around campus when she sees him around campus. Ghost him.

Another option would be *not* to avoid him. Go apple picking. Just . . . keep her mouth shut about the whole rape thing. Go about her business and hope she never bumps into Richard and Jenny and Jordan and, wow, Carrie all at the same time.

Because that would be beyond awkward, bordering on cataclysmic, actually.

And fairly likely, given what a small campus this is.

So the only option is . . . candor.

As she waits for him outside the union, she feels a little nauseous. She can't decide whether it's nerves because this is sort of a date or dread because of what she has to say. Or both.

He pulls up in a battered blue Subaru wagon. Her hands are full (she thought it would be a nice gesture to pick up some good coffee), and he leans over to open her door. It's warm for an October morning, and he wears a T-shirt and jeans. Old running shoes. As she climbs into the car she thinks he looks tired.

"Good morning, sunshine!" she says, slipping one of the coffees into the cup holder next to him. "I went to the corner store and got us pumpkin lattes." Is it her imagination, or does he wince?

He pulls away from the curb. "So I have to ask you," he begins, "are you always this bright-eyed and bushy-tailed in the morning?"

"Morning is the best time of day," she says, laughing.

He looks stricken. "Oh god," he replies. "She's one of those."

"And this morning," she continues, "was the first in two weeks that I didn't wake up with a headache. So watch out, Math Dude."

Richard smiles, but it seems to require some effort.

"Rough night?" she asks.

"No excuses. It's my own damn fault," he says. He wears an embarrassed-with-a-hint-of-wise-ass expression. "Nothing a little fresh air and good company can't cure."

Haley feels the warmth spread across her cheeks when he refers to her as good company. *Yeah, let's see how long that lasts.*

She'll wait as long as possible. She deserves a little fun with this boy. Because depending on how he reacts, it may be the last time they speak.

The orchard is part of a family-owned farm twenty minutes from campus. Bright orange, red, and gold flags line a long gravel driveway leading to a big barn spilling children and their parents. A sea of pumpkins, gourds, and mums for sale takes over one side of the lawn; on the other, fields of gnarly trees bend, heavy with apples.

Rows are labeled: Macs, Cortlands, Red Delicious, all the same price. Haley and Richard each grab a grocery store–size paper bag and head out.

The sky is a clear, intense blue. They walk to the far end of the field, passing from shade to sun, away from the exuberant family groups.

"Smells like fall," Richard says. "Cider. Mown hay."

"Rotten apples," Haley says. The ground beneath each tree is littered with them.

Richard laughs. "One woman's rotten apple is another man's cider."

She breathes in deeply, filling her lungs. "Donuts," she adds. "Something baking."

"They have fantastic cider donuts here," Richard says. "And apple pie. They serve it with their own homemade vanilla ice cream."

Haley stops in her tracks. She breathes deeply again. She can smell the fry oil from the donut maker. Damp, fallen leaves. Manure from the dairy farm next door. It's a bright morning. And it doesn't hurt.

"This is so cool," she says. "The light doesn't bother me. I don't have the slightest headache."

He looks relieved. As if someone has just delivered the good news he's been waiting for. Before she realizes what's happening, Richard steps in close, wraps one arm around her shoulders, and continues their walk through the field.

He smells like cotton and soap. And him. His warm guy smell.

Oh god. Maybe she shouldn't say anything. *Don't wreck this, Haley.*

"It's good to know one of us doesn't have a splitting headache this morning," he says.

• • •

*Marliese knows where Conundrum House is, so they follow her.
The trippy, laughing pack weaves across the dark campus.*

*They don't need coats; Tamra's bottle warms them. They
stumble in shoes not meant for walking, their heels a syncopated
scrape and click as they pass through a wooded labyrinth of winding sidewalks.*

*They hear the party before they see it. Distant voices obscured
by drumming. Will they ever get there? But then a smudge of light
glows behind the trees, they round a corner, and the house—bright,
teeming—appears.*

• • •

16

RICHARD

Richard may fall asleep.

That would be nice. A nap, right here, stretched out on the warm, sloping grass, sun lightly toasting his closed eyelids. Dry whisper of the trees. They're at the quiet end of the orchard, farthest from the barn.

Then Haley says, "There's something I need to talk to you about."

Her tone. Not good. He sits up.

Their bags, stuffed full with every variety of apple, are propped behind her. She stares out into the distance, the full length of field visible from the slight rise where they sit. She speaks without looking at him.

"So the other night, when we were at the Grille? You probably wondered why I sort of . . . left."

"Yeah, now that you mention it," he says. *I thought you were a complete snot*, he doesn't say. "What was up with that?"

"Your housemate," she says. "Jordan."

Something dark gathers in Richard's chest. His heart drums just a little harder, a little faster. *What? What now?*

"I figured he said something obnoxious to you," he says. "Haley, the guy's a jerk. Don't pay attention to anything that comes out of his mouth."

She pivots and faces him now as she speaks. "Actually, it's not anything he said to me. It's something he did. Something I know about, and if you and I are going to hang out, you need to know, too."

Hang out. He wants to stop her there and further explore what she means by that. He definitely has some ideas that extend beyond apple picking.

"A couple weeks ago," she continues, "my roommate was attacked. Raped. It happened the night of my concussion, a Saturday, at that house near yours. Conundrum. She hasn't told me any of the details, and I only know the name of the guy by accident. She was waving some papers around and I saw it. And it's him. Jordan Bockus. That's why I asked you his last name the other night. It sort of freaked me out when I realized who it was."

Richard blinks. A minute ago he was dozing off. Now he is definitely awake.

"Jenny," he says reflexively. "Your roommate is Jenny?"

Haley's eyes widen. "You know about this," she breathes. "*You* know about this."

"Shit," she says. She stands. Arms crossed tightly, she stares down at him.

"Jenny the freshman," he says. "The girl who is charging Jordan with rape. That's *your* roommate?"

"She's not 'Jenny the freshman.' She's Jenny James. And yes. My roommate. The woman I live with."

"Shit," he echoes. He rubs his hands over his eyes. "This is unbelievable."

"You think?" She's standing with her back to the sun, and it hurts to twist his neck and look up at her.

"Would you sit? I can't talk like this," he says.

She returns to the grass beside him. "How long have you known?"

He squints, thinking. "Known about them hooking up or about her charging him?"

The instant the words are out of his mouth, he realizes his mistake. It's like getting smacked in the back of the head with a snowball: a thud, followed by glass-sharp prickles of dread melting down your neck.

He has just told the woman who lives with Jenny that he knows Jordan hooked up with her. He said the one thing Jordan asked him not to say to possibly the worst person he could have said it to.

This is bad.

"Oh, is that what he told you?" Haley says. "That it was a hookup? That's rich. Trust me: if you knew my roommate, you'd know that isn't even remotely possible. She does homework and hangs out in the lab. Before the other night, I doubt she'd ever even held a guy's hand, much less had sex."

"So what was she doing at a Conundrum party?" Richard responds. "Everyone knows you go there to throw down."

"Wow." She stares at him. "Are you hearing yourself?"

"What?"

"That's like . . . she was looking for it. Or she should've known better? Throw down or get raped, ladies, take your pick." The stare has morphed into a glare.

It occurs to him that he has an uncanny talent for pissing off women he likes. And for being misunderstood.

"No! That's not it. I'm just saying maybe your roommate isn't as naive as you think. And even if she was? Take two steps into one of those parties and it's pretty apparent what everyone came for. And it's not mocktails and swing dancing, okay?"

"Were you at that party?" Haley says. A crack in her voice. Like she doesn't really want to ask.

"That's not my scene. I was somewhere else that night." He can tell by her expression that she knows precisely where he was and who he was with.

Which is when it hits him. Ton of bricks. Hello, dumbass.

"That's how your roommate knows Carrie," he says. "How *you* know her."

Haley doesn't register surprise. "Carrie was the first person Jenny spoke to about it," she admits. "She was actually the one who told me what happened. Jenny could barely say it."

"So Carrie said it for her," he says. "Why am I not surprised? Haley, the woman is a militant feminist. She sees a stalker behind every tree. Men are amusements at best, enemies at worst. Don't believe everything she tells you."

"So? You think Carrie is making up Jenny's rape?"

"I'm not saying she's making it up. But she's characterizing it for her, isn't she? Let me ask you something: did your roommate run right out and report this? Or did Carrie convince her to?"

Haley hesitates. "She didn't tell anyone for a few days," she says. "Then, after she started talking to Carrie on the hotline, it took a few more days before she reported it. But Richard, you don't know Jenny. Something bad happened to her. She was okay and now she's . . . wrecked. People don't act like this unless something awful happened to them."

Richard puts his hands up in surrender, conceding the point. "I'm not saying it did, and I'm not saying it didn't. I wasn't in the room with them. What do I know? But I do know Jordan, and while he's definitely a douche, I don't think he'd attack some girl. It's probably more likely that things went further than Jenny expected, she felt yucky about it the next day, and now Carrie has her convinced it was rape."

Reasonable. That's what he is. Completely balanced and reasonable. Not taking any particular side or demonizing anyone (except maybe Carrie, but that's okay) and putting the whole thing in perspective.

So why does Haley look like he's just killed somebody?

"You know what?" she says. "This was a bad idea. I'm not even supposed to be talking about this. I don't know what I was thinking." She stands.

Richard scrambles to his feet. "What? What did I say?"

But Haley has grabbed one of the bags and strides toward the barn.

He picks up the other and follows. "Haley!"

"It's not really what you said, but what you *think*. That's the problem, Richard," she says over her shoulder.

"What I think? Oh, so you're a mind reader?"

She stops. Whirls on him. "Yucky? Did you actually say

yucky?" She practically yells this. A few trees down the row, he sees a father-type turn his head in their direction. "Sex without consent is not *yucky*, Richard. It's a crime."

"I'm not a caveman, Haley. I'm fully aware that no means no. But I'm also one of those guys who thinks when yes the night before turns into no the morning after, it's a little unfair to call it rape!"

"Who said she ever said yes?!" She's actually yelling at this point.

"He did!" Richard is yelling, too. Saying stuff he absolutely should not be saying, but at this point, what the hell? "He won't back down. He absolutely insists she was good with it that night."

"Excuse me? Are we talking about the same guy who, a few minutes ago, you said, 'Don't pay attention to anything that comes out of his mouth'?"

She's got him there. He said that. And he meant it. He usually only half believes Jordan's bullshit. The rest he attributes to swagger.

So Richard is arguing for him ... why?

He likes this girl. So much. They need to get past this. He can't blow this because of freakin' Jordan Bockus.

"Haley." He feels deflated. Like she just stuck a pin in him. He presses his fingers against his temples. His head pounds. "Yes. I said that. Guess I should follow my own advice. The fact is, I don't have the first clue what happened at Conundrum that night, or what went on between Jordan and Jenny. Only they do. Those two people. So why are we mad at each other?"

"I'm not mad," she says angrily. She resumes her march to the barn.

After a moment, he follows, a few paces behind. "You sure do a great imitation of mad," he says as they quickstep down the row of apple trees.

No response.

"Can we talk? Please?" They've drawn even with an apple-picking family, and without breaking stride, Haley holds up one hand, signaling Richard to keep his mouth shut. As they hurry past, the children stop what they're doing and watch them pass with wide eyes. Their voices must have carried.

At the barn, Haley moves straight to the checkout with the scale. Richard gets in line behind her. He stands just short of touching her, speaks quietly into her ear.

"Let me buy you a piece of pie."

She shifts slightly forward, away from him.

No response.

"Cider donut? Cup of coffee? They sell Wicked Joe here. I could really use some Wicked Joe."

"I need to get back to campus." She turns her face only slightly in his direction as she speaks. "Ton of work to do." It's her turn at the scale, and she places her bag on it. When she pulls out her wallet, Richard reaches around and places one hand on hers. "I've got this," he says.

She proceeds as if he's invisible. "Seventeen fifty," the woman at the scale says. Haley hands her a twenty, pockets the change, and without a backward glance stomps off with her apples to where they've parked the Subaru beneath a bright orange maple.

Richard heaves his bag onto the scale and tosses two tens on the counter. His apples weigh pretty much the same as Haley's. "Keep it," he says before the woman hands him change. He grabs his bag and heads to the car.

It's going to be a long drive back.

. . .

There's a line at the door. Raised voices.

"Sorry, man," they hear. "No entry without a freshman female."

"Are you kidding?"

"I don't make the rules. You want to come in, you have to be accompanied by a freshman female."

There's a scuffle. Elbows, pushing. Tamra jumps to the head of the line, the cluster of red-faced guys. "Hey." They all turn. "Six freshmen, right here," she says.

Once inside, they lose the guys.

. . .

17

Haley

Tamra, known as "T" to her friends, corners Haley at breakfast.

She's just sat down, is looking forward to tucking in to some seriously good banana pancakes drenched with syrup, when Tamra slides her tray across the table.

"May I join you?" she asks as she settles into a chair.

I have a choice? Haley refrains from asking. Instead, she smiles politely.

Soccer and all its demands had insulated her from the Tamras of MacCallum College. Haley had arrived for preseason, two weeks before freshman orientation, to a team full of insta-friends, unlike the NARPs on her hall, all searching for their tribe. Haley watched as they spent weeks trying on different people, sorting out where they fit in. They'd all been warned that this was part of the process of going to college and they had to be patient. But knowing didn't make it easier.

And people like T definitely made it harder.

It was like they spoke some secret language, or knew the club handshake that signaled One of Us. It wasn't spoken. It wasn't seen. You might think it was money, but there were rich girls who didn't make the cut, and you might think it was looks, but several of T's besties were practically barking. It was something more akin to unquestioned confidence. Entitlement you could practically smell, like a fragrance.

And like a fragrance, it was impossible to grasp. You just waited to see if you were one of the anointed, one of the Pack of T.

Or not.

"So how are you?" Tamra begins. She rips open a Splenda and tips the contents into her black coffee.

"Good. You?"

Tamra raises one finely arched eyebrow. "That makes one of us. So I guess it's true? You didn't get the letter?"

Haley wills her face into a Carole Patterson–like expression of blankness. You want to keep the upper hand with T. "What letter?"

Tamra glances around, then leans in closer. "About the investigation. What Jenny is saying?" The second eyebrow arches.

That was quick.

Jenny had warned her: stuff was about to get real. Jenny had to make a list of "witnesses," anyone who could shed light on what happened at Conundrum that night. Those names would be given to an investigator, who would interview each person individually.

Those interviews probably wouldn't happen for a while.

But the notifications that you were on the list for questioning? Right away.

Haley imagines someone like Tamra would be none too pleased to find herself on that list.

"No," Haley says, "I didn't get a letter. But I do know about the investigation."

Tamra's face lights up. She gets out of her chair and moves to the other side of the table, alongside Haley. "So what's going on? The letter was sort of vague. A lot of stuff about violating community standards, blah blah, but it *definitely* mentioned Jenny's name and that she's charging somebody with . . . what? I think it said 'sexual misconduct'?"

Haley's mind races. Is even this, simply acknowledging the fact of the investigation, off-limits? As Jenny's advisor, is she supposed to get up and walk away right now, or tell Tamra, "Sorry, sworn to secrecy"?

There's only one surefire way to get the Ts of MacCallum to ignore you: make them think you've got nothing they want.

"Like I said, Tamra, I didn't get the letter, so I don't know what's in it."

"But you *do* know what's going on." Not a question. Tamra waits.

"Actually, you probably know a lot more than I do," Haley says. "Remember, I was getting my head examined while you were all at that party with her. So you tell me. What went down?"

Tamra scowls. "Here's what went down: Jenny disappeared. Poof! We all pregamed in my room, walked together to Conundrum, and at some point everyone lost track of her.

152

Vivian wanted to move on to a different party, we couldn't find Jenny *anywhere*, so we left."

Haley feels a warm flush on her cheeks. "What, you didn't text her? Find out where she was?"

Tamra seems unfazed by this question. "None of us has her number."

"So you ditched her? At an upperclassmen party across campus, practically back in the woods?"

"Hey, we figured she ditched us! We thought she got mad and left."

"Why would she be mad?"

Tamra rolls her eyes. "Oh . . . drama. Marliese hooked up with the guy Jenny had her eye on. This sophomore named Brandon Exley? He's the one who invited Jenny, but he barely paid any attention to her once we got there. So when we couldn't find her, we figured she'd gotten pissed and left. But hey, all's fair, you know? Not Marliese's fault the guy preferred her."

"Jenny and Marliese competing for the same guy? In what universe?"

Tamra looks confused.

"Let me get this straight," Haley continues. "You came together and left without her? Left without knowing where she was? You broke the number one rule, the I-got-your-back-at-a-party rule. It's like deserting a man behind enemy lines. If you were an Army Ranger, they'd probably court-martial you."

Tamra's eyes narrow. "Yeah, well, you know what? I'm not an Army Ranger. And I'm not a babysitter. If Jenny can't handle playing with the big kids, she should stay home."

"No one expects you to be a babysitter, Tamra. But next time? Try being a friend. Even if it's just for one night."

The pancakes are cold, but she's lost her appetite anyway. She doesn't like imagining Jenny off with these girls. Counting on these girls. They look out for each other, but everyone else? They don't even see them.

Tamra should be mad right now. No one talks to T this way. So this is the part where she huffs off and ignores Haley for the next four years.

Unfortunately, T keeps talking.

She wants something.

"So, what exactly happened? Do you know?"

Haley flashes her best fake smile. "Sorry. I'm not supposed to talk about it."

"Haley. Let me lay this out for you: We pregamed in my room that night. I'm the one with the fake ID. I bought the vodka. Now I'm about to get called before an investigator, so I'd like to know what I'm walking into."

Cry me a river. The fake smile disappears. She is hanging on to self-control by a fingernail.

"Totally. God forbid somebody was underage drinking in college, Tamra. My advice would be to keep your mouth shut, let the rapist get away, and Mommy and Daddy will never find out you got drunk one night."

The surprise on Tamra's face lets Haley know she slipped. "Somebody *raped* her? Oh my god. Who was it?"

On cue, as if sensing from somewhere across campus that Haley desperately wants to tear herself away from this conversation, Jenny texts. Her phone is on the table, and she can see the message.

Can u come to the room? I need u.

"This has been fun, but I have to go," Haley says, gathering her things.

Tamra jumps up. "Oh, c'mon. You can't drop that and just walk away!"

Watch me.

"I get why you're mad," Tamra continues. "And you're right, we shouldn't have left the party without Jenny. My god. Rape. That's awful! But we honestly didn't know anything bad had happened to her. We were all pretty wrecked."

Haley hoists her pack over one shoulder and picks up her tray with the cold pancakes. She sidesteps around Tamra, toward the exit, but T is on her.

"Just . . . do you think you could talk to her?" Urgency in Tamra's voice. "Ask her to take me off the list? I don't have anything to tell them. I barely remember what happened at the party."

"Ask her yourself," Haley says shortly. She walks toward the bussing station and the revolving conveyor belt where you load trays.

Tamra follows. "I've already tried." Pleading now. Very un-T-like. "She won't talk to me. Barely makes eye contact."

"Can you blame her? You ditch her at a party and she gets attacked? You know what: I don't want to talk to you, either. You suck."

They've reached the bussing station, where Haley shoves the tray into the rotating carousel, grabs the plate, and begins furiously scraping her wasted breakfast into the compost bucket.

It's crowded, and Tamra, insistent, presses close. "Oh, so you're saying this is somehow my fault?" she hisses into Haley's ear. Finally, angry. "For your information, nobody 'ditched' anybody. *She* wandered off. The rest of us all managed to stay together; what's up with her? So if you want to know what *sucks*, I think it *sucks* that she didn't come to me before reporting everyone and dragging us into some investigation."

Haley stops scraping. "It's all about you, isn't it? Unbelievable." She tosses the now-empty plastic plate onto a tray, pushes past Tamra, and exits the dining room. T, thankfully, doesn't follow. As Haley walks quickly through the throng of students in the lobby, her phone sounds again.

Haley? Please.

She moves to one side, begins typing a quick response— *coming*—and feels someone tap her shoulder.

Eric something-or-other, who lives on the floor below her. She barely knows him.

"Hey. Did that guy ever catch up with you?" he says.

She presses send. "What guy?" They begin walking toward the door.

"I don't know him. He was leaving a message on your whiteboard. I was a few doors away and told him you were at breakfast."

Haley sighs. Richard has been texting plus leaving her voice messages. She's ignored them all. "Light brown hair? Blue eyes? A little taller than me?"

Eric hefts his pack a bit higher on his shoulder. "I don't know. He was wearing a baseball cap. No clue about his eyes."

They step outside and separate as Haley heads toward the dorm. Of course. She could only avoid Richard for so long.

Eventually they were going to have to talk. Figures he might actually come by. Didn't Carrie call him a stalker?

She scrolls back in her mind to his last text. He'd asked to meet her at the math lounge. Neutral territory, he'd called it. He said they could talk right after his tutoring shift. This afternoon, in fact. Weird that he'd stop by while she was at breakfast, when he'd suggested meeting later. And him not a morning person.

But Eric didn't say "the guy" was looking for *her*. It might not have been Richard.

Haley picks up the pace. For the first time in a long time, she's running.

* * *

He sees them across the crowded room. They enter as a pack, tentative in the dim light. He recognizes the one from class.

He skirts the wall, avoiding the crush of bodies, to reach them. They stand, transfixed, at the entrance. They look nice. All dressed up.

Her face lights, relieved, when he approaches.

"You came," he says.

She laughs. Says something he can't hear.

He lowers his head, ear close to her mouth.

"This is crazy!" she says loudly.

He nods, looks up. One of her companions, tall, dark eye makeup, stares at him.

"You brought friends," he says, staring back.

"I'm Tamra," she says.

"Brandon Exley."

* * *

18

RICHARD

Quadratic equations. Really? Did this kid even graduate from high school? But that's what Richard's explaining for the umpteenth time to some hapless freshman when he hears a shuffle near the lounge entrance and Haley enters.

He'd just about given up hope that she'd show. She'd never answered his text suggesting they meet. She'd never answered any of his texts. But here she is, her eyes darting in his direction before she beelines it to her regular chair by the ficus. She makes a big show of unzipping her pack, pulling out a fat textbook.

The nanosecond the clock registers four, he abandons the still-confused freshman—"Good luck," he mutters to the next tutor—shrugs into his jacket, and crosses the room. She looks up. Which he takes as encouragement. He'd half expected the big book to become a missile aimed at his head.

"Want to get a coffee?" he asks quietly.

She nods, collects her stuff. Follows him from the lounge, retracing their earlier descent to the basement snack bar, their steps echoing in the stairwell. She doesn't speak, and he follows suit. He's determined not to say the wrong thing. Even if that means saying nothing at all.

They get coffee, no brownies today, and automatically move to the quietest spot at the farthest corner of the room. He leans forward, elbows resting on the table, both hands wrapping the warm mug. He waits.

"By any chance," she begins, "did you drop by my room this morning?"

He smiles. "No. Thought about it, though."

Her eyes narrow, questioning. "Thought about it?"

"Yeah. When you didn't answer my forty thousand texts and voicemails, I considered leaving gifts outside your door."

A corner of her mouth turns up. She's fighting the impulse to smile. More encouragement.

"What sort of gifts?"

"Not flowers. Too cliché. And not chocolate. Too predictable."

"For the record: chocolate is never unwelcome. You can't go wrong with chocolate."

"I'll keep that in mind next time I make you mad. No, I was thinking something a little more creative. Can you guess?"

Something about her expression suggests she's not in the mood to play games. "Just tell me."

"A slice of pie."

She does not look impressed. "You just won't let go of that pie."

"That's because it's amazing."

"Tell me: were you planning to drive all the way back to the farm to get the pie, or was this going to be something you nicked from the dining hall?"

"Would you have known the difference?"

"Probably not."

The blue eyes look hard and there's ice in her voice. Does she get that he's trying?

"It's not really the pie," he says. "It's what the pie represents. A missed opportunity. We were having a good time. At least, I was, can't speak for you. And then . . ."

He pauses. Gives her a chance to fill in the blank. But she stares at her coffee mug, which seems suddenly fascinating to her.

"Here's the thing, Haley," he continues, leaning forward a little more. "I'm not a bad guy."

"I know. You just play one on TV."

"I'm being serious now."

"Okay. Sorry."

"I know I pissed you off last Saturday and I'm really sorry about that. I'm really sorry that we've ended up on opposite sides in somebody else's war. The fact is, I'm not on a side. But I've only heard one. Side, that is. So how about this: tell me what I don't know. Tell me what I don't get. Then, let's move on. Because *whatever* went down between Jordan and Jenny doesn't have to do with us. And I'm interested in us. In you. I like you. I'd like to spend time with you."

He had rehearsed, in his head, some version of this little speech. It comes out pretty close to what he intended. Maybe a little more heartfelt than it needs to be, but hell. He's probably better off sounding more sincere than less.

He knows he's taking a chance. A huge one. Not only in terms of rejection, which is a very real possibility, but in terms of opening his big mouth. Again. He's not supposed to be talking about this, but he doesn't see a way around it. If he wants to have anything to do with Haley, things need to be said.

He just has to be careful what those things are.

Haley buries her face in her hands. Not the reaction he was hoping for.

"Why," she says, groaning, "do you have to make it so hard to hate you?"

A true green light of encouragement. He grins. "I'm that sort of guy."

She lowers her hands. Looks exasperated. "This is way more complicated than you realize."

"Actually, it's not. Okay, the Jenny and Jordan thing is. That's extremely complicated. But you and me? Very simple. Boy meets girl. Boy likes girl. Girl . . . hopefully . . . likes boy? Boy and girl drink coffee, pick apples, maybe—"

She cuts him off. "Stop, Richard. Okay? I need a turn."

He nods. Sits back.

Her shoulders rise and fall as she takes a deep breath. "You're right. We need to talk about this. Unfortunately, that's exactly what I can't do."

Yellow light. He waits for her to continue.

"The fact is, I'm involved. Jenny has asked me to be her advisor. It's this support role, I don't completely get it, but it means I have to go with her to a lot of meetings and be with her when she's questioned. The biggest thing is that I can't talk about it. Not any of it. Especially not to one of Jordan's friends."

He concentrates on his face. The expression he imagines playing out there. *Don't react*, he wills his mouth, his eyes. But her words jolt him.

Jenny's advisor.

Jordan's friend.

He has to correct the record on that last one. Even though he's supposed to be listening.

"Housemate," he says. "Not friend."

"Whatever," she says. "He tells you stuff, right? I mean, he told you he hooked up with Jenny."

"He's a big talker, and most of it's crap," Richard says. "Like I said, who knows what really happened?"

"Even so. He did tell you, and you did repeat it to me, and I did react, and all of it is so, so totally *not* what I'm supposed to do. I probably shouldn't even be at this table with you. I mean, think about it. What if the other night, Jordan had sat down with us, and Jenny walked into the Grille at the same time? This is . . . not possible." Her eyes move to the exit. She seems poised to get up and leave.

He reaches across the table and places one hand over her wrist. He doesn't grip, just lays his fingers there gently. She doesn't jerk away.

"We can't see each other until this thing is over," she says quietly.

"I can't accept that."

"It's worse than you know."

"How? How can it be worse?"

"Now that the witness lists have gone out? Jenny's getting harassed. While we were at breakfast this morning, someone wrote 'Lying Bitch' on our whiteboard."

The earlier part of their conversation comes back to him now. First words out of her mouth. He pulls his hand away, having second thoughts. Like he placed a bet, but decides to yank the stack of chips off the table before the roulette ball settles.

"Wait a minute. Is that why you asked if I'd been by your room?"

The familiar flush spreads across her cheeks. "Someone saw a guy in a baseball cap writing on our board this morning."

"And you assumed it was me? What the hell, Haley?" His raised voice turns heads.

"I assumed it was you *before* I knew what he wrote. I thought because I wasn't answering your texts, you came by. Then, Jenny told me about the message and . . . I had to ask, Richard."

"Really?" he says sarcastically. "Well, you know, I have to ask: what have I done to make you think I would ever . . . *ever* . . . do something like that?"

"Nothing," she stammers. Her face is completely red. "That wasn't fair. I'm sorry."

He stands. Stares down at her. Even Carrie, whose opinion of him was fairly low, had never insulted him like this.

"No, *I'm* sorry," he says, and walks out.

• • •

They follow him along the edge of the room. They reach a table stacked with red cups. Bodies pack tightly at one end, as if the floor had tilted and the people all rolled together, like little metal balls in a handheld child's toy. Exley shoulders through, clearing a path for them.

A plastic garbage can half-full of liquid reveals itself as the magnet. A tall boy fills red cups from the can and passes them to eager hands. Exley plucks two, dips, then extends them toward Tamra and Marliese. His eyes alight on Jenny.

"Want some punch?"

• • •

19

Haley

After Richard storms out, Haley realizes she might cry. Which she deserves. A big, fat crying jag, complete with tissues, chocolate, and crap television bingeing.

Because the day keeps getting worse. And it started out pretty badly.

This morning, responding to Jenny's text, she'd arrived back at the room, winded, to a locked door. Jenny was tucked atop her bed, at the corner where the walls meet, knees drawn up to her chest.

"Where's the fire?" Haley announced, only half joking, then dead-stopped when she saw Jenny's agonized expression. "Oh no. What?"

"He's stalking me!" Jenny said. Strangled voice. Like someone wrapped a hand around her throat.

"Who is? What happened?" Haley lowered herself on the bed beside Jenny.

"Jordan! Who else? He wrote on our whiteboard. While I left to get breakfast! He must have been watching, outside, waiting for me to leave the building!"

Haley rose, went to the door, and opened it. The whiteboard adhered to the outside was completely blank. Which was odd; it was usually peppered with messages she and Jenny didn't bother erasing.

"There's nothing here," Haley said. She closed the door.

"I wiped it."

"Why?" She couldn't help the exasperation in her voice. Her mind had already made the immediate leap to evidence. Something to show when they reported this.

"I couldn't leave it! It was awful!"

"What did it say?"

"'Lying Bitch.' Oh god. I am so freaked out. I just keep thinking of him outside the building, waiting!"

Haley sat beside her again. "How do you know it was him? Did you see him?"

"Who else would it be?"

"I know, but did you *see him*?" Haley repeated.

Jenny stared. "Why are you asking like that? Like you don't believe me?"

"Of course I believe you! But how do you know it's Jordan?"

"Who else would it be?" Jenny's voice had grown shrill with repetition.

"Oh . . . I don't know. Any of a dozen guys on Jordan's witness list? At this point you know he's told his friends what's going on. Maybe one of them got mad?"

"But we're not supposed to be talking about it! He's not

supposed to talk about it!" Her breath came in gasps. Her eyes were wide, wild.

"Jen." Haley tried to counter the rising hysteria in her roommate's voice by speaking calmly. "Talk is inevitable. People are going to ask him why they're being called by an investigator. You should have heard Tamra this morning: a zillion questions. You said yourself things were going to start happening."

"But not this! Not stalking! My father is right. They should have thrown him off campus."

Haley took a deep breath. Glanced at her watch. Here's what wasn't happening: class. She couldn't leave her like this.

"Okay. Let's think. When I left for breakfast, you were still here." Jenny nodded. "When did you leave?"

"Maybe ten minutes after you."

"Did you notice the board on your way out?"

A thin line formed between Jenny's eyebrows, as if she didn't understand Haley's question. "Notice the board?"

"Did you notice whether the words were written there when you were leaving for breakfast?"

Jenny blanched. "You mean, did he write them while I was inside the room?"

"Yeah, that's what I'm wondering. Did you even notice?"

"I don't know." Jenny's eyes filled. "I don't remember looking at the board on my way out, so I don't know. Maybe he did. Oh god. That's really creepy. Him standing outside my door while I'm in here?" Jenny grabbed her pillow. Buried her face in it. Yelled into it. "I want this to be over!"

"I know, I know you do," Haley said quietly. "Listen: that was a dumb question. I didn't notice the board, either. I'll bet he wasn't outside the door while you were in here. You would have heard him, you know? We have a pretty squeaky pen. I always hear Madison writing stuff."

Jenny lowered the pillow. Her eyes were red with tears, but she attempted to smile.

"Definitely squeakiest pen on the hall," she agreed.

"So let's not worry about when you noticed it. All that matters is that you saw it when you came back from breakfast. Now, here's something: does Jordan usually wear a baseball cap?"

"How would I know that?"

"Did you notice a guy with a baseball cap on our hall, or just outside our building?"

"Half the guys on this campus wear baseball caps. Why?"

"Eric from downstairs says a guy with a cap was writing on our door this morning."

"That was him." Jenny said this definitively. No room for argument.

"Well . . . maybe," Haley said. "Might have been someone else. This guy I know from math? He's been trying to reach me." Haley summoned a mental image of Richard's hair. She'd spent a lot of time lately wondering if it was blond or brown. She couldn't remember ever seeing it cap-covered.

"But what difference does it make who did it?" Jenny moaned, suddenly tearful again. "Just the fact that *someone*—"

"Of course it makes a difference! When we report this, we'll tell them what Eric saw. Jordan's not supposed to be anywhere near you, right? Not even in the same dining hall? If Eric saw him in our building, looking for our room, they will definitely make him leave. You'll feel safer then."

Jenny's expression was anything but reassured. "Report this?"

"Right now. I'll go with you to Carole."

"I don't want to report this."

Haley was silent. Jenny's words could have been a door slamming. Within an inch of her nose.

"If I make a big deal about this, it'll just get worse," Jenny said. "I can't let him know he upset me. That's what he wants! He'll just do it again."

"Jen," Haley said. "You have to report this."

"No! I don't have to. I don't *have to* do anything I don't want to, Haley."

"Well, yeah, you do. You reported somebody for rape, and so now you have to follow through. You can't pick and choose what you tell them, Jen. If he's still bothering you, you have to report it."

"Don't bully me!"

Where had Haley heard Jenny say that before?

Then she remembered: on the phone. With her parents. Her father, specifically. Who can't decide whether he's more furious with MacCallum for not expelling Jordan on the spot or with Jenny for choosing Haley as her advisor. He'd been insisting she needed a lawyer instead.

When she first heard about his objections to her, Haley had felt a little insulted. Did Mr. James think she was some jerk who wouldn't look out for his daughter? But as this thing has gone on, she'd begun to suspect the man had a point.

Haley was in over her head. And Jenny was complicated.

"I'm not bullying you," Haley replied. "I'm trying to help! You texted *me*, remember?"

"Then be a friend and please respect what I want. And I don't want to report this!"

"Fine." Haley stood. She was through. "Then I hope you'll respect my need to get to class. I've already missed too many." She grabbed her pack and marched out, slamming the door behind her for effect.

All this happened, what, five hours ago? But it feels like days. Her still-bruised brain, struggling simply to keep up with her reading assignments, feels overwhelmed by Jenny's problems.

As Haley sits at the now-empty table, Richard's still-full mug in front of her, she plucks a brown paper napkin from the dispenser between the salt and pepper shakers and blows her nose. Maybe it's for the best. The two of them were doomed anyway. Not only is it a matter of time before Carrie sees them, but the coincidences here are too much. He's Jenny's rapist's housemate. She's Jordan's accuser's roommate. Just breathing together in the same room is probably some code of conduct violation.

Definitely for the best.

So why does she feel so bad?

She pushes back her chair with a loud scrape . . . and startles when someone slips into Richard's just-vacated seat.

The someone wears a café apron. One of the work-study students who bakes and serves coffee.

"What's your hurry?" Gail says to her.

．．．

Exley makes sure they all have drinks. Then he watches.

Tamra with the smudgy eyes and her friend Marliese. They drain their cups and elbow their way to the center of the room. Laughing, arms over their heads, hips in a slow, suggestive swivel, they dance together.

Marliese is pretty. A good dancer. She smiles as if she's having so much fun.

Tamra knows he's watching. She knows without looking his way. She dances and she laughs because he's watching.

．．．

20

RICHARD

Anger is like caffeine. It fuels you.

And right now Richard rides a four-pack-of-Red-Bull buzz.

His mind flies over the possibilities, a heat-seeking drone on a quest. Library? Class? Dining hall? But, of course, he tracks Jordan down at the house. He's in the Taylor common room.

He's not alone. He sits on the couch next to Exley. The two of them, heads close together, laugh at something on Exley's phone. They glance up quickly when he enters.

"Hey," Jordan says, smile at the ready. "Just the man I was hoping to see."

"That so?" Richard says. "And I thought I was looking for you." Something in his tone melts the smile right off Jordan's face. "We need to talk. Alone." He aims the last word in Exley's direction. The Doctor rises, slipping the phone into his back pocket.

"Great seeing you, too, man," he says, slapping Richard on

the arm as he passes out of the room. A little too hard. Richard chooses to ignore it. "Have fun," Exley says. Is it his imagination, or does he wink at Jordan when he says that? Such an asshole. Richard waits to hear his retreating steps down the hall before he begins.

He doesn't sit.

"Tell me," Richard says quietly, "you did *not* go to that girl's room this morning."

To his credit, Jordan looks genuinely puzzled. "What girl?"

"Jenny."

Jordan makes this noise like a snort. "You think I'm that stupid?"

Richard feels the tiniest hint of relief. "I don't know. You tell me. Because someone went by her room this morning and wrote 'Lying Bitch' on her whiteboard."

Jordan's eyes open wide. He looks surprised.

And amused.

"Wasn't me," he says. "But if you find out who it was, let me know. I'd like to shake his hand."

Richard's disgust rises like vomit at the back of his throat. The guy's not just annoying. He's an asshole.

And yes: stupid.

"I can't believe I'm going to say this, but I wish your uncle were here right now," Richard says. "He'd rip you a new one."

Jordan no longer looks amused. He stands. He's shorter than Richard. "Something bothering you, Richard? You seem a little worked up."

"You think? Well, I'll tell you something, Jordan. I am. And for some reason, you're not. Which confuses me. Because you're the one on trial for rape, while I haven't done a damn thing! But somehow, I'm caught up in it! So yeah, I guess I'm a little worked up!" He's surprised by his own voice, rising.

Jordan takes another step closer. Richard can practically feel his breath. "Number one," he says, "I'm not on trial. For anything. This is a college hearing. Number two, I didn't do anything wrong, either. And number three, you're being a douche." Jordan stumbles on the word *douche*. Almost stammers. He's trying to sound tough.

What an incredible jerk. It occurs to Richard that it would feel really, really good to hit something right now. A wall. A punching bag.

Jordan's face.

Somehow, Jordan can tell. He steps back, putting up both hands. "What the hell, man?" he says. "Seriously, what has gotten *into* you?"

"Guilt by association. That's what. Do you know, someone asked me if *I* wrote on her whiteboard?"

Jordan suddenly looks very interested. "Who?"

He's said too much. Anger has made him sloppy, and he's firing in any direction. And the fact is, even though he pretty much can't stand Jordan, he's only half-mad at him. The other half is furious with Haley.

At least Carrie had reasons to be pissed with him: he said stuff that annoyed her. And she told him. Very up-front about all her issues with him, he had to give her that. But Haley? Suspecting him of bullying her roommate? Randomly unfair.

"Doesn't matter who," he says. "Somebody who knows what's going on, knows I know you, and connected the dots. And here's the thing: I don't want to be connected with your crap anymore."

Jordan connects the dots. "Hot math girl," he says knowingly. "The one at the Grille. She knows Jenny?"

"I'm not in the mood to play guessing games with you," Richard says. "Unless you want to play Who Wrote On Jenny's Whiteboard? Oh, wait: you'd win that game, wouldn't you?"

"I told you," Jordan says, glowering, "I don't know anything about that."

"Yeah, right," Richard says, shaking his head in disgust. "You're just this swell guy who happens to always be in the center of some shit storm. Not your fault, right? Pardon me if I want to get out of the rain."

Richard turns to leave the common room. He needs to leave before his anger explodes in ways that hurt him.

"So once you cool off," Jordan calls after him, "my uncle's in town. He wants to meet with us. I was planning to tell you: our interview with the investigator is the day after tomorrow."

Richard wheels around. "You mean *your* interview. And please give my regrets to Uncle Hard-ass. I'm conveniently unavailable."

Jordan's expression darkens. "I don't think that's an option."

"Sure it is. It's my option and I'm exercising it."

"Richard, you agreed to do this. You can't back out now."

"I agreed to sit there looking like an upstanding citizen while people grill you, but that doesn't mean I have to jump every time your family cruises into town. Tell him hi from me."

He leaves the room for real now, expecting to hear Jordan call him back, reply in some way. But he's silent.

For Richard, that's good enough for now.

. . .

Jenny doesn't drift to the center with the dancers. But the red cup gives her something to do.

Because no one talks. No one can. They yell into each other's ears, but even then they have no idea what was said.

She's not sure what to say anyhow. So she stands to the side, watching the dancing, sipping. Sipping. Lemony, fizzy. Supersweet.

She pushes through the crowd, back to the can, which takes some time. The tall boy is still there. Friendly smile when he refills her cup.

. . .

21

Haley

"Tell me I didn't just see what I just saw," Gail says to Haley from across the café table.

The older girl wears this expression—head tilted, one eyebrow arched—that challenges Haley to say anything but the truth, the whole truth, and nothing but the truth.

But Haley is a complete idiot about guys. "He's my math tutor," she explains.

Gail snorts.

"Seriously. I met him at math help," Haley insists.

"That didn't look like calculus to me."

"No," Haley admits.

Gail's eyes narrow. "You do know he's Carrie's latest, right?"

"I thought that was over."

Gail pauses, thinking. "It is. But she's . . . territorial. Just because she doesn't want him doesn't mean anyone else can have him. Especially her friends."

"I'm not her friend," Haley says quickly.

"Hmmm," Gail responds. She looks at Haley critically. Assessing. "She's not a bad person to have in your corner. And she likes you."

"Unless I start dating her old boyfriend," Haley adds. "Not that it's even a remote possibility. I just messed that up for good."

"He didn't look like a happy camper," Gail agrees. "Want to talk about it?"

You have no idea how much I don't.

The look on his face. Anger. Hurt. He's absolutely right: he'd done nothing to deserve her suspicion. It's just . . . she's heard so much negative stuff about him. Plus he *lives* with the damn rapist! Does she buy his insistence that they're not friends?

"No. But thanks," Haley says.

"Well, for the record, I always thought he was a nice guy. Definitely gets failing grades for political correctness, but his heart's in the right place. So are a lot of his other parts. Which compensates, know what I mean?" Haley smiles, as if she knows. "But just in case you two *do* kiss and make up, your secret's safe with me. I won't say anything to Carrie."

"Thanks," Haley repeats.

Gail glances at the wall clock behind the counter. "My break's almost over. How's life treating you otherwise?"

"Actually, there is something."

Gail leans back in her seat, arms folded across her chest. "Five minutes. Shoot."

"It's Jenny. I don't know, Gail, it's strange. But I think she's being stalked, and for some reason she won't report it. We pretty much had a fight over it this morning."

Gail sits up straight. A thin line forms between her eyebrows. "I don't know anything about this."

Haley describes the morning's drama. Leaving out, of course, her conversation with Richard. More omissions. As she speaks, Gail reaches into her café apron pocket and pulls out her cell phone. Her fingers fly over the screen. She scrolls, reads.

"Damn. Damn!" Gail stands. "It's on The Board." She tugs at her apron strings. Yanks the thing off. "We've got to go."

Haley stares at her. "I thought you were working?"

"It's on The Board!" Gail repeats angrily.

"I have no idea what you're talking about."

Gail looks at her like she's too stupid to live. She thrusts her phone at Haley's face.

"The Board," she explains. "It's an app. People share whatever garbage pops into their heads. You can read whatever's posted within a ten-mile radius. Oh, and did I mention? No one uses real names."

On the screen, Haley sees a cartoon of an old-fashioned bulletin board. Alongside, in glowing blue, a column of Twitter-length comments, each marked by a thumbtack-shaped icon. She manages to read a few lines before Gail snatches it away.

Someone oughta take the no-good c*** out and rape her again
She's nasty as shit
Bitch is psycho. She's not hot enuf to rape

For a moment, Haley wonders if she might actually vomit. The words are like a kick to her gut.

"Oh Gail. Oh no," is all she manages.

Gail grabs her mug and Haley's from the table and practically hurls them into the nearby bussing tray.

"Carrie and I call it 'The Bored,' as in haters who don't have anything better to do with their lives," she explains. "But this is beyond bored losers. It's totally the same person who wrote on your door. C'mon!" She strides to the café counter, tossing her apron in a plastic bin near the bussing cart. She disappears into the small kitchen out back, and Haley hears her urgent conversation with someone. When she emerges, she carries her backpack and a jacket.

"How do you know it's the same person?" Haley asks, hurrying to keep up as Gail exits the café.

Gail's got her phone out, reading as she racewalks. "Damn!" she repeats. "The comment field is huge. God, people are sick."

Haley stops. "How do you *know* it's the same person?"

Gail interrupts her sprint to explain. "When you start a thread, you label it," she says. "This one's called 'Lying Bitch.'"

Haley feels the vomit threaten to rise again. Gail resumes jogging, and this time Haley follows.

"Where are we going?" she asks.

"Carole Patterson's office," Gail replies. "Whether Jenny likes it or not, we're reporting this."

. . .

"Having fun?" he shouts.

"Jenny," she shouts back.

Tall Boy leans closer. Motions for her to repeat herself.

"Jenny!" She's practically yelling. How funny is that? She laughs.

He smiles down at her.

"What's your name?"

He replies. She points to her ear, shakes her head, laughing. Tall Boy laughs, too. They abandon conversation.

He serves punch as she stands alongside, listening to the music, sipping.

. . .

22

RICHARD

The khakis are wrinkled, the starched shirt stiff. It makes for an interesting contrast. Not that Richard gives a damn how he looks. But Uncle Bruce had been very clear about what they should wear when they meet with the investigator.

"No ties or blazers," he said. "You'll look like you're trying too hard. But you do want to appear respectful, so go with button-down shirts, nice pants. No sneakers: wear real shoes. Loafers, if you have them. *With* socks. Nothing screams 'douche bag' louder than loafers without socks."

You would know, Richard didn't say.

As he sits in the reception room of the Dean of Students Office waiting for Jordan—is the guy really going to be late for his own inquisition?—he almost feels relieved. An hour, maybe two, and it'll be over. All he has to do is keep his mouth shut and look clean-cut while Jordan answers questions. Then he can wash his hands of this whole deal. Plus the entire Bockus clan.

He'd gone out for dinner with them the night before: Jordan, his mom, and his dad. They'd surprised him. Literally. There he was in his room, attempting homework—actually, he was stalking Haley on Facebook; she has bad privacy settings and he could check out photos going back to her sophomore year in high school—when there was a knock. He opened it to find Jordan, flanked by two adults who looked creepily like him.

"Hey," Jordan said, nervous fake smile on his face. "My folks are in town and wanted to meet you."

He got up from his chair. He'd wanted to push the door shut and lock it; instead, he invited the "Bocki" into his cell of a room and shook their hands. Made small talk. Couldn't think of a single excuse when they asked him, on the spot, to join them for dinner at the inn where they were staying.

Which just happened to be the same bed and breakfast where Uncle Bruce had checked in. Two days earlier, it turns out. He didn't join them for burgers and steaks, but "would really like to chat before you head back to campus," Mrs. Bockus told Richard when the coffee came. Hand on his forearm. Red lacquered fingernails. They'd sandbagged him, totally.

At least he'd gotten a decent sirloin out of it.

Later, in Uncle Bruce's room, Mrs. Bockus explained they had all driven in to "support" Jordan. Well . . . *support* was her word. Flutter-nervously-and-bug-the-crap-out-of-everyone was more her thing. Richard thought she was nice enough, but Jordan was barely civil to her, especially when she lapsed into tearful, random comments.

"You'll do great! It'll all be fine! We'll be through this soon!" After a while, you tuned her out, like a mosquito buzzing in the corner of the room. This thin woman in stretchy black pants.

Jordan's dad, in contrast, barely spoke. He glowered, Jabba the Hutt–like, from where he sat in a deep armchair, the folds of his thick neck swaddling his face and his eyes gleaming like blue pinpricks. He scarcely reacted to his wife, but Richard could tell he registered, critically, everything Uncle Bruce had to say.

Which was plenty.

"So, the investigator," Uncle Bruce explained, "is a Mac-Callum dean. Rather than hire a pro from outside, the college has decided to save money. Although my sources say this dean—his name is Elliot Hunt—has actually taken an investigator training course, so he might not be a total bozo. Let's just hope he's not a crusader."

"Crusader?" Jordan asked.

"Out to cleanse the campus of predators like you," Uncle Bruce said.

Jordan's mom turned a color approximating her nails. "No one finds that amusing, Bruce."

"Sorry. But in my experience, these folks are either incompetent or out to get you. It blows my mind when colleges don't cough up the cash to pay a pro to get the job done right. But, that aside . . ." He trained his eyes on Jordan. "This guy could be one of the Marx Brothers. Or, he could be the Terminator. We can't predict what you'll get. So stick to the script."

As Richard sits in the reception room waiting for Jordan, he imagines the dean dismissing them from his office with

185

"Hasta la vista, baby." He laughs to himself. Definitely not the script Uncle Bruce has in mind.

Just then, he sees Jordan enter and announce himself to the young woman at the front desk. His wet hair is slicked back, and his trousers have been ironed to a neat pleat running down the front of each leg. Uncle Bruce must have advised him to abandon his usual Vineyard Vines and go for the Young Republican look. His expression is grim as he crosses the room toward Richard.

"Something funny?" Jordan asks.

Richard realizes he's still grinning and attempts a somber expression. "No. How's it going?"

"How do you think it's going? Rest of my life pretty much depends on what I say in the next hour." Jordan runs his fingers across his scalp, his eyes darting toward the stairs at the back of the lobby. "The girl at the desk said we could go right up."

Richard rises.

"One sec," Jordan says. He seems reluctant to leave the room. "I told my folks I didn't want them sitting down here, waiting. I think that would make me nuts."

Richard nods. He can see that. He waits, but Jordan is still rooted to the floor.

"So, you're good?" Jordan asks suddenly. His eyes bore into Richard's.

Richard doesn't flinch. "Why wouldn't I be? I'm just supposed to sit there and look respectable."

He's petrified. All that swagger. Guy's just a little chickenshit.

Richard almost feels sorry for him.

They mount the stairs to Dean Hunt's office on the second floor. Jordan knocks.

"Come in," a deep voice beckons.

Richard's first impression is . . . wood. Polished wood. Cherry bookcases line every inch of wall space that isn't taken up by windows, while a dark wood desk dominates an entire corner of the room. Two gleaming college chairs, the ones your parents might buy you as a graduation gift, are positioned before the desk.

A man who looks around his father's age, with a close-trimmed beard and wire-rimmed glasses, sits backlit by a tall window. A stack of papers and a blank yellow pad of paper are lined up neatly on the smooth surface before him. He stands, walks around the side of the desk, and extends his hand.

"Good morning. Elliot Hunt," he says.

"Good morning, Dean Hunt," Jordan begins. "I'm Jordan Bockus. This is Richard Brandt, who will be my advisor today."

Elliot Hunt's eyes flit down the length of Jordan's pleats. When he shakes Richard's hand his grasp is warm, firm. But not overly firm. His smile is polite. He gestures toward the two chairs, returns to his own.

He doesn't seem ridiculous. Or menacing. He seems utterly at ease.

This should be interesting.

"Thank you," Dean Hunt begins, "for being punctual. You'd be amazed how many students think an appointed time is merely a suggestion."

Jordan laughs, shaking his head in disbelief. As if he couldn't possibly imagine ever being late for anything.

"Before we begin," Dean Hunt says, glancing at the papers

on his desk, "we have a few formalities. I'm going to ask several preliminary questions, Mr. Bockus, just to confirm that you are fully informed about our proceedings today. First: have you been apprised as to the nature of this meeting?"

"Uh . . . you want to interview me?" Jordan replies.

The dean stares at him for a moment, then nods. "I'll take that as a yes. Have you been informed about the complaint made against you?"

"Yes."

"Including the amendment to that complaint, which includes cyberbullying as well as violating the college's protection order that bars you from entering Ms. James's dormitory?"

"Yes," Jordan says without hesitation.

Richard can't help it—he sort of gasps. Audibly. Jordan hadn't said anything about new charges. What the hell?

"And I understand you have responded to that amendment?"

"I responded that she's out of her mind. No way would I go near her dorm, and I have *not* been posting stuff about her. I don't even have that app."

"Just a simple yes or no would be fine, Mr. Bockus."

"Yes. I responded."

"And do you understand that I have been appointed as the college's sole investigator in this matter?"

"Yes."

"And have you been informed that during today's meeting I will ask you questions related to the claim against you for the purposes of filing a report with the MacCallum College Judiciary Committee and making a recommendation as to whether sanctions against you are warranted?"

Jordan shifts uncomfortably in his chair. "Excuse me?"

Richard detects a sigh from Dean Hunt. "I'm going to ask you questions today, Mr. Bockus. I'm going to take notes. I'm going to use these notes in my report to the committee. I'm going to tell them whether I think you have violated the college's code of conduct. I'm going to suggest whether they should sanction you. Then they'll decide what happens. Is that your understanding as well?"

The furrow on Jordan's forehead smooths. "Oh. Yeah. Yes."

Dean Hunt pushes a sheet of paper and a pen across the desk toward Jordan. "Would you please sign this, attesting that you have responded affirmatively to each question."

As Jordan signs, Richard's eyes trail over the book spines displayed in the cases. There's a lot of literature. Poetry. More like a professor's office. Not that he knows what a dean's book collection is like.

He meets Dean Hunt's gaze.

"How are you doing today, Mr. Brandt?"

He's not sure what he thinks about the way Dean Hunt keeps calling him and Jordan Mr. So-and-So. Is he old-school or ironic?

"I'm well, thanks. You?"

Dean Hunt does not respond to the question. "It's quite a responsibility you've signed on for, advising Mr. Bockus. And unusual. It's actually never happened before. Respondents usually ask a faculty member or lawyer to accompany them."

It's an opening. Disguised as small talk. *Go on*, he's inviting Richard. *Tell me something I don't know. Explain to me why this kid, who must be lawyered up, because there's no way in hell his family would send him into the lion's den unprepared, is dragging you into this meeting.*

Dean Hunt is smart. He smells a rat.

"It's not a problem," Richard replies, rejecting the bait.

Dean Hunt smiles with his mouth closed, his eyes narrowing slightly as he watches Richard.

Jordan clicks the pen shut and drops it on top of the desk. "Richard's a close friend," he interjects. "We've known each other since, what? Freshman year? And now we live in the same house. It may be a little out of the box to ask another student to do this, but the fact is, Dean Hunt, I'm getting plenty of advice from my family. I wanted a friend to come with me to these meetings. And Richard is a solid guy. Math tutor. Honors student. He's a . . . really solid guy."

Richard tries to imagine the expression on Uncle Bruce's face if he were witnessing Jordan right now. This is what the guy was worried about. His nephew spontaneously combusting. It's a possibility.

Dean Hunt raises his eyebrows. "Well. A math tutor. Imagine that. Shall we begin?" He picks up the yellow pad and the pen, crosses one ankle over the opposite knee, and leans back comfortably in his chair. "Mr. Bockus, did you read Ms. James's statement concerning the events of October seventh?"

"Yes."

"And how do you respond to that statement?"

"I don't agree with it."

"What parts don't you agree with?"

Jordan's face looks frozen. "Parts?"

"Yes, Mr. Bockus. Ms. James gives a very detailed account of the night in question. Which parts of that statement do you disagree with?"

Two lines form across Jordan's forehead. He was doing semi-okay until now.

"You say one thing. One thing." Uncle Bruce had beat that point like a drum the night before. "*I did not rape Jenny James.* That's the answer to every single question. If he asks what you ate for breakfast, you say, *I did not rape Jenny James.* If he asks what color the sky is, you say, *I did not rape Jenny James.* He will not be happy with you. But that's not our concern. He has to walk out of there empty-handed. Don't give him even an inch of rope to hang you with."

Last night, watching Uncle Bruce make his point again and again, Richard thought it seemed simple enough. Now, as Jordan is effectively backed into a corner—because he can't just say it's all a lie, since some of it, like their having been at the Conundrum party, is not—he realizes that this is hard. You can get tripped up.

Dean Hunt has played a great opening move.

"Mr. Bockus?" he prompts.

"I . . . disagree with all of it." Dean Hunt tilts forward in his chair and pulls a couple sheets of paper from the stack on his desk. The room is silent as he scans the sheets.

"You do not agree that you were at a party at Conundrum House the night of October seventh?"

"Excuse me?"

"You do not agree that members of your residence, Taylor House, hosted that party at Conundrum House?"

Jordan's jaw tightens. Two red patches begin to appear on his cheeks.

"You do not agree that a highly alcoholic punch was served to underage guests, among them Ms. James, at that party?"

Still, Jordan does not reply.

Dean Hunt tosses the papers onto the desk and leans back again. "Taylor residence members subverted a ban on house parties by hosting an event at Conundrum. You and Ms. James both attended that event on October seventh. These facts are all contained in her statement. So I'm curious: which parts of her statement do you disagree with?"

Richard sees Jordan's shoulders rise and fall as he takes a deep breath. "Dean Hunt, I did not rape Jenny James."

"Actually, Mr. Bockus, Ms. James does not use the word *rape* anywhere in her statement. She says the two of you engaged in 'nonconsensual sexual intercourse.' "

"I don't agree with that."

"Are you saying it was consensual?" Dean Hunt asks smoothly. His expression is bland. The guy could be watching a public television documentary on butterflies for all the emotion he reveals.

But even Richard knows: he just asked the key question. If Jordan says anything that confirms that he and Jenny had sex, he's cooked.

It took, what? Sixty seconds to get to this point?

Then, Jordan surprises him.

"Dean Hunt, I did not rape Jenny James."

A flicker, just a flicker, of irritation passes over the dean's face. He thought he had this fish on the line.

"Well, why don't we move on from Ms. James's statement to your version of events. Why don't you tell me what happened that night."

Jordan clears his throat. "I don't have anything to say except I did not rape Jenny James."

"Yes, I understand that. Tell me what *did* transpire between you and Ms. James."

"I have nothing to add."

"You refuse to answer my questions?"

"Not at all. I will answer every question. But I'll answer them the same way."

"My record is going to show that you have been uncooperative, Mr. Bockus. This will not help you. Would you like to reconsider?"

Richard sees Jordan clench his jaw.

"Dean Hunt, I mean no disrespect to you or to the college," he says carefully. Like he's practiced the lines. "But if she decides to pursue this criminally, everything I say here can be used against me in court. From your point of view, and the college's point of view, it probably seems like I'm uncooperative. But from a legal point of view, it's what I have to do. I hope you understand."

"Jordan." The switch to the first name surprises Richard. So does the tone. He's changing tactics. "I'm not out to get you. I want to hear your side of the story. If you refuse to tell me, then the only side I've heard is Jenny's."

For a nanosecond, Jordan hesitates. It's so incredibly obvious that he wants to talk. He's so full of self-justification, he could burst. He wants to talk and talk and talk. Richard sees him, hovering at the brink of a deep abyss of words that will sink him.

Then, as if there were an invisible rope wrapped around his waist, pulling him back—Uncle Bruce's voice in his ear?—he recovers.

"I'm sorry, Dean Hunt, but that's all I'm prepared to say about that night."

The dean's gaze lingers over Jordan as he considers his next move. He seems to make a decision and returns to the pile on his desk. He pulls out another sheet. Reads it over, puts it down.

"All right then. Why don't we move on to the amended portion of the complaint. Ms. James says you went by her room and wrote obscenities on her door. She's also claiming that you started a cyberbullying campaign against her using a smartphone application. Now, I know you've met with the college's human resources officer, Carole Patterson, and also responded to these new charges in writing, but why don't you tell me what's going on?"

Jordan leans forward. Like a dog, moments before the leash comes off. "I have not gone anywhere near her room. I haven't stepped foot in that building all semester, actually. As for the phone thing, wasn't me. When Ms. Patterson called me into her office and told me about it, I handed my phone to her on the spot. She could see I don't have that app, so I couldn't possibly have done it."

"Well, you could have used your computer, couldn't you?"

"Not without first having the phone app."

Dean Hunt scribbles something on his pad. "Do you have any idea who would have done this?"

"No."

"None of your friends? No one you know is talking about this?"

"I can't control what people say. Since those witness lists went out, everyone is talking."

Dean Hunt drums his pen lightly on the pad as he thinks. Changes direction abruptly.

"Which of your friends has the app?"

"I don't know. You'd have to ask them yourself."

The dean nods. As if this is an excellent idea he had never considered before.

"Well, I think we're done for today, Mr. Bockus. But do know I intend to meet with you again. I'm nothing if not hopeful."

The boys stand, Jordan leaning over the wide desk to shake the dean's hand. Richard follows suit. But Dean Hunt waves him back to his chair.

"Actually, as long as you're here, Mr. Brandt, why don't you and I chat now? Saves us the trouble of scheduling something later."

Jordan doesn't even attempt to disguise his panicked expression.

"I'm not on the witness list. I wasn't there that night," Richard says.

Dean Hunt looks at him with wide, innocent eyes. "The investigation is not limited to the names Mr. Bockus and Ms. James provided," he says. "And as Mr. Bockus points out, I should ask his friends myself." Dean Hunt's eyes move to the door, willing Jordan to follow suit.

For a moment, it looks like he won't budge. When Jordan finally does turn to leave the room, he flashes Richard a severe look.

Don't screw me over, it communicates in no uncertain terms. He strides to the door, closes it loudly.

Dean Hunt smiles pleasantly. "Well. Richard. I hope this will be a more productive conversation."

• • •

Exley drains his cup. He tosses the empty.

He shoulders through the crowd. She has her back to him, but the friend sees him approach. She signals with a glance, a smile, assenting tilt of the head. Look, it says.

Tamra turns.

As if on cue, as if in time to the music, as if choreographed, as if rehearsed . . . Marliese fades into the others.

Exley and Tamra begin their dance.

• • •

23

Haley

The three insistent raps on the door don't surprise Haley; she's been waiting for Gail and Carrie. They're moving Jenny to a different room today.

The short woman planted on the other side, red dreadlocks sprinkled with small brass clips, is completely unexpected.

"Wow," escapes Haley, who feels her cheeks instantly blush. Will she *ever* learn to control what pops from her mouth?

"Hey," the woman says, smiling. As if she didn't hear. Or is used to it. "Haley, right? I'm Carrie's friend Mona." Freckles that match the hair spatter her nose and cheeks like rust-colored paint. "I'm part of the moving crew."

Haley steps back and motions the Mona person inside. The room looks like thieves broke in and didn't find what they wanted. She's been trying to collect Jenny's things without the aid of boxes or duffels or even Jenny, for that matter, and all she's managed to do is yank stuff from drawers and closets and heap it on the vacant bed. Her roommate hasn't stepped foot in the building since Gail and Carrie hustled her out the other night. Right after the three of them met with Carole Patterson.

"I *begged* you not to report it!" Jenny practically shrieked. Not at the older girls; at Haley. They'd found Jenny wrapped in a blanket, curled on her bed, windows shut and blinds drawn. Even in the dim light Haley could read betrayal in her furious eyes.

"Jen, we had no choice," Haley began, but stopped when she felt Gail's foot pressing on hers. *Let us do the talking*, that foot said.

Carrie moved right to the bed and wound her arms around Jenny. "Girl, we've got this. We've *got* this."

Jenny squirmed, trying to free herself from the embrace. "*This* will only make it worse! Don't you see?"

"This will make it better," Carrie continued, her voice a smooth contrast to Jenny's. Haley could see Carrie tighten her hold. "This is how you fight back."

"That's what you said before," Jenny accused. "You told me if I reported the rape, things would get better. So I reported, and now he's stalking me! What'll he do now that you've reported the stalking?"

Gail pulled one of the desk chairs next to the bed and sat. Haley still hadn't budged from her spot near the door.

"Jen, there's more going on than you realize," Gail began.

Carrie widened her eyes, shaking her head slightly at Gail. *No*, Haley could see her mouth. *Not now.*

"Hell yeah," Haley said, surprising herself. "She needs to know!" Something about the older girl swooping in, her body a wrapped barrier between them and Jenny, had bugged her. And now spoon-feeding Jenny information in bits? Like she was some child in a high chair? It loosened Haley's frozen feet and silent tongue. Carrie didn't look pleased, but she released her hold on Jenny and didn't argue as Haley moved to her own bed and sat.

"Jen," Haley began, "have you ever heard of an app called The Board?"

"No," Jenny said. Quieter. She'd ratcheted the yelling down to something more like nervous suspicion.

"Me neither, until this afternoon," Haley said. "It's an online bulletin board where people post anonymously about random stuff. A topic is usually started as a thread by someone to get a conversation going."

"That's one way to put it," Carrie commented, unable to help herself.

"Shh," Gail warned her.

"You put a topic out there," Haley continued, ignoring Carrie, "and people weigh in. Like the comments section for a blog or online newspaper. Anyway, it can get rough. You know how those comments sections are."

"Why are you telling me this?" Jenny asked.

Haley took a deep breath. "Someone has started a thread about you."

"About *me*? Why?"

"Because of the investigation. The thread is called 'Lying Bitch.' "

It was hard to look at the expression on Jenny's face. Torqued. Like she'd just been kicked in the stomach.

"Show me," she said, her voice small, but her hand held out, insistent. Gail glanced at Carrie, who turned her head, refusing to make eye contact. Gail passed Jenny the phone anyway.

Thirty seconds into scanning the posts, Jenny's eyes grew round and she gasped. She tossed the phone on the bed as if it were hot.

"Why?" she exclaimed. She stared at it, then stared at them. "I get *him*. He's mad. He wants to intimidate me. But everyone else? They don't know what happened! They don't even know me!" She began to sob. Wild, choking cries that shook her.

As if on cue, all three moved toward her. Jenny waved them off, lifting one arm in a blocking motion, sharp elbow pointed out. As if their touch would be another violation she just couldn't bear at that moment.

"Now, finally, *now*, are they going to *do* something?" she demanded.

Haley knew exactly the "they" Jenny was talking about. "They're trying. Carole called the college's IT office as soon as we told her, and they blocked The Board from the server, but anyone with a data plan can still access it."

"They're also asking the company that runs The Board to put a virtual fence around MacCallum," Gail added. "But that might take a couple days."

Jenny turned to Carrie. "He'll go now, won't he? Jordan? They'll have to throw him out after this, right?"

Carrie looked grim. "Carole's supposedly interrogating his sorry ass right now. We'll see what happens."

Jenny didn't respond, but collapsed on her bed again, knees pulled up to her chest.

"We should get her out of here," Gail murmured. "It feels—and smells—like a cave."

Carrie nodded.

Things moved quickly from there. Jenny needed little convincing to spend the night with Carrie at Out House. By the next morning, Carole had not only met with Jordan (and discovered he didn't have the app on his phone, so . . . still no expulsion for him), but also had issued a campus-wide e-mail condemning The Board and threatening sanctions against anyone traced to the online attacks.

She also told them she was "looking into" a different room for Jenny. But it would take time, she said.

"Yeah. Time's up," Carrie declared when she heard that.

Hence the moving crew.

As they take stock of the messy room, Mona wastes no time telling Haley what *she* thinks of Carole. And her e-mail. Mona has brought a roll of faux-plastic garbage bags with her ("Biodegradable, made from cornstarch," she'd informed Haley, as if she needed reassurance), and while they stuff the items heaped on the bed into the environmentally correct bags, she vents.

"I mean, you've got to wonder: did she take how-to-be-stupid lessons? Because anyone who didn't have The Board app before sure does now! Carrie says an hour after that e-mail went out, comments on the thread doubled. Doubled! A lot more of them were for our side, calling out the haters. But still.

"And this room thing? Bullshit. You know there's space *somewhere*. If you ask me, Carole Patterson is good for nothing."

Haley holds a many-jointed collapsible desk lamp in her

hand. Will it rip through if she tries to bag it? "She's good at lists."

Mona looks puzzled. "Lists?"

"Yep. Bullet points. To-do lists. Every meeting I go to with her, she's created a new one. It's her superpower. She's Action Item Woman."

A short, sharp laugh escapes Mona. It punctuates the air like a bark. "Okay. You're hilarious," she says. No trace of irony.

Haley decides the lamp is not a faux-bag item and places it on top of Jenny's desk. Carrie and Gail are due to arrive with a car, so maybe they'll bring boxes?

"So, I don't get something," Haley says. "If Carole says there are no free rooms anywhere, how is it we're moving Jenny permanently to Out House?"

Mona grins. "That's thanks to yours truly," she says. "I'm giving her my room. Action Item Woman has no clue."

"But where will you go?"

"Just downstairs," Mona says. "I have a friend who doesn't mind making space for me."

Haley gets the impression this is not much of a hardship.

"And you can thank me, too," Mona adds. "I'm sure you don't mind having a single, right?" She winks at Haley.

Mom will be thrilled. Haley hasn't spoken to her family in days. They have no idea what's been going on.

"I would have killed for a single my freshman year," Mona continues. "Every weekend and most weeknights I was sexiled to the couch in the lounge. Sucked."

"Not an issue with me and Jen," Haley says quietly. *Not for either of us*, she doesn't add.

Mona stands gazing at the growing collection of filled

bags, hands on hips. She seems to be thinking. "When people ask where she's gone, don't say," Mona tells her.

Haley's shoulders drop. "Ugh. I mentioned it to Madison. Not good, huh?"

Mona looks severe. "Well, get hold of Madison and make sure it *ends* there. You know he's still on campus, right? Her attacker-slash-online-harasser?"

"Yeah, Carrie's pretty furious," Haley says.

Mona rolls her eyes. She can tell from Mona's reaction that she's up to speed with what's going on: no one has been able to link Jordan to the whiteboard or the online Board. Carole's promise to "get to the bottom of this" has done nothing except reveal a bottomless pit of questions.

Mona opens a bag with an impatient snap. "Well, Carrie's one of those no-red-tape types. She thinks all this stuff about hearings and evidence is bureaucratic nonsense and you need to protect victims regardless of little things like due process."

"What do you think?"

"Me? I'm pre-law. I'm all *about* process. But here's the thing: this is a private college. They can do whatever the hell they want. For example, that stuff on The Board? Out in the real world, that's protected speech. Here in MacCallum Land, it's a violation of community standards and they can have you gone in a heartbeat if they find out you did it. So I don't know which of this rapist's great grandfathers built the place, but they're tiptoeing around the dude."

At this moment, shadows appear in the door. Gail and Carrie. Who both, thankfully, carry cardboard boxes.

"Hey, we're parked on the sidewalk illegally," Carrie says. "Let's make this quick." She drops an empty box, seizes four bags, and stalks out. Gail does the same.

Mona glances at Haley and rolls her eyes again. She begins packing Jenny's textbooks into a box.

"*Such* a bossy boots," Mona mutters.

Haley grins. She grabs the jointed lamp and deposits it in a box.

．　．　．

Jordan sees them leaving, the girls Exley invited. Except for the tall one he's dancing with, their group moves toward the door.

Jordan follows, drink in hand. "Hey!" They're down the stairs, moving along the sidewalk. His ears ring from the party. The night air is cool. "Leaving so soon?"

Marliese turns. "It's too crowded!" she calls back, laughing.

He takes two steps down, but they are gone, slipping into the dark woods, the winding paths. Jordan turns to go back inside. A guy, standing at the head of a line he only just notices, blocks him with his arm.

"Can't go in without a freshman female."

"I was just in there."

"Sorry, back of the line."

"You saw me! I was just in there!"

"Yeah, and four girls left ahead of you. Get in line."

Jordan stares at him, stunned. He moves toward the door. The guy stands in his way. He tries to push forward; the guy pushes back.

Something rises in his chest, like a wave. He hurls his full cup at the door, swearing. It hits the side of the house and splatters. To the sound of angry voices, Jordan retreats into the dark night, away from the house.

．　．　．

24

RICHARD

Richard manages to avoid Jordan and his uncle most of the day, which is no small thing.

He'd expected them to be lying in wait in the lobby, ready to pounce the moment he emerged from Dean Hunt's office. But apparently Jordan had class, and Dean Hunt had gone on for a while. Which explains the texts.

Three from Jordan pop up the second Richard turns on his phone.

The first: *Went to history. Text when ur done.*

The second: *Done yet? Text me.*

The third: *WTF?? get out of there*

A fourth chimes as he escapes the building and strides across campus: *????????????*

Richard silences the phone. *Let him twist*, he decides. *Might do him some good.*

Besides. He needs time to figure out what he'll tell them.

"I don't know how 'productive' I can be," Richard had said after the door closed. "I don't know a whole lot."

"We always know more than we realize," Dean Hunt said. He sat back. Regarded Richard in a not-unfriendly way. "It's interesting," he said. "I received such long witness lists. Not only from Ms. James, who included everyone who lives on her hall, but also from Mr. Bockus. Especially from him. He listed every single resident in Taylor House, most of those from Conundrum House, and everyone he could think of who attended that party. The list is so comprehensive, it strikes me as odd that you're not on it."

Richard stuck to the script. "I didn't go to the party."

"Several people on Mr. Bockus's list didn't go to the party," Dean Hunt said. Which was not a question.

So Richard didn't answer.

"Let's be honest," Dean Hunt continued. "These are not 'witnesses' in the traditional sense. These lists are about . . . point of view. Who tells the story. Ms. James gives us a list of narrators and Mr. Bockus gives us a different one. All in an attempt to grasp that great, elusive, bothersome thing: the truth. I wonder, Richard, why Mr. Bockus doesn't want you to tell his side of the story?"

"I'm a math major. I suck at stories."

The words were out of his mouth before he had time to consider the wisdom of saying "suck" to Dean Hunt.

But he laughed. "I'll remember that," he said. "Fiction is not your natural inclination."

Richard smiled. "You were an English prof."

"Am I that obvious?"

Richard gestured to the walls. "Your library gives you away."

Dean Hunt's eyes automatically trailed to the bookshelves. Richard recognized a few titles he had to read in high school.

"Why did you stop teaching?"

The dean looked thoughtful. "I haven't. They throw the odd course my way. I fill in when someone's on sabbatical. But the real answer is: they're paying me more."

"Plus you don't have to grade papers," Richard said.

"Or read them," Dean Hunt added. "I lost patience with those endless pages of bull. Admittedly, I got some gorgeous work. Real quality. But more and more it felt like students were writing papers at three a.m. the night before they were due, about books they'd only half read. It amazed me that they thought I wouldn't notice."

Richard didn't say anything. He wasn't so sure he didn't fall into that category himself.

"I don't imagine you would insult my intelligence that way, Richard," Dean Hunt said.

"If you mean would I try to pull something over on you, no," Richard said. "But I've definitely handed in some fairly lame papers." They both laughed. It occurred to Richard that this was friendlier than it needed to be.

And no accident.

"So, why do you think you're not on his witness list?" Dean Hunt finally asked. In his back-to-business voice.

"Probably because I wasn't around that night."

"Where were you?"

"At my girlfriend's. She lives in Out House."

"How long were you there?"

"All night. I didn't get back to Taylor until the next day."

"And your girlfriend is . . . ?" Dean Hunt waited.

"You want her name?"

"Sure."

"Carrie Mason."

Dean Hunt stilled. "Why is that name familiar?" He leaned forward, shuffled through the stack.

"She's sort of a campus activist. Everyone knows her."

Dean Hunt found what he was looking for.

"She took the initial call reporting the rape," he said, his eyes scanning a sheet he'd pulled. "She's on the college's Sexual Assault Response Team."

Richard nodded.

"Have the two of you discussed this case?" Dean Hunt asked sharply.

"No," Richard said. "Actually, we broke up. I haven't spoken to her since the night of the party."

"You broke up the night of the party?" Not even bothering to mask the skepticism in his voice.

"Well . . . the morning after."

"May I ask why?"

Because I joked that she raped me, Richard managed to not say.

"Does it matter? We were always fighting. Things came to a head, now it's over. Why do you care?" He felt himself getting annoyed.

"I don't care about your personal issues with your girlfriend.

But I do care about *connections*. That's what an investigation is all about: connecting the dots. Putting the pieces of the puzzle together. And now I'm told the best friend of the accused is seeing the SART leader who counseled the victim? I'd say it matters."

"For the record: he is *not* my best friend. We're housemates. That's it."

Dean Hunt shook his head, as if he were trying to clear his thoughts. "We'll get back to your . . . uneasy relationship with Mr. Bockus. For right now, I want to know: did you and Ms. Mason discuss this case?"

"Absolutely not."

"Think carefully, Richard. Pillow talk is a tricky thing."

A harsh laugh escaped Richard. "Carrie's not the pillow talk type," he said. "Listen, Dean Hunt, she and I hung out at her house that night, fought in the morning, and broke up. We didn't have a chance to talk about the case. Jenny didn't even report it until days after the party, and Carrie and I were long past speaking terms by then."

"And you know that . . . how?" Dean Hunt asked quietly.

The room moves. It swirls. It whirls. Like an amusement park ride that doesn't stop.

"Do you want to dance?"

Tall Boy, in her ear. His lips brush her ear. Jenny looks up at him, staggers slightly. He laughs, takes her hand, pulls her along with him to the center of the room.

When they reach the middle, he tries to let go, but she grasps his arm. She's not floating anymore; she's spinning. The music buffets them, tiny piano hammers at her temples. Tall Boy bobs his head in time to it, smiles at her, moves his shoulders. She holds on.

This is dancing, she thinks.

25

Haley

Richard is waiting for Haley on the chapel steps. It's late. A few stragglers wandering back from the library are out, but otherwise the sidewalks are deserted.

"Hey," he says as she approaches.

She sits beside him. "This is pretty stealth," she observes. "You know, the Grille is open for another hour. It's warm. They sell cocoa. What do you think?"

"I need to talk to you alone and not get interrupted," he says. He sounds serious.

"We could have gone to my room," she observes wryly. "Jenny's moved out."

"Really?" he says. "Like, left college or just moved to a different room?"

"Different room, different building. I was helping carry her stuff, which is why I couldn't meet you until now." She leaves out telling him how tired she is. Hauling Jenny's things

213

took longer than expected, not only because Jen insisted on not leaving so much as a pencil behind, but also because they had to move Mona's furniture to a room downstairs.

"Good for her," he comments. "Wish I could change rooms."

This surprises her. She thought he liked Taylor.

"So." Haley takes a deep breath. "On a scale of one to still furious with me, where are you?" In the dark, she can't quite make out his expression.

"Annoyed," he finally says. "I don't stay furious for long."

"That's a nice quality."

"I'm a nice guy. Not that women notice."

"I noticed," she says quietly.

"Yeah. Well," he says. She sees his breath mist in the cold night air. "I didn't drag you out here to get into all that."

She waits. What *did* he drag her out here for, then?

"I met with the college investigator today," he begins abruptly. "I told him you and I talked about Jordan and Jenny."

Haley startles. She didn't expect that. "Richard . . . why? Are you *trying* to get me in trouble?" She feels tears coming.

"No! Nothing like that. I wasn't intending to talk to him at all! I was already there. See . . . and here's something else I need to tell you . . . I'm Jordan's advisor. Was, actually. He fired me a couple hours ago. But this morning, I still was, and had to go to this meeting with him and the investigator. The guy decided to question me, too, and . . . I told him. About us. It just slipped out."

Her mind whirls. She's trying to remember what exactly she and Richard said about Jenny and Jordan. But she's too tired and it's elbowed out by the other, bigger thing: he's Jordan's advisor. Was. Whatever. It's all bad.

214

"There's more," he continues. "I told the investigator I used to date Carrie. Which made him all suspicious that I've been talking to *her* about the case, which is pretty hilarous when you think about it, but since she answered the phone when Jenny called the hotline, naturally he's going to question her, and it's pretty likely I'll get brought up in that conversation, so . . . it's only a matter of a day or two until Carrie knows you and I have been seeing each other."

"Seeing each other?" she remarks sarcastically. She can't help it. "Oh, you mean sitting outside on the stairs in the cold? Actually, I can barely see you. It's that dark."

"How about we don't start sniping at each other again?"

"And since when are you and Jordan such great friends?" she continues. "I thought you didn't like the guy."

"We're not. I don't."

"Richard. You're his *advisor*. Someone he trusts to help him through this totally awful, potentially life-wrecking . . . thing. I'd say you're one of his best friends."

"Haley, I can't explain this to you without talking about the case, and we're not supposed to be talking about the case—"

"But of course we're talking about the case," she can't help saying.

"The advisor thing is complicated," he says. "I pretty much got maneuvered into it. But it's over now and I'm *so* done."

"Done?" she says. "It's barely started. And that's just the case. Wait until Carrie, and Jenny, and . . . oh my god, Mona . . . hear about this." She sees him flinch, as if she stuck him with a pin.

"Mona? You mean from Out House?"

Haley nods. "She helped us move Jenny."

Richard puts his head in his hands and says something she can't quite hear. Something about hippies?

"Can I ask you something?" she says. "Why even bother to tell me? I mean, if you wanted to screw me over by getting me charged with an honor code violation, you've succeeded. Why the secret meeting?"

"I'm not trying to screw you over! I'm trying to give you a heads-up."

"Like that will help!" She doesn't know what she dreads more: the investigator coming after her for discussing the case, or Carrie swooping down on her for tiptoeing around with her ex-boyfriend. Or Jenny, horrified that she's been talking to Jordan's "side."

She feels Richard's hand on hers. It's surprisingly warm. She jerks away.

"I'm not the enemy," he says.

"You are totally the enemy. You lied to me about being Jordan's advisor."

"No. I neglected to tell you I was Jordan's advisor."

"Same thing as a lie. Trust me; I know."

"I was afraid you wouldn't speak to me."

"You would have been right."

They sit in silence. She considers marching off, but that hasn't worked with him in the past.

And strangely enough, mad as she is, she doesn't *want* to walk away. So they sit, in the cold, shivering.

"I feel like we keep breaking up," he finally comments, ending the stalemate.

She snorts. "That assumes we have a relationship."

"We do have a relationship."

"What? Enemies with no benefits?"

He laughs.

"I was being serious," she says.

"I know. So was I. Listen, Haley: we talk. We fight. We try to work it out. That's a relationship. Benefits is easy. Talking is hard. And we've got that down."

She decides not to share that she has no clue about benefits, easy or otherwise. Unless you count Seven Minutes of Heaven in the broom closet with Bill Brown back in seventh grade. Which was far from beneficial. His rotating tongue practically down her throat, all that saliva . . . she'd almost gagged.

Luckily, Richard interrupts her gross memories.

"On a scale of one to furious with me, where are you?" he asks quietly.

"Extremely furious," she says.

He doesn't respond.

"Really mad."

Still no reaction from him.

"Okay: annoyed. Deeply, profoundly annoyed."

"I'll take it," he says. She realizes he's shifted closer to her. Their shoulders brush.

"Jenny meets with the investigator tomorrow," she says. "Tomorrow! I'm supposed to be there. What do I do?"

"Go with her," he says. "If the investigator keeps you after, like he did me, just answer his questions. Keep it simple. When you tell him the same story I did, he'll know it's the truth and move on. He's investigating Jordan, not us."

"So that's the truth?" Haley wonders out loud. "The same story?" She doesn't see, but can feel, Richard's shrug.

"The story told the same way," he amends.

She sighs. "I suck at stories."

He laughs. "Something else we have in common."

She doesn't get why he thinks that's funny.

It's late. She should go. She moves as if to stand, but Richard speaks again.

"You know what I really want?" he says. "A do-over."

"What sort of do-over?" she asks. "Like, your whole life? Lunch yesterday? The choices are endless."

"You," he says firmly. "I wish we could start over. I wish we were meeting for the first time. Clean slate."

Haley considers this. It's such a little-kid term. "Do-over!" they'd shriek on the four-square court. The kickball field. Back when there was no mistake you couldn't fix, no hurt you couldn't heal with Band-Aids, hugs, and snacks. She'd love a do-over as well.

Which makes her a little sad.

"I think we're too old for do-overs," she says.

Richard holds out his hand.

"Hi," he says. "I'm Richard Brandt." When Haley hesitates, he places her hand in his and squeezes. "And you are?"

"Haley Dougherty."

"It's very nice to meet you, Haley Dougherty."

Their faces are so close, she can feel his breath on her cheeks and make out the way his lashes curl.

"I promise to never, ever *not* tell you something again," he says softly.

"Okay."

"We're never too old for do-overs," he whispers. His eyes, in the dark, are colorless but bright with moonlight. Neither of them move.

"Okay," she says again.

. . .

Someone—not Marliese—realizes.

"Wait. Where's Jenny?"

They pause, consider. Conundrum . . . too crowded, too dark, too loud, now only a persistent thudding beyond the dark trees. It feels, like Jenny, too distant. They are on their way to the next party.

"I think she left."

"Text her and check."

"Anyone have her number?"

"We should go back."

"There's a line!"

"We're freshmen. They'll let us back in."

"She's fine. She knows Exley. Let's go." Marliese. The girl you follow. She knows the way through the woods, and she leads them now, away from Conundrum, on to the next light, bright thing. She pulls them. Like magnets. Like moths. Airy, powder-dusted. As if they had no will of their own.

As if.

. . .

26

RICHARD

Pool shots is well underway in the basement when Richard returns to the house; he can hear the hilarity through the floorboards. Smell it, too. Sugary whiskey. Those cheap flavored vodkas. Entering Taylor these days is like stepping into an aged bourbon cask. The ban on hosting parties has only increased the underground, in-house drinking.

Richard is heading for the stairs when he hears his name. Someone in the common room.

Joe. His friend he hasn't spoken to in what feels like ages. Even though Conundrum and Taylor are next door, he and Joe have been orbiting in different circles this semester. It's too bad, really. Joe's a good guy.

"Hey, how's it going?" Richard says.

Joe sits in an armchair. In the dimly lit room, Joe reminds

Richard of an illustration he'd once seen of that character Ichabod Crane: he's that tall and scarecrow-thin.

"Got a minute?" Joe asks.

Richard glances at his watch. "A minute, man. I'm shattered."

He'd lost track of time with Haley. At some point, he realized his feet were numb but he decided to ignore them. Only when the chapel bells struck one and her eyes grew wide and she exclaimed that seriously, she had to go, she had an eight a.m. class, could he drag himself from the steps.

Adrenaline spent, he feels every bit of his long day now. He wants sleep. Bed. He'd prefer to catch up with Joe some other night.

Even so, Richard flops into a corner of the couch. Wills his eyes to widen, focus.

Joe doesn't look so great.

"I hear you and Bockus met with the investigator today," Joe begins.

Richard lowers his head into his hands and groans. "No, not that. Anything but that!" When he looks up, Joe seems startled. "Can't talk about it. Sorry, dude."

"I know," Joe says earnestly. "But I'm asking as a friend. It'll stay between you and me."

Richard stands. "Anything you want to know, go to Jordan."

"I did," Joe says. "He won't talk. But somebody said you're, like, his student rep who goes to all the meetings with him."

"Not anymore," Richard says shortly.

Fired. That's how he described to Haley the pyrotechnics that erupted when Jordan and Uncle Bruce finally caught up with him. She hadn't asked for details, and he was happy to not relive them.

"That's *it*?" Jordan had exclaimed after he'd described his conversation with Dean Hunt. "You were in there for an hour discussing your love life?"

"I think he was trying to figure out who said what to who," Richard explained. "Especially when he realized I know Haley."

Jordan threw himself back in his chair. "Freakin' math girl is Jenny's roommate! You never mentioned this *why*?"

"You never asked," Richard said, leveling his gaze at him. "And I only answer direct questions."

Jordan fired a can-you-believe-this look at his uncle. Who ignored him.

"How did it come up?" Uncle Bruce asked quietly.

"I mentioned that Jenny hadn't called the hotline until a few days after the party. He wanted to know how I knew that, and . . . it was Haley. She told me."

"How many days after the party?" Uncle Bruce asked.

"I have no idea."

"Think, Richard. Is there anything Haley said, any little offhand comment, that gives you a *sense* of how much time might have passed?" Richard didn't like how the conversation veered from what he had discussed with the investigator to what he had discussed with Haley.

"I don't know."

Uncle Bruce began pacing around the room. Like he was thinking. Then, he stopped.

"There's no rape kit," he finally declared. To no one in particular, or to both of them, Richard couldn't tell. "Evidence disappears after seventy-two hours, and she delayed. Jordan wasn't notified for more than a week. There's no rape kit. They've got nothing!" The guy looked like he was going to break out in a dance.

Uncle Bruce returned to his seat in front of Richard. He pulled his chair close. "What did he ask you about the night of the party?"

"Nothing. I told him I was with Carrie and he moved on."

"Did he ask you about Jordan and Jenny?"

"It never came up."

"Did you tell him Jordan told you that he'd had sex with Jenny?"

"No. He never asked. He was more interested in the online bullying stuff. Which, by the way, I never heard of until I was sitting there. Thanks for that heads-up." He directed the last comment at Jordan.

Uncle Bruce nodded a couple of times, got up, started pacing again. "This is good. This is really, really good," he said. "And you haven't repeated it to anyone else." Not a question, really. More like a statement.

But Richard decided to treat it like a question. "I, uh, did say it to Haley."

The pacing stopped. Uncle Bruce and Jordan stared at him.

"Yeah," Richard said nervously. "That same day, when she told me Jenny hadn't called right away? I told her Jordan described the whole thing as a hookup."

Stunned silence. Then, Jordan.

"You asshole," he breathed. "You stupid asshole!" He looked like he was going to strangle Richard.

Uncle Bruce put up a hand. "When was this?" he asked

calmly. The more intense his question, the quieter his voice seemed to get.

"The day we picked apples."

"When was *that*?"

"What the hell difference does it make?" Jordan demanded. "He told Jenny's roommate that I said we hooked up! I'm freakin' *toast*!"

Uncle Bruce, his expression placid, held up one hand toward Jordan. "Not necessarily. It's only a problem if Haley tells the investigator Richard repeated it coming from you." It took Richard a second to sort out what that meant. "In a real trial, it's hearsay and wouldn't be considered. But a hearing like this? Anything goes. We have to hope she doesn't say that. If asked."

Silence in the room.

"Do you think you could suggest to Haley that she not repeat your private conversation to the investigator?" Uncle Bruce asked. Matter-of-factly. Like it was no big deal.

Richard stood. "You people are unbelievable," he said. "You know what? No. Go to hell. I'm done." He grabbed his backpack from the floor and began his march to the door.

Jordan looked wildly at his uncle. "You can't just walk out! He can't do that!"

Uncle Bruce shrugged. "Sure he can," he said. "The question is why. Before you leave, Richard." Hand on knob, Richard turned. "What's the problem?"

The range of answers was so vast, he didn't know where to begin. He decided to go with the biggest thing that was bothering him.

"The problem," Richard said, "is that you think I'm the

sort of guy who would even ask her to do that. Not that she would. Makes me wonder: how far have I sunk?" He felt disgusted. Mostly with himself. He should never have agreed to get involved with these people.

As he opened the door, Uncle Bruce made one last request. "Please let *us* contact the college and let them know Jordan will be changing advisors," he said. "Can we count on that much from you, Richard?"

"Sure, you can tell them I quit," Richard said.

Uncle Bruce smiled. "We'll tell them we released you," he corrected.

It occurs to Richard now that this "release" might give him a little space—just a little—to talk to Joe about the case. It might feel good, actually. To finally unburden himself to someone he trusts.

Then again, it could be an honor code violation that bites him on the ass. Better to say nothing.

"I'm sorry," Richard repeats. "I'm not trying to blow you off. I actually *can't* talk about this."

Slumped in his armchair, Joe doesn't look at all satisfied with Richard. He looks a little sick. "Guys in the house told me she reported Bockus for rape."

Richard stands. He's so done with this tonight. "Like I told you, direct all questions to Jordan."

To his surprise, Joe stands, too. Seizes his arm. "I was serving that night. I was handing out punch to whoever wanted it. And I'm pretty sure I gave some to that girl."

Richard glances at the hand gripping his arm, and Joe lets go. He wouldn't have pegged Joe to react like this. All people can worry about is whether they'll get nailed for underage drinking. "So what? You'll get a citation. No worries; they don't call your parents until you get five."

Joe shifts his feet. Like he can't decide whether to run or kick something. "It's not that," he insists. "I just . . . Do you know what she looked like? There was one girl that night who was really wrecked." Joe's voice trails off for a moment. "I feel like shit thinking I might have served the girl who then went off and got hurt."

Richard glances toward the stairs. What can he tell him? Joe probably did serve Jenny. There's nothing Richard can say to make this guy feel better.

"I'm sorry," Richard repeats. "I can't talk about it." He walks out of the room and heads up to bed.

• • •

She loses track of Tall Boy. The music is like something she can touch.

umph umph umph umph

Blurred bodies packed around her bump, pulse, swirl. Vaguely familiar strangers' faces. Eyes closed, heads bounce. They look at everything and nothing, see everyone and no one. Not even her. No one sees her.

umph umph umph umph

She can't breathe this close air. She presses against the circle, searching with her hands for the way out. Her foot rolls. One face, livid, whirls.

Tamra.

"Bitch! That was my foot!"

umph umph umph umph

Then Tamra disappears into the not-light, dissolves in the throbbing haze of shadows and music that concusses the air, the floor.

She doesn't know Jenny. Doesn't see it was Jenny.

• • •

27

Haley

"Whoa. Where's the fire?"

Haley's crash landing at the dining hall table startles even full-throttle Madison. Half Haley's coffee sloshes onto the tray when she plunks it down. Madison, nursing a second cup, stares, amused, as Haley sits and takes an enormous bite of her bagel.

"I have," Haley says, mouth full, glancing at her phone, "ten minutes to eat and get across campus before Jenny's meeting with the investigator."

Madison's eyes widen. "Didn't you set the alarm, Miss Punctuality?"

"Of course! Then I get a knock on the door this morning, and it's Jenny's parents. Plus their lawyer. Looking for her! They wanted to take her out for breakfast before the interview, but apparently she never told them she'd changed rooms."

"Weird," Madison comments.

"I tried to describe to them where Out House is, but they looked all confused, so finally I *walked* them over. And I'm getting the third degree the whole time, you know? How's she doing, why'd she move? I said as little as possible because I don't know what Jenny wants them to know. Anyhow, I had to go all the way over *there*, then race over *here* . . ." She takes another big bite, with a coffee chaser. She could have used the caffeine *before* this morning's James Interrogation.

It was interesting: while the parents couldn't shut up, the lawyer (introduced to Haley as "Mr. Talbot") had been silent. And he was the very person Jenny had asked them not to bring. *Insisted* they not bring. He and her dad were still pushing for Jenny to file a report with the local police.

"My father thinks he knows me better than I know myself," Jenny had once commented to Haley. They were comparing notes on their parents. Sort of a mine's-worse-than-yours competition. "'You'll like this, sweetheart,'" Jenny had said, dropping her chin to her chest and lowering her voice in a dead-on imitation of her father. "'You won't want to do *that*. You'll want to do *this*.' Sometimes I just want to say to him, 'How do *you* know? Because I'm still figuring out what I like. Or what I want to do!'"

Haley had been unimpressed. Her mom, she felt, was infinitely more controlling. "So why don't you? Say it, that is. What's the worst that could happen?"

Jenny scoffed. "No one crosses Dad," she said. "Life is way more pleasant when things go his way."

Haley's wide eyes prompted Jenny to explain what she meant.

"He's not abusive or anything. But when you are what he wants you to be? Do what he wants you to do? He's amazing. It's like he's the sun and it just can't shine brightly enough. But when you don't? He's totally . . . not. And life's totally *not*."

As Haley hurriedly gulps her breakfast with Madison, it occurs to her that this morning's meeting with the investigator will be the first time she'll hear, from Jenny's mouth, what actually happened the night of the Conundrum party. Jenny's never told her directly.

Indirection—like setting Haley up to tell her parents she'd moved—is more her thing.

"Did you catch a glimpse of that cute lumbersexual Kyle who lives at Out House?" Madison asks.

Haley almost chokes. "Lumber *what*?"

Madison leans forward. "Lumbersexual. Think outdoorsy metrosexual. Bearded. Hikes *and* cooks. Wears Patagucci."

"I thought that was a joke. Patagucci is a thing?"

"No, but Kyle is. A very hot thing. Remind me to visit Jenny sometime this week after practice."

Haley takes another big bite, shaking her head at Madison. "You are so lame," she says, mouth full. "Pretending to care about Jenny so you can scope out guys at Out House."

Madison looks hurt. "Of course I care! Why would you say that?"

"Fine. What one thing have you asked me about her since the night she was raped?"

"I thought you weren't supposed to talk about it!"

"Not the details of the case. But 'Hey, how's Jenny doing?' is perfectly all right. Better yet: why not ask her yourself?"

231

To Madison's credit, she actually looks embarrassed. "Okay, you're right," she says. "Not that I don't care. But that I don't ask. Now I feel like an awful person."

Haley wraps the last of the bagel in a napkin and gathers her things. "You're not awful. You're typical. No one asks her. I get that it's awkward, but it just makes her feel . . . shamed. As if she's done something wrong, or she's stained in some way."

Madison grimaces. This strikes a chord. "T and Company have been . . ." Madison trails off.

"Bitches?" Haley supplies. "Yeah, I know. They ignore her when they see her and whine that they're going to get in trouble because of the vodka. I even think they posted some of those comments on The Board."

"Well, I don't know if they would do *that*," Madison says. "But I get it. About supporting her." Haley slings her pack over her shoulder. "Tell her I said good luck today, okay?"

Haley smiles. "Go see her," she urges. "Bring her chocolates. While you're there, maybe Kyle the lumberjack will wander by."

When Haley gets to the Dean of Students Office and beelines it for the front desk, she can't help glancing into the waiting room to her right: Mr. and Mrs. James, plus the lawyer, occupy two low couches. The student receptionist directs Haley upstairs where Jenny and the dean wait.

She finds the two of them seated on either side of a wide desk. Dean Hunt looks . . . professorial. About her dad's age. Bearded. Not in that lumbersexual-hot way Madison was going on about. He's too preppy. And old. But he looks fit. And familiar.

232

Dean Hunt greets Haley and they get started.

"So, Jenny," he says. Leaning back in his chair, like they're settling in for a pleasant conversation. "I've read your statement. But I'd like you to walk me through it. Tell me what happened, from the beginning, and take as long as you need. We're in no rush. I might ask a few questions as we go along."

Jenny sits up straight in her chair. "Well, I arrived at the party with the girls from my hall. There was a line—"

Dean Hunt puts up one hand, stopping her. "I mean start at the beginning."

Jenny hesitates. "Arriving at the party isn't the beginning?"

"Go back further. Start with the student who invited you."

"Oh. Brandon Exley invited me. That's in my statement."

"I know, Jenny, but I'd like to hear it again. I want to make absolutely sure I've got my facts straight."

The same story. Told the same way. That's how he'll know it's the truth. Richard was dead right about this guy.

Jenny begins again. And Haley hears about Brandon Exley. The older boy Jenny occasionally spoke to in Econ, who invited her to the party and said she could bring friends. How the girls in the hall were all for it, and everyone got ready together. How she'd never gone to an upperclassmen party before and borrowed a dress. How they pregamed in Tamra's room.

Dean Hunt doesn't comment. He just nods when she mentions the booze.

"You were all drinking?" he asks matter-of-factly.

Jenny nods.

"Do you recall how much?"

Jenny hesitates. "Tamra just handed me a cup. I have no idea what was in it."

Dean Hunt writes something on a yellow pad. It's the first time he's written anything. "Can you describe how you felt at that point? Dizzy, clearheaded, tired . . . ?"

"Happy," Jenny says quietly. "We were all listening to music and singing and having a lot of fun. I wish we'd never left."

"If you had to rate your clarity of mind from one to ten, with one being completely sober and alert and ten being unconscious, what would you rate your clarity as you left Tamra's and started for Conundrum House?"

Jenny looks pleasantly surprised. Something about assigning numbers, as if the events of that night could be measured, their acidity calculated along a pH scale, appeals to her.

"Three," she says.

Dean Hunt writes. "What happened next?"

"There was a line when we got there," Jenny continues. "Mostly guys. They couldn't get in without a woman. A freshman. That was the rule the party organizers made up."

Dean Hunt looks surprised. "Not just any woman?" he asks. "A freshman?"

"That's how Tamra got us right in," she says. "She cut to the front. The guys at the head of the line were pretty happy when we all walked up."

"Do you remember who the guys were?"

"I have no idea. They disappeared once we got in. It was crowded and pretty dark."

"Did you know about this rule before you went?"

"No, but it explains a lot."

Dean Hunt tilts his head. "Explains what?"

"Why Brandon Exley invited me," she says. Just above a whisper. A catch in her voice. The first so far. "I'm a freshman. And he knew I'd bring others."

There's a box of tissues on Dean Hunt's desk, but he doesn't make a move toward it. Haley reaches over and plucks a few, hands them to Jenny.

"Thanks," Jenny says.

"Did you see Brandon Exley at the party?" Dean Hunt asks.

Jenny dabs at her nose before answering. "Not at first. It was so crowded. But eventually he saw us and came over. I introduced him to everyone and then he sort of . . . cleared a path for us. To the drinks."

Dean Hunt writes. Haley wishes she could see what, exactly. She's fascinated by what he chooses to record and what he just listens to.

"Tell me about that. The drinks."

"There was this garbage can full of something. It was really sweet. They were handing out cups of that."

"Who was?"

"Some guys. I don't know their names."

"They were handing you cups that were already full?"

"Yes."

"You didn't fill the cup yourself?"

"No."

"Did you actually see them fill your cup from the garbage can?"

"Uh . . . yes. They would dip them in and hand them out."

"Did anyone hand you a full cup that you did *not* see filled from that garbage can?"

Jenny pauses, narrows her eyes. As if she's trying to focus on a blurred image. "I don't think so."

"And you don't know who served you?"

"Well, Brandon Exley. Once. Then there was this guy who was sort of working the can, serving a lot of people. He gave me a few. I don't know him."

"Can you be more specific than 'a few'?"

Jenny pauses. Bites her lip. "No. I never exactly emptied my cup."

"Because you didn't drink from it?"

"Because he kept putting more in."

Dean Hunt jots. His jawline tightens. "Can you rate your clarity at that point?" he asks, his eyes glued to his notepad.

"After a while it might have been . . . five. Six, maybe."

She started dancing, Jenny explains. At first it was fun, but then she felt dizzy. She felt like the room was spinning and she couldn't really make out faces. She lost track of the girls; they seemed to drift away on the dance floor. Marliese was grinding with some guy, and Tamra disappeared. She suddenly realized she was alone and tried to push her way out, but she was still holding her cup and she spilled punch on some girl.

"'Watch it, bitch!' That's what she screamed at me," Jenny says. "It felt like . . . I don't know. Hell? It was dark and loud and someone was screaming at me, and I felt like I was going to throw up or cry or both."

Jenny needed air. She wanted to leave. But she couldn't find the exit. It was so dark, and there were so many people in the way.

"It was a seven," she says quietly to Dean Hunt, even though he didn't ask for a rating.

"That's pretty high," he says. "Are you sure?"

She nods. "I threw up," she continues. "In a wastebasket. Somehow I wandered into a quiet room and just . . . barfed."

"Can you describe the basket?" he asks gently.

Jenny draws back, straightening. "Describe it? You mean, what it looked like?"

Dean Hunt reaches behind him and pulls out a wastebasket. It's a metallic cylinder, lined with a white plastic bag. "Did it look like this?"

Jenny's eyes widen. "No," she says. "It was red. And plastic. Actually, it wasn't a wastebasket—it was a recycling tub! And there were bottles in it. Empty water bottles. I remember . . . Oh my gosh, this is coming back now . . . I remember feeling sorry. So sorry. Because somebody was going to have to rinse out the gross tub and deal with the bottles."

Those are returnables. You don't put returnable bottles in the recycling tubs. Even Haley knows that.

You also don't keep tubs in the common areas. Only the bedrooms.

Dean Hunt returns the cylinder to its place behind his desk. He writes some more. "What happened after that?"

"I managed to get outside," Jenny says. "I remember the fresh air felt so good. I walked a little. Not far, because I could still see the house and hear the party. I remember thinking I would walk back to the dorm, by myself, and I was about to leave when someone said hello. And it was him. Jordan."

"He followed you?" Dean Hunt asks.

"Maybe. I don't know. He was just there. Standing under a tree."

Haley can't help it: she shivers. This creeps her out. Poor Jenny.

"What did you do?" Dean Hunt asks.

"I said hi. He asked me my name. I remember thinking it was strange. That he was out there all by himself. Drinking. Not the same thing. It was a bottle of something."

"Did he offer it to you?"

"No." She pauses. She seems to retreat into herself as she scrolls through the memories of that night. She wears the saddest expression. "He asked if I was having a good time, and I told him no. He said he wasn't having a good time, either." She looks at Dean Hunt. "I remember we both sort of laughed."

"Did he say why he wasn't having a good time?"

"I don't really remember," Jenny replies. "Maybe something about it being too crowded? He didn't like the music."

"What do you remember next?"

Jenny swallows. Her shoulders rise and fall.

Here it comes.

"We walked. Nowhere in particular. Along the sidewalks around the houses."

"Did you pass anyone? Anyone you know or who greeted Jordan?" Dean Hunt asks.

"I don't remember."

They talked, Jenny continues. Or she did, at least. Jordan asked her about herself. Where she was from, her major, how she liked MacCallum. At some point, she says, it started to feel weavy.

"Weavy?" Dean Hunt asks.

"Like we weren't walking. We were weaving. Through the trees, in the dark. I didn't feel right. And I told him that."

"What did he say?"

"He said, 'Do you want to lie down for a minute? I live right here.' "

Dean Hunt doesn't say anything. He just looks at Jenny and waits.

"I know how that sounds," she whispers. "I shouldn't have gone with him. I didn't know him. I should have gone back to the party, found the girls, told . . ."

"Jenny. Just tell me what happened next."

"We went to his room. It was upstairs. I remember climbing stairs. I remember it was quiet. He said everyone was still at the party. I remember two beds. He sat on one and sort of grabbed my hand and pulled me down so we were sitting next to each other. I remember my feet hurt. I had borrowed Marliese's shoes and I never wear heels. So I took off the shoes. I don't know, maybe that was it? He thought I was getting undressed? I should never have—"

"Jenny?" Dean Hunt interrupts. "Just so I'm clear: you walked into Taylor House with Jordan?"

"Yes. Taylor. He said it was where he lived, and he lives in Taylor."

"And you went upstairs?"

"Yes."

"And you remember the room?"

"Yes."

"Can you describe it a bit more?"

"Typical dorm room. Two beds, one on each side. One desk was at the foot of a bed, the other in front of the window. A lot of posters on the walls. Junk on the floor. I remember kicking a stray shoe."

"Did you or Jordan turn on the lights?"

"He turned on a desk lamp. Not the overhead. I remember that because he had a picture, a framed photo of his dog. On the desk. He has a really cute dog. I actually picked up the picture for a better look."

"What kind of dog?" Dean Hunt asks.

Seriously? You're asking about some damn dog?

"A golden retriever," Jenny says without hesitation. "I love goldens."

"Did he tell you the dog's name?"

"Oscar," she says, smiling slightly. "I thought it was a great name."

"Jenny, did you talk about the dog and hold the picture before or after you sat on the bed?"

The smile fades. "I guess before. Definitely not after. When we were on the bed, it was dark. So he must have turned the light out, then pulled me onto the bed."

Dean Hunt nods and scribbles, quickly. Jenny pauses as he writes.

"And can you describe what happened next?" he finally prompts.

There's a window behind Dean Hunt's desk. Haley sees Jenny stare out that window. Hears her take a long, deep, slow breath in, then out.

"It will be hard," Carrie had told her, "telling a complete stranger. A man, at that. They should really get a woman to ask these questions, but . . . that's another story."

They were sitting in Mona's-now-Jenny's room. Right after they'd hauled the last of her stuff. Carrie had handed out cookies and was talking about what Jenny might face from the investigator. Gail protested, saying give it a rest, it's late, but Jen said no, it's okay. That she needed to hear this. So Carrie went on.

"You'll want to focus," Carrie said. "Get in the zone. Don't look at him, but pick a point, maybe a tree outside? Or a painting on the wall? And talk to that point. Tell the tree. Tell the painting. Keep it simple and clear and it'll be over before you know it."

Watching now, Haley can tell: Jenny's picked her point.

"We sat on the bed. He told me I was so pretty," she says. "He asked me if I had a boyfriend. I told him no. He acted all surprised.

"He kissed me. It was nice. Nothing awful. He's good-looking and it was a nice kiss. And I kissed him back. We started to make out, and at first it was fine. But then I started to feel sick again. I told him I needed to slow down. That I felt swirly."

"Swirly?" Dean Hunt asks.

Jenny swallowed. "Like the room was swirling around. It was making me sick. He said, 'Want to lie down?' And we did. We stretched out on his bed, and he sort of had his arms around me. He told me to close my eyes, that that would help.

But it didn't. It actually felt worse. Like the room was spinning. I wanted to go back to my dorm, but I didn't think I could walk there."

"Did you tell him you wanted to leave?"

"I didn't say anything. He did all the talking. I thought I'd just lie there until the swirling passed, then walk home. Meanwhile, he was just . . . talking. I can barely remember it all. Stuff about him and his friends. I couldn't concentrate. I fell asleep."

Jenny pulls her eyes from the window. She looks straight at the dean.

"I guess that's ten," she says quietly.

Dean Hunt is silent. He waits for her to continue.

"When I woke up," she says, eyes riveted on the window again, "he was inside me. At first I thought I was dreaming. But I couldn't breathe; there was this pressure on my chest. It was like a dream of drowning, and I was suffocating."

"Jenny," Dean Hunt interrupts. Her eyes move to his face. "I'm going to ask you a difficult question. But I have to ask, and you need to be specific. What do you mean 'he was inside me'?"

Jenny nods. She stares out the window once again. Carrie had warned her Dean Hunt would ask this question and there was only one way to answer it.

"His penis was inside my vagina," Jenny says. Robotically. As if she were peering into a microscope and describing what she saw at the end of the lens.

Dean Hunt nods, jots. Waits.

"I remember saying, 'Jordan, no!' He was hurting me. Pushing inside me so hard, the bed made a sound each time.

His head was pressed against my face and his hair was in my mouth." Jenny grimaces. "I could almost taste him. His shampoo. I feel sick if I smell it on someone else. I tried to push him off. I remember being surprised at how heavy he was."

Jenny stops talking. The room is loud with her silence. Haley, holding her breath, doesn't move. It seems to her that neither does Dean Hunt.

"But it was too late," Jenny finally continues. "Right when I said 'no' he made this . . . sound. He was finished. I know because he sort of collapsed. This dead weight on top of me, and I remember thinking, 'I'm going to die, I can't breathe.' But then he rolled off. And just . . . lay there. I could hear him breathing. He said I was sweet, or that was sweet, I don't know. I remember 'sweet.'" Jenny's voice breaks. Her eyes, which have remained dry up to this moment, suddenly fill. Spill over. "How could he say that?" she whispers.

Dean Hunt doesn't respond. He waits.

"I don't know how long went by. A few minutes?" Jenny finally continues. "I didn't move. I think I was in shock. At some point he got up. I do remember that. I have no idea where he went. I remember sitting up.

"I was dressed, but my underwear was around my ankles. I pulled it on, found Marliese's shoes, and left. I didn't see him on the way out. Somehow I made it back to our dorm by myself, although I don't remember that walk. I do remember there was a big party going on in our hall. I remember waking you up." She directs this last comment at Haley. "That was it. I haven't spoken to him since. He's never contacted me. Never tried to find out where I went that night. He was done with me."

Dean Hunt doesn't say anything right away. As if he's waiting to see if Jenny has anything more to add.

Then, after a long silence, Dean Hunt asks, "Did Jordan Bockus have sexual intercourse with you while you were unconscious?"

"Yes."

"At any point, before he penetrated you, did you indicate that you did *not* want to have intercourse?"

"I told you, I was passed out!"

"But before you passed out, do you recall saying no, stop, I want to leave, anything like that?"

"I said no when I realized what was happening, but it was too late."

"Jenny, it is never too late. Consent can be withdrawn at any time. When you said no, did Jordan stop?"

Two bright patches appear on Jenny's cheeks. "So what are you saying? It's my fault? If I'd yelled louder he would have said, 'Oh, sorry! Excuse me!' and stopped?"

"I'm trying to determine how he responded to what you said."

"Well, he didn't."

"Is it possible that Jordan might have believed you wanted intercourse?"

"Just because I kissed him doesn't mean I wanted intercourse. Although, for a rapist, I guess passing out is one way to let them know you want sex."

The venom in Jenny's reply startles Haley. She's never heard this tone from her.

Dean Hunt doesn't back down. "I'm going to assume

you're being sarcastic. Please understand that the purpose of these questions is to ascertain consent, or lack of consent."

"Then let me be clear: Jordan Bockus had sex with me while I was passed out on his bed. I did not consent to that. It was rape."

Dean Hunt does not respond. He picks up his yellow pad, glances at his notes. "Do you remember walking down the stairs when you were leaving Taylor House?"

"I don't remember much about that walk back."

"You said you climbed the stairs to his room when you arrived. So do you remember walking down the stairs when you left?"

"Well, I must have."

"But do you remember it?"

"Why are you asking me this?"

"Please just answer the question."

"What's the problem?" Jenny sounds shrill.

"Please answer the question," he repeats.

"You don't believe me. You think I'm lying," she snaps. "You think I led him on and actually wanted to have sex with him! Why else are you asking me these ridiculous questions?"

Dean Hunt lays his pen and notebook carefully on his desk. He sits up straight in his chair. For the first time he looks disapproving, his lips pressed tightly together. Like she's crossed some line with him.

"I do not think you are lying to me. I think you absolutely believe every word you have said here this afternoon. Your testimony is consistent with what you wrote in your complaint. But you're right: there's a problem. My job is to determine the facts. And the fact is Jordan Bockus has a first-floor single in Taylor House. There is only one bed in his room, and you don't climb stairs to reach it. I'm not sure where you were that night, but I'm concerned it's not where you think."

Jenny's hands grip the arms of the chairs. Her chest heaves with rapid breaths. "So . . . what? You're saying I'm crazy?"

Dean Hunt raises his eyebrows. "No. But by your own account, you were highly intoxicated. Jenny, after you entered your statement, I walked the route you detailed. I walked from your dorm to Conundrum. I looked for the trash cans. I wandered outside. I also went to Taylor. A public safety officer accompanied me into Jordan's room. Here's what I found: not one single picture of a dog. I made some inquiries. The Bockuses don't have *any* pets."

Jenny stares at him, a stunned expression on her face.

"So if you're not lying and not crazy," he says, "the logical next question is: where's Oscar?"

. . .

"I need to go."

Tall Boy, his face reappearing. He doesn't hear. Jenny barely hears herself. He's so tall, thin. Like a tree. She considers saying that to him. Crazy. It would be funny if she didn't feel so sick. Like she wants to cry. Tamra. So mean.

The walls around her rotate. She grabs his arm. It stops her fall.

"I need to go!" she shouts. It comes out "oh," but he realizes. Sees. She feels herself moving, pushed, propelled, and hears the music fade and light brighten and air cool. A wall. She leans against it. A wave cuts her through the middle. Bucks her.

"Where are your friends?" she hears.

Tamra. Bitch. She wants to cry.

"Can you make it upstairs?"

Floating, flying, climbing. Another buck. In her gut.

She sits. In a chair, at a desk. This lamp is not hers. And this picture, not hers.

"What a cute dog," she hears herself say. The dog makes her want to cry. She wants to hold the dog—big, furry, gold dog—wrap herself around him.

"That's Oscar."

Oscar.

"Stay here. I'll be back."

The room, when the door closes, rings. Her ears ring. Oscar. She reaches across the desk and with one finger strokes the glass over the dog's face.

Then her stomach bucks hard, insistent, and her hand flies to her mouth.

• • •

28

RICHARD

Richard can usually count on the Taylor common room to be deserted at one in the afternoon. It's a good place to knock out some work.

Today, Exley hunts him down there.

"Knock knock," Richard hears. He's in an alcove off the main room, his textbook and papers spread out on a long table. He looks up to see Exley saunter in, backpack slung over one shoulder, jacket unzipped.

Exley pushes back the chair at the head of the table with one foot and lowers himself into it. The pack hits the floor with a thud.

"Can I help you?" Richard asks, fake-politely. He hates the guy's eyes. They register no emotion, ever. Roaring over beer pong, laughing at someone's joke, dancing with a girl—the eyes are the same, even if the mouth smiles or shouts.

Here's one thing they do convey: intent. Richard imagines

that if you zoomed in on a lion's eyes as he stalked his prey, they would look like Exley's.

"I hear you and Bockus aren't speaking," Exley says.

"That would be true," Richard says.

"Mind telling me why?"

"Yeah, I do. Ask him yourself."

Exley's brow furrows. "Why the hostility, Richard?" he asks quietly.

"No hostility, Exley. I'm just done talking about it."

"That so? I hear you had no problem talking about it with Jenny's roommate."

Something cold forms in Richard's gut. He doesn't like Exley mentioning Haley, even if not by name. "I see you've already been talking to Jordan. Which means you can't have much to say to me."

"Did you screw him over with the investigator?" Exley continues.

Richard laughs. "Didn't need to. He managed that all by himself. This strategy of his? Not answering questions? Complete fail. That dean is going to nail his ass. And not because of anything I said."

"I hope for your sake it's not."

Richard stares at him. The guy doesn't blink. "That sounds like a threat," Richard says. He wills his voice into nonchalance, but his skin crawls.

"You can take it any way you want. I'm just saying: you don't want to be known as the guy who sold out another guy."

Richard pauses, trying to make sense of this. "Known as? How would I be 'known as' anything?"

Exley stands. His mouth twists into a mocking smile.

"Beats me. People have ways of finding out. And talking about it." He hefts the pack from the floor with one hand. He begins to walk out.

Richard rises from his chair. Two can play this game. "True," he says. "Like, we wouldn't want that investigator finding out what Jordan told you. You know. About hooking up with Jenny."

Exley turns. "Did he say that? To me? First I've heard of it," Exley says, faking a wide-eyed, innocent smile. He can't pull it off, and it's creepy.

"Or the Doctor's bartending skills," Richard continues. "Wouldn't Dean Hunt be surprised to hear you've got a PhD."

Exley takes a step closer to him. "People hafta drink," he says softly. "They want to feel good, and that's what the Doctor's there for."

"So I hear," Richard replies. "Tell me, Doc: is it true you mixed a little something special in the barrel that night at Conundrum?"

Exley squints. The dead eyes are like slits. "Are you threatening me?"

Richard laughs softly. "You can take it any way you want."

Exley lifts. Word is he's obsessed. Competitive about it, too, always asking the other guys how much they press, making sure they know he did more. The results are intimidating, and standing inches away from him right now, Richard senses the inadequacy of his own lean runner's frame.

And unlike his past confrontations with Exley, there's no one around to step in between.

Then, inexplicably, Exley blinks.

"Don't play games you can't win, Richie," he sneers, and walks out.

*   *   *

Joe is tired of yelling in people's ears. No one knows who she is.

Until, finally, someone remembers the small girl at the drinks table.

"That crowd left," he shouts over the music. "Except for . . ." His eyes dart. They settle. He points. She's tall, dark eyes. She's heading for the exit. She walks with one arm wrapped around a boy's waist, his around hers.

Exley. They disappear into the night.

"Shoot," Joe says.

Maybe she can sleep it off, he thinks. Maybe she's better now. He goes to check.

The stink of vomit rolls out of his room when he opens the door.

*   *   *

29

Haley

"What the hell happened in there?"

Mr. James, his face mottled purple with rage, fires this question at Haley. On one of the reception room couches, her mother's arms encircling her, Jenny weeps. Her gasping cries draw attention from students arriving for other appointments. They peer in from the hall, their concerned whispers audible.

The lawyer, Mr. Talbot, places one hand on Mr. James's arm. "Dan, let's take this somewhere else," he says. "Back to the hotel?"

Mr. James nods, but refuses to decouple his gaze from Haley's.

She doesn't know where to begin.

Things pretty much fell apart after Oscar.

"I'm telling you the truth!" Jenny kept insisting.

Dean Hunt nodded. "Yes, I believe you are," he'd said,

which, if it were an attempt to reassure her, had the opposite effect. The calmer his tone, the angrier and more frantic she grew. Finally, he suggested they were done for the day; he might ask her back for some follow-up. Jenny, barely civil, practically fled the room.

"He asked tough questions," Haley stammers. "It shook her up." *It shook me up*, she doesn't add.

"She needs a lawyer in there," Mr. James seethes. He re-directs his glare at Mr. Talbot. "I don't know what to do!"

"We can start by getting your deeply upset daughter out of here," the lawyer says. He walks over to Jenny's mom and places a hand on her shoulder, murmuring something.

"Help us out, Haley," Mr. James says. "You were in there. You see . . . this." He gestures toward Jenny and her mom. "She needs a lawyer! But she insists on keeping you. Do her a favor: quit. If they call her in again, tell her you won't do it. Maybe then she'll listen to reason."

Jenny, her cries now replaced by breathy hiccups, unfolds from the couch, her mother half lifting her. Haley decides this is not the time to tell Mr. James it doesn't matter. That regardless of who sits alongside Jenny, she'll recall the same nonexistent dog. The same mysterious second-floor bedroom. The same vodka-soaked partying.

Jenny's wrong about Dean Hunt. He *doesn't* think she's lying. And he doesn't think she's nuts.

He thinks she was too drunk to remember where she was.

So what else does Jenny . . . misremember?

The Residence Inn where the Jameses are staying is walking distance from campus, but the drive over seems to take forever. Haley and Jenny sit in the backseat of a superclean car as Mr. James drives.

"Rental car smell," Haley murmurs to Jenny. It's nothing like Haley's mom's station wagon. Typically strewn with half-full Gatorade bottles, outgrown shin guards, random socks, and discarded protein bar wrappers, the Doughertys' car is a rolling Dumpster in comparison.

Jenny doesn't respond to Haley's attempt to coax a smile out of her. Instead, Jenny buckles her seat belt and stares out the window. Mr. Talbot follows in his car.

Mr. James doesn't waste any time. "You were going to tell us why you changed rooms," he begins.

"Dan, can we wait until we get back to the hotel?" Mrs. James implores. She glances at her daughter who, unspeaking, aims her tear-streaked face at the buildings whishing past. Mr. James ignores his wife.

"Why do I get the impression there's some conspiracy of silence here?" he persists. "We show up this morning, and not only are you nowhere to be found, but Haley's shocked to see us. We find you living in this . . . fleabag on the outskirts of campus, no explanation. What's going on?"

Jenny continues to stare out the window.

"Have you girls had a fight?" he presses.

Jenny makes this sound, like a short laugh. "No, Dad. We're getting along just fine," she says to the window glass.

"You know, it's bad enough the college tells us nothing, but for god's sake, Jen, we're your parents! We're on your side!" he says. It's as if he can't make himself stop.

They slow for a red light. *How bad would it be to jump out*

255

here? Haley does a quick risk assessment, calculates the odds of successfully dodging traffic and making it to the sidewalk without injury. Her chances aren't good, but faced with being trapped in this box with the Jameses . . .

The light turns green. Haley makes a different decision.

"Want me to tell them?" Her voice is low, intended only for the backseat.

Jenny's head swivels forward. Her furious eyes meet her father's in the rearview mirror.

"He's stalking me," she says. "He ignored the protection order, came into our dorm, and wrote on our door. He's also cyber-harassing me. It's all over campus. I'm notorious. That's why I changed rooms. I don't want him to know where I am."

Jenny's parents don't react. Both stare in shocked silence at the oncoming traffic.

"So guess what, Dad?" Jenny continues. Her voice is loud in the closed car. "You were right. As usual. And I was wrong. As usual. Guess I should have gone to the cops. He'd have been hauled off campus in cuffs by now. But stupid me! I wanted to protect my privacy and handle this quietly. Instead, I'm the campus skank. Hiding in some random group house and wondering, every time I walk through the dining hall, which of my wonderful classmates just posted cruel, obscene lies about me on the Internet!"

Mr. James almost misses the entrance to the inn.

"*What* are you talking about?" he demands. "Internet?"

"Enough! Both of you," Mrs. James says. She whirls on her husband. "Not here, okay? We will talk when we get out of the car and back to the room."

Something in her tone finally convinces him to shut up. He closes his mouth in a tight line.

In their room, Jenny heads straight for the bathroom and clicks the lock. It's one of those places with a living area and kitchen as soon as you enter, the bedroom and bathroom in back. Mr. James throws himself into one of the living room armchairs; Mrs. James follows Jenny. They can hear her talking to her daughter through the closed door. Mr. Talbot, who'd followed them into the room, drops his briefcase on the breakfast bar and loosens his tie. He sits on the couch.

Haley isn't sure where to go.

"Will *you* tell us what's going on?" Mr. James asks Haley.

"Do you want to know about the stalking? Or what happened with the investigator?" She's not trying to be a smart-ass, but realizes it might sound that way. "Sorry, I—"

"Stalking?" Mr. Talbot's eyes grow wide.

Mr. James throws up his hands. "What can I tell you, Bob? It just gets better and better."

The lawyer turns to Haley. "Just . . . start at the beginning."

At some point during her description of The Board, Mr. Talbot takes out his phone and attempts to download the app. He wants to read the posts.

"It may not work," Haley warns him. "The company might have put up the fence by now."

"Fence?" he asks.

"Virtual fence," she explains. "MacCallum was going to report the bullying and ask the company to block the app within a certain radius of the campus. Like a fence."

"Is it that bad?" Mrs. James asks. At some point in the

conversation she must have abandoned her post outside the bathroom door.

Haley nods.

Mrs. James turns to her husband. "She needs to come home." Finality in her voice. As if the subject of Jenny's return is a running debate between them. "All this talk about lawyers and the police and what the college is or isn't doing is beside the point. She's a wreck. She can't concentrate on her studies like this! Let's get her home, regroup—"

"Crazy or not, here I come," they hear.

Jenny has emerged. Her face is puffy but she's not crying. She glances around the circle of them. "What'd I miss?"

They all look at one another. As if no one wants to go first.

Mrs. James begins. "Sweetheart, no one thinks you're crazy." She walks briskly to the kitchenette. She grabs an aluminum kettle off the stove and begins filling it with water. "I'm making tea. Who wants some?"

No one answers her.

Jenny sits. She crosses her legs and folds her hands neatly in her lap. Her mouth forms a pleasant, tight-lipped smile. Her eyes are bright with anger.

"The investigator does," she says. "Not want tea—thinks I'm crazy. He thinks I'm absolutely out of my mind. Tell them, Haley."

Haley doesn't speak. The urge to escape is overwhelming her again.

"Jenny, what gave you that impression?" Mr. Talbot asks her. "Did the man *say* 'Hey, you're nuts'?"

"Not in so many words," Jenny tells him. "But when I

distinctly remember certain rooms and objects and stairs that he says don't exist, what else should I conclude? Especially since he doesn't think I'm lying? I guess 'delusional' would be one way to put it." She looks at her father. "Sorry to disappoint you, Dad. *It didn't go well.*" She says the last in a hushed, confidential tone.

"Actually, Jenny, it might not have gone as badly as you think," Mr. Talbot says, jumping in before Mr. James can respond.

Jenny levels an iron-eyes smile at him. "With all due respect, Mr. Talbot, it did."

Mr. Talbot is unfazed. "Haley tells us he asked a lot of questions about your drinking that night."

"Drinking from the mystery punch garbage can," she confirms. "Lost count, lost consciousness. Next question?"

Haley can't help it—she gasps. But Mr. Talbot waves one hand, batting away her sarcasm like it was a fly. "Probably nothing the investigator hasn't heard before. I wouldn't worry about it."

Jenny blinks. She doesn't comment.

"It's called 'conflating,'" Mr. Talbot explains. "You lose bits of the story, and also confuse the sequence. As you try to remember, your mind stitches it together into one seamless line, but in fact the pieces are out of order. Very common after a night of heavy drinking."

As they speak, Mrs. James places steaming mugs of tea in front of everyone. Haley forgets she didn't want any and clutches hers.

"What's important, Jenny," Mr. Talbot continues, "is that you *stick* to your story. Start changing it up at this point and he won't think you're crazy; he'll think you're lying." He looks at her steadily.

This, Jenny hears. Instead of a snarky comment, she nods.

"Now, about this other thing. On the phone." Mr. Talbot looks down at the coffee table in search of his smartphone. He'd placed it there while the app was installing.

It's in Mr. James's hands. He's squinting at the screen, as if it's hard to read. But then . . . he stands. He pitches the phone onto the couch. Like it's a baseball.

The virtual "fence" is not up yet.

"This should never have been allowed to happen!" Something in his voice chills Haley. This is the not-sunshine Jenny was talking about.

Mr. Talbot, lips pursed, retrieves his phone from the cushions. After satisfying himself that it still works, he glances up at Mr. James. "You should unburden yourself, Dan, from the notion that you could have done anything to prevent this."

"Hauling this creep before a judge would have prevented it," Mr. James counters.

Jenny turns to Haley. "See? All my fault. I didn't go to the police."

"Stop it! This is *not* your fault!" Mrs. James insists.

"What are our options at this point?" Mr. James asks Mr. Talbot, ignoring them both. "Legally."

"Well, we can start with the company that manages this application," the lawyer says, thinking out loud. "Fast-track this 'fence' Haley was talking about. I don't know if they can or will tell you who started the thread—"

"Can we get at him that way? Charge him that way?"

"I'm not. Going. To the police," Jenny says.

Only Haley seems to hear her.

"Can I see that? Now?" Mrs. James holds her hand out for Mr. Talbot's phone.

"Mom. Don't," Jenny says.

"I have no idea. I'll need to see if there's any precedent for that," Mr. Talbot says as he passes Mrs. James his phone.

"In the meantime, what the *hell* has the college been doing about this?" Mr. James demands. He looks at Haley. Her heart sinks. When did she become the stand-in for the college?

That's when Jenny finally, completely, totally, loses it.

"LISTEN TO ME!" she shrieks.

It has the effect of a mute button. The silence that follows practically rings.

Jenny stands. Her hair, untethered, flies about her face. Even her forehead is red. "What part of 'No!' 'Don't!' 'Stop!' do people not *get*?" she demands. "Or is it just me? Are the words *Ignore This Bitch* tattooed on my face?" She snatches the phone from her mother and thrusts it at Mr. Talbot. "Don't read it!" she yells at her. "I don't want you to see what it says!" She whirls on her father. "Stop trying to turn me into some rape victim poster child! I know you want me to be strong and brave and . . . and . . . *avenging*, somehow, but I'm not! I'm tired and sad and for once in my life, I want to do what I want! Not what *you* want."

Mrs. James, in tears, holds her hands out toward her daughter. Jenny literally steps back, as if dreading the suffocating embrace. She covers her face, stamps her foot.

"Sweetheart. Say it," Mrs. James tells her. "Say what you want."

Jenny lowers her hands. "I want you to stop telling me to leave college and move back home! That would kill me!" she hurls at her mother. "Dad, I want you to stop talking about the police! How many times do I have to tell you: *no.*" She looks at Mr. Talbot. "I want you to stop talking to my father. Talk to me. I'll listen. But just so you know: Haley is my advisor." She turns to Haley. "If you still want to be."

"Absolutely," Haley says. She avoids Mr. James's eyes.

Jenny sits. She suddenly seems exhausted. The room is quiet but laden, as if some tropical storm swept through and left unspoken thoughts behind, floating in the air like a humid stillness.

"I want this all to go away," Jenny says to no one in particular. "I want him to leave me alone. I want people to not stare at me as if I've got some scarlet *V* for *victim* embroidered on my shirt." She looks at Haley. "I want friends to believe me and not just feel sorry for me."

Haley feels a cool prickle of guilt down the back of her neck.

"Jen—" her father begins, but the girl holds up one staying hand.

"No, Dad. You're done. You've said it all, and I've heard it all. I know you want to help, I know you and Mom love me, but here's the thing: you can't fix this. I've got to work it out for myself." She glances around the room. Her eyes rest on the ginormous pack she's dropped near the door. She moves to it now, heaving it over her shoulders with an ease that never ceases to impress Haley. She crosses the room to her mother and wraps her in a tight, brief squeeze.

"I'm going to go now," she says. "I have class."

"No one expects you to go to class today—" her mother begins.

Jenny cuts her off. "I *want* to go," she says. "I want to feel normal. I'm sure I won't, but I have to try."

"Fake it 'til you make it," Haley agrees.

Everyone turns to her. Jenny's parents look horrified.

Duct tape. Permanently adhered to my mouth. It's the only way to save myself—and others—from the things I say.

Thankfully, Jenny doesn't look horrified. It's not entirely clear, but . . . a hint, a suggestion of a smile seems to cross her face. Haley can't be sure whether Jen is laughing with her or at her.

But it's a beginning.

"Let's go," Jenny says.

Haley, relieved, grabs her pack. Heads for the door. Exit: stage right.

．　．　．

Jordan tries the back of the house. The doors are locked from the inside. He peers through the window. People holding red cups stand in the kitchen, talking. He raps on the glass. A few heads turn.

"Bockus," someone says. "What the hell is he doing out there?" They see Jordan point to the door. They see him mimic turning a knob.

"Dude's playing charades."

Everyone laughs.

"Hey!" they hear Jordan shout. "Open up."

One guy gestures, pointing to the other side of the house. "Go around front!"

Jordan, expression dark, slams his hand against the door.

"What an asshole," someone says, giving him the finger.

Everyone laughs.

They turn away from the window, from the banging and yelling, and eventually the noise stops.

．　．　．

30

RICHARD

Richard agrees to meet with Joe and two of his Conundrum housemates. He doesn't know why they want to talk to him so badly. He's told them he won't discuss the case. But Dean Hunt is calling in five, six witnesses a day, and these guys are up next.

People are tense.

They wait for him in the pool room at the student union. They've claimed a corner booth where one of them, Jasper, attempts to eat a massive wrap that can't make up its mind: explode or disintegrate?

"What *is* that?" Richard can't help asking as he slides into the booth.

Jasper's cheeks bulge as he chews.

His buddy Henry answers for him. "Chicken tenders, bacon, cheddar, sour cream, and jalapeños," he says. "With a little lettuce and tomato."

"Heart-healthy," Richard observes. Jasper belches. Richard catches a whiff of bacon.

"You know it," Jasper says.

"So, what can I do you for?" Richard asks. He'd like to make this quick.

"We know you're not supposed to talk about this rape case," Joe begins. "But the fact is, everybody is talking about it. And there are a lot of rumors."

Richard looks around the table. "Such as?"

"Such as Jordan roofied that girl. Such as he wasn't the one who raped her. Such as she wasn't roofied but the punch was drugged. It's wild, man. Nobody knows what's real."

"Which is the point of the investigation," Richard says. "You don't need to worry about it. It's the investigator's problem."

"Not if it involves us," Joe says.

This is unexpected. Richard leans forward. "How does it involve you?"

"Shit," Jasper exclaims. The back of the wrap has split and a huge gob of the innards has landed in his lap.

"That thing is disgusting," Henry comments. "Even your dog wouldn't eat it."

"Oscar would love this," Jasper says. He attempts mopping his jeans with a fistful of paper napkins.

"Listen, Richard," Joe continues, ignoring Jasper and his wrap. He looks serious. "When you wouldn't talk to me the other night, I did some asking around. And now I'm pretty sure the girl I was wondering about is the one who's accusing Bockus. Anyway, there's something I didn't tell you: I brought her up to my room that night."

Richard's surprise feels cold. *What the hell?*

"I was worried about her," Joe explains. "She was hammered. She told me she didn't feel good, so I took her to my room to lie down—where, by the way, she threw up while I went to find her friends. I come back, my room smells like vomit, and she's gone. It was the last I saw of her all night."

The muscles in Richard's jaw relax. "So if that's the truth, what's the problem? Just tell that to the investigator."

"She was in *my* room," Joe repeats.

"*Our* room," Jasper corrects. "I live there, too."

"What if she decides to accuse me?" Joe continues. "I have no idea what she's saying. We aren't allowed to read her statement. My lawyer is really frustrated. He says I'm walking in there blind."

"You have a lawyer?" Richard asks. All three of them nod. He's stunned. "Why?"

"C'mon, Richard," Henry says. "Half the people at that party were freshman girls. And we were handing them Skippy. You bet my parents hired a lawyer. Think I want to get thrown out for serving minors?"

Richard looks at Jasper. "Why do *you* have a lawyer?"

Jasper belches again. "She was in my room."

Richard looks at them in amazement. "First of all," he says, "I think you're all overreacting. I get why Bockus is lawyered up, but trust me, no one is coming after you guys. Second, I don't get why you're telling me this."

"We were sort of hoping you might have some idea what she's saying," Joe says.

Richard throws up his hands. "I haven't read her statement, either. I'm in the dark, just like you."

"Yeah, but you date her roommate," Jasper says.

Richard is so surprised, he doesn't know what to say.

"Actually, I wish that was true," he finally manages. Even if it were, he'd still wonder where these three had heard about it. "Where are you guys getting your information?"

"People talk," Joe says. "But mostly The Board."

"It's lit up about this," Henry agrees.

"Haley and I are on *The Board*?" Richard says. Instantly sorry he spoke her name.

"Everyone's on The Board," Jasper says, wiping his mouth. He's abandoned the sodden remains of his wrap on a paper plate.

"You *post* on The Board?" Richard continues. "Dude, not cool. Delete that shit from your phone."

"I don't post. But I do read. Can't help it. It's addictive." Joe looks ruefully at the other two guys.

Richard leans forward a bit more. He wants to get in their faces. "Want to know what's going to screw you up?" he says. "The Board. They are going *after* whoever's been bullying that girl. If you know anything about it, or if you've had anything to do with it, I suggest you talk to your lawyers about *that*. And if you know who's responsible, tell them to knock it off."

"Dr. Feelgood," Jasper says.

"What?" Richard says. *Random.*

"He's the big poster," Jasper explains. "Ten, twenty a day. He's the one who started the Lying Bitch thread."

"It's a made-up name," Henry explains.

"I know that," Richard says impatiently. Dr. Feelgood. Where else has he heard that?

"Listen, we don't post on that thread," Henry reassures

him. "I agree, it's nasty. But we're getting away from the point here. Do you have any idea what's in that girl's statement?"

"Yeah, like, insider information?" Jasper adds.

Richard looks at them in disgust. He stands. "What part of 'I can't talk about this' do you not get?" He shoulders his pack.

As he turns to leave, Henry tosses a final comment at him. "Yeah, Exley warned us you'd be a total douche."

Richard freezes.

Jordan and Exley, seated close together on the couch, looking at something on Exley's phone. *He's got a PhD*, Jordan said. *People Hafta Drink.*

They want to feel good, and that's what the Doctor's there for. How could he have missed it?

As Richard quick-steps away from the booth, he texts Haley.

Where r u?

She replies immediately.

Library. Y?

Meet me at ur room now?

K. ??

see u there

The library is closer to Haley's dorm than the union, so Richard fully expects her to beat him there. When he reaches her door, he knocks.

"It's open," he hears.

The shock Richard feels is reflected on Carrie's face when he steps into the room. She's sitting up, reading on the bed with the bare mattress. Haley is nowhere in sight.

"Well," Carrie says once she recovers from her surprise. "If it isn't loverboy."

· · ·

Joe flicks on the light. She's not there.

He searches for the stench. Checks the sheets, the wastebasket. Inside the closet. Shoes.

He finds it in the recycle bin where Jasper stores his empties. It's yellow-green, strewn with chunks. It coats the bottles, the bottom and sides of the bin. Joe gags.

He carries the thing out of his room, downstairs to the kitchen. His eyes dart the halls, scan the teeming dance room, but there's no sign of her. In the kitchen, people move quickly out of his way when he heads for the industrial sink with the hose.

He breathes through his mouth, rinsing the gunk from the tub. As he aims the spray, he hears shouts, glass rattling.

"What's that?" he asks.

"Bockus got locked out," someone says.

Joe laughs, shaking his head. "What a tool."

· · ·

31

Haley

Haley hears raised voices in her supposedly empty room.

"Honestly, Richard. Do you expect me to believe that?" Carrie's voice drips sarcasm as Haley pushes open her door.

I should do a better job remembering to lock. It was one of the few things that caused friction when she and Jenny were still living together: Haley liked windows open and doors unlocked; Jenny always closed and bolted.

Haley feels a stupid expression form on her face as she walks in on Carrie and Richard. Feels embarrassed, as if she's interrupting. As if this isn't her room.

They seem like a couple to Haley, even though she knows they're not.

"Hey," Richard says. He looks upset.

Carrie looks pissed.

Haley drops her pack. "Okay. This is awkward."

Carrie, who half reclines on Jen's bare bed, swings her legs over the side and sits up.

"She was in here when I got here," and "The room was unlocked," they say simultaneously.

"Would you like me to step out? It's no problem," Haley offers, moving toward the door.

"No!" they both exclaim.

Richard, who has been leaning against one of the desks, passes a hand tiredly over his face. He pulls out the desk chair and sits. "You're the *last* one who should go."

"You're the first," Carrie mutters.

"Actually, I think maybe it should be you, Carrie," Haley says sharply.

Richard and Carrie look surprised.

Haley's surprised, too. But she's sick of these women picking on Richard.

They'd been piling on the night before. She'd stopped by Out House to visit Jenny, and they were all there: Mona, Carrie, and Gail. They were "discussing" the speaker the college had just scheduled for a campus event, a guy named Matt Trainor who did assemblies on sexual consent.

Carrie wasn't pleased. Since The Board thing happened, she'd been pushing for a whole day of canceled classes, replaced by workshops focused on rape prevention. Like the old-fashioned teach-ins of the '60s, she said. Matt Trainor fell way short of her expectations.

"The guy's an entertainer," she'd insisted. She had Jenny's bare foot in her lap and was painting her toenails as she spoke. Jenny flashed Haley a contented smile when she walked in. She held a large brown mug in both hands and wore a bright, dragon-pattern kimono Haley didn't recognize. "His videos remind me of the hypnotist that visited campus a couple years back."

"Oh, I remember him! That guy was a riot," Mona said.

Carrie glared at her.

"First," Gail parried, "we *need* an entertainer. Think Mary Poppins: a spoonful of sugar helps the medicine go down."

"These are adults. Not children," Carrie growled.

"This is a poorly evolved mob," Gail replied. "You start scolding them, they'll throw rocks. Second, he delivers the message we're after. We need to think beyond bystander intervention at parties or victim support the day after. We need to change the culture of sexuality on our campus. That begins with conversation. Trainor's program gets people talking."

"He turns serious issues into jokes," Carrie said.

"Laughter heals," Gail insisted.

"He reminds me of Richard," Carrie said. "Took nothing seriously."

"Who's Richard?" Jenny asked.

"This guy I used to hook up with," Carrie said.

Haley glanced at Gail, who winked at her.

"A *sophomore*," Gail added. "She dated him for most of this semester."

"'Dating' implies a relationship," Carrie said, then blew on Jenny's toes. She was applying deep purple polish. "This was purely physical."

Gail laughed. "Stop it. He's a sweet boy."

Mona snorted. "He was an entitled asshole," she corrected. "Hated that guy."

"Why?" Haley couldn't help asking.

273

Carrie patted Jenny on the leg, and she switched feet.

"Mona saw him naked," Carrie commented, grinning.

"And you're complaining?" Gail said, one eyebrow arched.

"He acted like he owned the place!" Mona exclaimed. "Couldn't be bothered to slip on his boxers when he went to the bathroom. As if I didn't live on the hall, too!"

"In all fairness," Carrie said, "he thought you were away that weekend. And he never did it again. Trust me, it's the least of his offenses."

"He called me names," Mona added.

Everyone looked at her.

"Hippie Witch," she supplied.

"I never should have told her." Carrie sighed.

"Oh," Jenny said. She looked thoughtful. "That's mean." She paused. "And . . . sort of funny."

There was a long silence, then everyone—except Mona—burst out laughing.

It went on from there. All the -ists, -isms, and -phobes that embodied Richard's deeply flawed character. Gail was silent, but Carrie and Mona seemed to have a can-you-top-this contest going. Haley could feel herself getting madder and madder. Finally, she just left.

Looking at Carrie now, sitting on Jenny's vacant bed, Haley feels the full weight of the older girl's superior attitude. What makes her always right and anyone who disagrees with her, or sees the world in a slightly different way, wrong?

"You know what?" Haley says. "He was invited. You let yourself in. Say what you want, then go."

Carrie's eyes narrow. "Is it true that you two are seeing

each other?" she demands. "Gail told me. Right after you got up and weirdly stormed off last night. Now I get it."

So much for "your secret's safe with me." Haley looks at Richard, who glares at Carrie. She can't help it; her cheeks grow hot.

"That's none of your business," he says evenly, a little aggressively.

Carrie whirls on Haley. "You *do* know who he is, right? *The* Richard? Who lives in the same house as Jenny's rapist?"

"You seem to think that makes me guilty of . . . what?" Richard demands.

"Did you know?" Carrie turns on him. "When you started targeting her, did you know she was Jenny's roommate?"

"That is *so* not what's going on here!" Haley bursts out.

Carrie laughs. "You sat there last night and said nothing! You let us go on and on. Then, what? Report back to him? Haley, wake up! Do you think it's a *coincidence* that he starts pursuing you at the same time Jenny reports his friend for rape?"

Richard slams his hand on the desk. They both jump.

"That is so freakin' unfair! It's sick, Carrie. It's paranoid!" He's yelling. Haley wonders if someone on the hall is going to call campus security.

"It's mean," Haley says, purposely lowering her voice. "What? I'm so out of *your* league that your ex-boyfriend couldn't possibly actually *like* me? Thanks."

A twinge of regret seems to pass over Carrie's face. Only a twinge. "Then why don't you explain it to me?" Carrie says. "Because on the surface, it looks pretty sketch."

Haley looks at Richard, but his mouth is shut in a tight line. He looks like he's struggling to control his anger.

"We met at math tutoring," Haley explains. "Neither of us made the Jenny-and-Jordan connection for a while. By the time we did it was . . . too late." She decides not to define "too late." She doesn't know if she can.

Carrie stands. She takes a step toward her. "Haley. Tell me you haven't said anything to him. Tell me you haven't compromised Jenny's case."

"Tell her nothing," Richard says sharply. "We've signed confidentiality agreements, which means we don't talk about it with each other, or with you."

"Why would you have to sign a confidentiality agreement, Richard?" Carrie asks. "How are you involved?"

"I was interviewed by the investigator," he says simply.

"You weren't at the party," Carrie says suspiciously.

"That's right," he says smoothly. "I was with you. Which, by the way, I told him."

Carrie folds her arms across her chest and glares at them. She looks far from satisfied. "This stinks," she finally declares. "I should report you. Both of you."

"For what?" Richard says. "And why? So *you* can compromise the investigation? That would be monumentally stupid. Carrie, this guy, Dean Hunt? He's smart. He's tough. Don't get in his way. He's doing a good job."

"How would you know that?"

For a moment, Richard hesitates.

Don't say anything else, Haley thinks. *Quit while you're ahead.*

Richard doesn't answer her. Instead he looks at Haley.

"Don't let her get in your head," he says to her. Pleading in his voice. "It's poison."

Haley turns to Carrie. "I think you should leave now."

Carrie doesn't move as she considers this. "I have one more question," she says. "Why are you quitting on Jenny? She was pretty upset after you left last night."

Haley freezes.

That had been the cherry on the great big sundae of an evening. When she was leaving Out House, Jenny had walked her to the front door.

"How're you doing?" Haley asked.

"Better," Jenny said. "My folks flew home. I feel calmer." She put her hand on Haley's arm. "Before they left my dad said you agreed with him that I should have a lawyer. I told him that's not true; you would have told me yourself." She looked at Haley a little accusingly.

Haley paused, stunned. The guy was a piece of work. "Not true. He asked me to quit; I said nothing."

Jenny looked relieved. "I knew it. I knew you wouldn't desert me." She moved toward Haley, intending a hug.

Haley stepped back. "But Jen, he's not wrong. I said I'd be your advisor, and I will. I'm here for you. But I *do* think you need a lawyer in there."

Jenny's face fell. "I don't want my dad's lawyer telling me what to say. I know what happened!"

"Jen, I know this is going to sound harsh, but Dean Hunt ripped holes in your story. You should have been better prepared."

"I told the truth!" Jenny said vehemently.

"I know," Haley insisted. "But a lawyer can help you. Like, he would have sorted out this Oscar stuff with you beforehand."

Jenny looked impatient. "The dog isn't important."

Haley couldn't quite believe what she was hearing. "Uh, the dog is very important," she said. "So are the stairs. So is the vodka. You passed out drunk, can't remember how you got home, and can't place the room you were in. You need a lawyer."

Jenny stepped away from her. She stared at Haley like she was seeing her for the first time. "You don't believe me," she said, her voice flat. It was a statement, not a question.

"Yes, I do," Haley replied, fatigued. "But what I think doesn't matter. You've got to convince Dean Hunt."

Jenny took another step back. "Just . . . go," she said, her tone still dead.

"Jen—" Haley began, moving toward her.

But Jenny put one hand up, stopping her. "Did you know," she said, "your mother called mine? Weeks ago, when this whole thing got started? Told her you were recovering from a head injury and couldn't get involved. Said you didn't want to get involved, but that you felt responsible for me."

Haley was stunned. She'd have thought Jenny was making it up, except . . . it sounded exactly like the sort of thing her mother would do. Behind her back. "I had no idea. I'm really sorry about that—"

"I finally get it now," Jenny interrupted. "You don't believe me. You just feel sorry for me." Jenny turned and ran up the stairs.

Here's what Haley now realizes: she doesn't feel one bit guilty. Well, about her mother she does. That was awful, and she'll have to deal with her at some point. But Jenny *does* need a lawyer. As she faces Carrie now, it occurs to her maybe she can convince her and Gail to second that message.

"I didn't quit. She just got upset when I told her she needs a lawyer. The investigator poked serious holes in her story. Maybe you could talk to her."

Carrie gets up in her face. She looks disgusted. "She needs a friend," she tells Haley. "Which you are not." Carrie glances over at Richard. Shoots him a dirty look as well, then heads for the door. "Watch out for this guy," she says to Haley. "The packaging is nice, but the box is full of worms." Carrie slams the door behind her.

Haley tries to sit, but actually collapses on her bed. She feels the tiny cat's paw beginnings of a headache behind her eyes. Richard sits next to her. He presses right up against her.

"You all right?" he asks.

She nods.

"About what she said? You know I would never use you for information."

"I know," Haley says quietly.

"Here's the truth, Haley: I sought you out, at first, because I saw you talking to Carrie. You know the day. Outside the history building? We'd just broken up. But then I got to know *you*. And you know the rest. How we realized the Jordan-and-Jenny connection. That's what matters: what *we* know is true."

"I know," she repeats.

"So are we okay?"

Haley puts her head on his shoulder. "I don't know what we are, but I think it's all right." She hears him laugh softly. "I hate to ask," she says, "but you texted me to meet you. What did *you* want to talk about?"

• • •

Jenny finds herself outside. The sounds of the house seem far away. The cool air, the quiet, feel good.

She had thrown up. It just came, jolted, bucked, up into her mouth, and she knew it had to go somewhere. She saw the familiar red bin. Filled with bottles.

When it was over she felt so sorry. She had to clean it up. Had to find Tall Boy, tell him, apologize. So she went looking for him.

Now she is outside. She feels better. The bucking has stopped. The air is like fresh water. The dress, airy, lifts, caresses her legs in the breeze. She closes her eyes, breathes deeply.

"Hello."

A boy, brown hair, holds a bottle. Smiles.

"Hello."

• • •

32

RICHARD

For something fairly simple, setting this up had not been simple.

First, Richard and Haley tried photos. But digging up a decent picture of Exley wasn't easy. He and Richard weren't Facebook friends, so access to his photos was limited. The few they could see were crap, and Exley's profile pics were all shots of his favorite bands.

"I really can't tell," said Eric, the guy from Haley's dorm who had seen the "guy in a baseball cap." Haley had asked him to meet with her and Richard. She didn't explain why, and he seemed a little surprised when they shoved the open laptop in front of him.

"I mean, maybe," he said, squinting at the blurry picture. "That could be a lot of guys."

Richard sighed. Coordinating with Eric, who not only

played a sport but had two labs, had taken days. In the meantime, Dean Hunt was tearing through the witness lists. Six, seven, sometimes as many as ten people were getting called in each day.

He felt like the window for speaking up was closing. But if he was going to narc on Dr. Feelgood to Dean Hunt, he needed to go on something more than gut instinct. He needed Eric to confirm Exley was the one outside Jenny's room.

"Why do we need a picture?" Eric asked. "Dude eats lunch at Lower dining hall on Tuesdays and Thursdays. I could point him out to you."

Richard and Haley looked at each other. "Yeah. Dumb and Dumber," she commented.

So here Richard sits, over a greasy Reuben sandwich and cold fries, with Eric the Freshman. As they watch the doors for Exley, Eric attacks a slab of sausage pizza. The pizza at Lower is notoriously terrible.

"Haley won't tell me why you're so interested in this guy," Eric says.

Richard tries not to watch him chew. "I'm not going to tell you, either."

"That's okay. I pretty much know. It has to do with her roommate who got raped, right?"

Richard levels an are-you-kidding-me? look at Eric. The kid doesn't even blush. He takes another bite of pizza.

"Whatever. I'm just happy to help. Sucks, what happened to her. She's a nice girl."

Richard eyes him curiously. "How do you know what happened?"

Eric laughs. "C'mon, man. Everyone talks. Half the girls

on her floor were called in to testify, plus there's all that crap on The Board."

"You believe The Board?" Richard laughs. His gaze returns to the door. Traffic is starting to pick up; it's almost noon.

"On the upside," Eric continues, "we have the morning off tomorrow."

Richard nods. MacCallum has canceled tomorrow's classes and replaced them with an assembly about consent. It would run three times so they could cycle every student through.

"You're going, right?" Haley had asked him.

He'd been taken aback by the question. "Isn't everybody going?"

"Ha," Haley said, no trace of laughter in her voice. "My dorm is already planning a rager for the night before because people plan to sleep in the next day."

Richard made a face. "People suck," he declared.

She didn't correct him on that count.

"Want to go together?" she asked.

He was surprised by the hesitance in her voice. He'd assumed they'd go together.

"Uh . . . yes," he said. She looked relieved. Did she think he'd say no? It occurs to him he's been preoccupied lately. Semi-obsessed with this Exley thing.

"So, are you going?" Eric asks him now.

"Yeah, somehow Haley convinced me to go to the first session with her. Bright and early."

"Are you two dating?"

"Why do people keep asking that question?" Richard wonders out loud.

"She's cute. People want to know if she's unattached."

Richard is about to comment on that remark when Exley enters the dining hall.

He's with Jordan.

"Okay, slowly. Try to be cool. I know that's difficult," Richard says. "But the guy I'm wondering about has just walked in. Turn and tell me if he's the one you spoke with."

Eric takes another bite of pizza for good measure, then nonchalantly pivots in his seat. He scans the cluster of students who have just entered, then turns back around. He finishes chewing.

"Guy in the red shirt. Dark brown hair. That's him."

Richard glances over Eric's shoulder to where Jordan and Exley have gotten in line for burgers. Jordan wears a light blue jacket, Exley a red shirt. No one else in sight wears red.

He stands and slaps Eric's hand. "Thanks, man. That's all I needed to know."

"Oh, c'mon. You're going to tell me, right? Was it him? What the hell did he do?"

Richard walks quickly away before people overhear Eric.

He knows where he has to go next.

• • •

"*Are you having fun?*"

Jenny hesitates. She was. Then she wasn't. She felt awful. She feels better. She looks at him.

He's not tall. He wears jeans. A blue shirt. He smiles at her.

"*I don't know. Are you?*"

He laughs. "Sure. That's why I'm out here."

Confusing. He doesn't sound happy.

"*I need to tell my friends where I am,*" *she says. Then she thinks: Tamra. Her eyes fill.*

"*Good luck getting back in,*" *he says.*

She turns toward the front of the house. The ground sways. The branches in the tree overhead sway. She feels a hand, strong, on her arm.

"*Steady there,*" *he says.*

She looks at him. The swaying stops.

"*Want to go for a walk?*" *he asks.*

• • •

33

Haley

Gail's not expecting her. Haley decides to skip the "hey I'm coming over" text and go for the element of surprise. See how she likes it.

Because like Carrie the other night in her room, Haley has things to say.

When she walks in, Gail is at her desk, laptop open. The only light is from a small desk lamp, the computer's blue glow, and strings of white bulbs lining the windows. Tablecloth-size tapestries and posters of black women—she recognizes older versions of Maya Angelou and Toni Morrison, their hair silver-marbled—conceal the tape- and tack-scarred walls. Haley can tell by Gail's expression that she's already heard about the Carrie-Richard conflagration.

"My bad," Gail says before Haley even speaks. She holds

her hands up in surrender. "Completely, totally. What can I say? I slipped. I never meant to tell her about you guys."

Haley drops onto Gail's bed. She throws her hands up and stares, challenging her to explain. "So why *did* you?"

Gail seems at a loss. "When you stormed out the other night, it was obvious something was bugging you. I was tired, didn't think, and said, 'Maybe you were all too mean about Richard,' and . . . whoops. You should have seen their faces. Then Jen comes back and she's in tears, saying you've sided with her father. Carrie was convinced you'd crossed over to the Dark Side."

"Of course she would! Because in Carrie World there are only two sides: hers and everyone who's wrong."

"Well, to be fair—"

"When is she ever fair?" Haley interrupts.

Gail is silent.

"A warning would have been nice."

"I thought I would see you before she did. I had no idea she would be so . . . quick."

Haley shakes her head. "The woman's a heat-seeking missile."

"Was it a direct hit?"

"She missed," Haley says. "We emerged from the wreckage."

Gail looks relieved. "I'm glad," she says. "I would be sorry if I'd messed that up. You guys are good together."

Haley snorts. She stands. "Together? What the hell is that? Seriously, define it for me."

Gail smiles hesitantly and cocks her head. "Excuse me?"

Haley paces. The urge to kick something borders on overwhelming. She could be on the sideline right now, moments before heading onto the field: that's what this adrenaline rush is like.

She misses that release. The heart-pounding run, the pure impact of her foot connecting with the ball. For all the drama with her mother, the demands, and the pressure, soccer had been so simple. There were accepted rules. A clearly marked goal.

"Just friends, or with benefits?" Haley wonders aloud. "And if you're friends with benefits, isn't that hooking up? And if you're hooking up more than once, like, for weeks, is that dating? And doesn't dating include talking and doing stuff together beyond the bedroom? Which sounds an awful lot like a relationship. Facebook-official. Which, let's be honest, is practically an *engagement* announcement around here! I mean, people are either joined at the hip or ignoring each other at the juice machine the morning after! I don't get it."

It's a rant. She hears herself. Doesn't particularly like the way she sounds. But it feels good to let it all out. Like a good kick from the corner.

"Actually, sounds like you do get it," Gail replies. No irony in her voice.

Haley flops onto Gail's bed. "I don't pretend to know what 'together' means," she says. "Between you and me? I'm failing College Love 101."

Gail laughs. "Oh, stop it. You must be doing something right. You've got one of the cutest guys on campus interested in you."

"Do I, though? And interested in what?" Haley presses

her. "What are his expectations? A guy getting great sex on the reg isn't going to be satisfied with holding hands and picking apples indefinitely. I can never measure up. She's the hottest, most beautiful woman in MacCallum history."

Gail waves one hand, dismissing the comment. "Don't even go there," she says. "Carrie is not beautiful. She is other-worldly. Mere mortals like us do not compare."

"I can't help it."

"And something else to keep in mind?" Gail continues. "She rips through men. She says she doesn't want them. But it might be that they want something she can't, or won't, give them."

Haley stares at her. The idea that guys want something Carrie can't give is foreign to her.

"Emotional intimacy?" Gail suggests. "Support? Encouragement?"

Haley raises her eyebrows.

"Friendship?"

"Guys want that, too? I thought it was just the women on my hall. Minus Tamra," Haley says.

Gail looks disapproving. "C'mon, Haley. Don't be like that. Bitterness isn't your thing."

Haley throws herself backward and stares at the ceiling tiles. Has bitterness become her thing? It used to be chocolate. Laughter. Playing hard. Blushing hard. Blurting the stupidest stuff.

So when did those things become not enough?

Haley told Gail she and Richard are fine, but in fact, Carrie's drone attack shook things up. Richard had been totally nice afterward and said all the right things, but once he told her about Exley and The Board and they arranged a meet-up with Eric, he just . . . left. No kiss, no nothing. And her in that big, empty single.

Was there something about seeing them side by side, the comparison inevitable, that prompted him to run the other way? They have plans to attend the assembly together, which is good, but still. Something is different.

"You know," Haley says, "I used to think I didn't like her because of the political correctness. She's such an activist, and I've never heard of half the things she's screaming about. Then, with the Richard stuff? I thought it was just . . . jealousy. Plain and simple. She's-prettier-and-the-cute-guy-likes-her. I know, really shallow. But I'm being honest." Haley sits up. It's as if her thoughts are taking shape in a clear stream. Bright, bracing, sweeping her along and out of some muddied eddy.

"But that wasn't it," she says. "The problem is how she makes me *feel*. Not only less experienced and less attractive, but just . . . less. Less intelligent. Less mature. Less *cool*."

"Don't be ridiculous," Gail begins.

But Haley's on a roll. "Face it, Gail, Carrie embodies cool. Women who are all about career, not relationships. Who take charge. Who insist they don't need a man to complete them. Someone like me? Still pretty much a third-grader when it comes to sex, and wishing for a boyfriend? I'm like the Disney princess to her Hillary Clinton."

Gail bursts out laughing. "May I remind you Hillary is also a wife and mother? *And* grandmother?"

"You know what I mean!"

Gail folds her arms across her chest. "No, I don't," she says. "I have a boyfriend. Does that make me uncool?"

Haley's shock is visible. She manages to keep her mouth shut, but she knows her face betrays her surprise. For some reason she'd put Gail in the "no commitments" box with Carrie.

"He graduated from MacCallum two years ago," Gail continues. "He's in medical school at Howard University. These days we mostly Skype. But we're making plans together for when I graduate."

"Okay, that's . . . cool," Haley tells her.

Gail shrugs. "Works for us. Listen: my friend Carrie—and she is my friend—doesn't want to be emotionally tied to a man. Sex is satisfying and impersonal to her. I respect that. But me? I'm all for partnership. Yeah, I want a career and a good education. Yes, I feel strong and beautiful on my own. But *doubly* so when a good man I respect values me. We have each other's backs."

Both of them are quiet for a while. They let their words and the emotions attached to them float gently in the room, finally settling, like feathers, on the floor. The furniture. The rumpled comforter. Haley realizes she's not mad anymore. Realizes there was never going to be a good way to tell Carrie about her and Richard. Whatever that is.

"You know," Gail says, as if something has just become clear to her, "I forgot, Ms. Soccer Star, that you're a competitor."

"Was," Haley corrects.

But Gail shakes her head. "You still are," she says. "Look at you. Worrying about how you compare to Carrie. Figuring out where you stand in the Game of Love. Piece of advice? Stop keeping score. Just do you and it'll all work out."

Haley stares at her. Then bursts out laughing. "Sounds good," she says. "Especially since I haven't figured out how to do anything else."

Gail smiles at her. "You could not," she finally says, "pay me enough to repeat freshman year."

"It sucks," Haley agrees.

. . .

Jordan talks. Jenny hears herself laughing. She hears him answering her questions.

She's not sure where they're going. Everything moves. The leaves—papery sound—the sidewalk, the street lamps. They come out of the woods, go back into the woods, her arm crooked through his. When she sways, he squeezes tighter.

Her dress is like gauze. Out of the woods, the breeze stronger, it puffs up. High.

"Your dress is beautiful," he tells her.

She doesn't answer.

"Do you have a boyfriend?" he asks. "You must have a boyfriend."

She doesn't answer.

"I feel swirly," she finally says.

. . .

34

RICHARD

Richard and Haley show up late and barely manage to grab two seats at the rear of the auditorium. The session is packed.

"I thought you said everyone was sleeping in," Richard comments.

"Not the teams," Haley says, pointing to rows packed with jersey-clad students. "Coaches were on this."

From their vantage point in the back they can check out the whole scene. The men's lacrosse team sits in the first three center rows. To their left, separated by an aisle, Carrie and Co. occupy seats: the Hippie Witch's unmistakable red dreads could be a placard announcing *Activists Sit Here*. Other campus cohorts (football players, whole freshman halls, hipsters) fill the place. A boisterous din of conversation floats to the ceiling.

The stage, in contrast, is stark. A couch he recognizes as

a theater department prop is positioned dead center. A guy, fortyish maybe, hard to tell, wearing jeans and a T-shirt emblazoned with red lips, as if a giant wearing lipstick had kissed his chest, stands to one side, big smile on his face.

"That's Matt Trainor," Haley tells him.

"And he is?" Richard asks.

"A one-man traveling sexual-consent road show," Haley explains. "He's a counselor *and* a stand-up comic. He does this thing at colleges and military bases."

The din fades as a student, looking professional in black slacks and a matching short jacket, walks toward the microphone at center stage. He recognizes her: it's that friend of Carrie's. Gail.

"Good morning," Gail says. She holds an oversize index card, probably containing notes. The buzz slowly dies as people realize the program is beginning. "I can't tell you how pleased I am to introduce Matt Trainor to MacCallum College today . . ."

As Gail runs through the list of Matt's accomplishments, places he's visited, the difference he's made in changing the dialogue of consent, Richard's eyes drift to Carrie's corner again. At the same moment, Carrie's white-blond head pivots and she twists in her seat to scan the audience behind her. Their eyes lock over the sea of students.

Her expression isn't friendly.

"Wow," Richard hears. For a second, he thinks he's said it. Then he realizes it's Haley. She's noticed Carrie, too. "If looks could kill, right?" she murmurs into his ear. Richard sees

Carrie whisper to the Witch, who twists around, glances at him and Haley, then turns back in her seat. Her face registers nothing. Not even surprise.

"Ignore them," he tells Haley. Then he makes a decision. He takes one of her hands in his, lacing his fingers through hers and squeezing tight. He doesn't look at her when he does this, but then he feels the pressure of her fingers squeezing back.

Richard hears applause. Gail is stepping back, and the Trainor guy is stepping forward. Skipping forward, actually.

The guy's pumped.

"Before we begin," he says, "I'm going to ask for two volunteers. One man, one woman. Right here, up on the stage. Anybody brave enough?"

There's a pause, nervous laughter and shuffling, as several hundred people shift in their seats and look around. *Brave my ass. More like stupid. To the tenth factorial.*

He feels a tug on his hand, a rush of cool air. Haley is standing, which strikes him as odd. Why would she leave? It's just beginning. But then she's pulling him up.

"We'll do it," Haley calls out to Matt Trainor.

Every head whips around in their direction.

Shit.

Richard hears a whoop from a pack of girls in team sweatshirts. One of them screeches, "It's Haley!" There's a ripple of applause, a wave of laughter, an undercurrent of whispers, and her hand, now relentless, pulling. He imagines what he looks like. A doe facing a Peterbilt?

Which is a complete contrast to her. Haley's eyes are bright. Her jaw is set, but her mouth twists in a barely suppressed laugh. She's as pumped as Trainor. With some serious business behind that grip.

It's her game face. He's never seen it before. It's . . . impressive.

"C'mon, Math Dude," she urges. "We've got this."

The applause in the room increases as he drags himself to his feet. He can smell the relief in the air, everyone so glad that some idiot just volunteered and Matt Trainor didn't have to select random victims.

"You do recognize the irony of not asking for my consent before volunteering us at an assembly about consent, right?" he says as they leave their seats and walk the gauntlet toward the stage.

"Duly noted," she tells him, not looking one bit sorry.

On stage, two students clip tiny remote microphones to their collars. Gail affixes his.

"I hope you know what you're doing," she says quietly to him.

"No clue," he answers grimly. The stage lights blind him to most of the audience; only the first few rows are visible. Carrie and Co. are in plain view to his right, Carrie's expression frozen, unreadable. Front and center are the lax bros, looking highly entertained. All the way to the left he glimpses MacCallum's president, sitting alongside her husband.

Gail flicks Richard's mike and the room resounds with the thud.

"Say something," she prompts.

"Testing one two three," he tries. He hears his voice bounce off the walls. Haley's does the same.

"Okay, you two," Gail whispers. "Breathe. Have fun. Good luck." She walks away.

The next few minutes are like a dream. Matt Trainor, exuding high-voltage enthusiasm, gets them to introduce themselves, then seats them on the couch while he delivers his opening lines. Richard tries to concentrate, but it's hard. He's disoriented by the warm, bright lights and the bursts of audience laughter breaking over them like waves.

Eventually, Trainor's words begin to resemble a language he understands.

"Here's the problem with 'No Means No,'" Richard hears. "It sets up this dynamic that basically says, 'I'm going to keep pushing until you say stop.' Well, what does that tell us? That silence means yes? That it's okay to go for it until someone draws the line? I want to suggest something more positive. More affirmative. More sexy, even. How about 'Yes Means Yes'?"

As if on cue, applause breaks out. Richard isn't sure why; he's still waiting to find out what the guy means.

"Here's my question," Trainor continues. "Do you ask? Before something as simple as"—he gestures to the lips on his shirt—"a kiss?" Uneasy laughter ripples through the room. Trainor doesn't wait for anyone to answer. Instead, he wheels around.

"Haley. Richard." Richard feels himself startle. Matt Trainor looks at them curiously. "You volunteered together. By any chance, are you a couple?"

"Couple of what?" Haley asks.

The audience cracks up. Trainor smiles, but definitely looks taken aback. He's used to making all the jokes, Richard realizes. And Haley's funny.

Then, Haley turns on him. "Actually, Matt, it's a good question," she continues before the laughter fully subsides. "I'm not really sure where we stand. We've only recently met. But we're spending time together. It's sort of a work-in-progress. What do you think, Richard?" She looks at him, eyes wide. Questioning.

But every word feels like a combat dagger hurled at Richard's head. He reads a challenge in her faux-innocent expression.

A protracted "ooooooh" rises from the student seats.

What the hell?

"Uh, yeah," he stammers. "Pretty much an early stage work. In progress." He feels his face burn.

Matt Trainor looks delighted. "Come on up here, Richard," he says enthusiastically. Richard hauls himself to his feet. Trainor drapes one arm over his shoulder.

"So, Richard," he begins. "Let's say you're with a woman you're just getting to know. A woman you're interested in . . . romantically."

Everyone suddenly bursts out laughing. Matt Trainor looks confused, until he sees where they're looking. He and Richard pivot and catch Haley pointing to herself with both hands. She stops when they turn, winking suggestively and giving Richard a little wave. Trainor shakes his head ruefully and returns to the crowd, playing along with her.

"Tell me, Richard, with *such a woman*"—he tilts his head in Haley's direction; more laughter—"how do you know when it's the right time to . . . *make your move?*" He lowers his voice dramatically.

The audience waits.

"Depends on the situation," Richard says. Weak answer, he knows. But hey, it does.

Trainor tries again. "Let's say you want to kiss her," he says. "How would you know if the feeling is mutual?"

"I guess body language," Richard says. "Like, if we're already touching? Holding hands, or sitting next to each other. You just kind of know if the moment is right."

Behind them, they hear Haley make this high-pitched, breathy "oooohhh" sound. They turn to see that this time she's collapsed on the couch in a fake faint, a smile on her face, hands clutched to her chest.

The audience loves it.

Richard redirects his gaze to Trainor. "If she swoons, that's also a good sign," Richard says, deadpan. "Although you want to wait until she wakes up before you kiss her."

"Totally," someone shouts from Carrie's corner. Richard wills himself not to look in that direction.

"What about just asking?" Trainor says. "Why not say, 'Can I kiss you?'"

Richard squinches his face, puckering his lips like he tastes something sour. "I don't know. Kind of messes with the mood. Seems awkward."

This is exactly the opening Matt Trainor was hoping for.

"Does it, though?" he asks. "Isn't it more awkward to move in for the big kiss and have her push you away?"

"That would suck," Richard agrees.

"As a matter of fact," Trainor says, stepping back and addressing his comments directly to the audience, "I would suggest that rather than wrecking the mood, building up to the big 'ask' can be romantic. It's a mood enhancer. It's *hot*." He faces Richard again. "Let's give it a try."

This was a bad idea. Richard returns to the couch. The undercurrent of conversation throughout the auditorium sounds like a swarming hive. The lax bros can barely contain themselves; they think this is hysterical.

"There are better and worse ways to ask, 'Can I kiss you?'" Trainor begins. "For example, you don't want to startle them. 'Oh my god! Can I kiss you?'" He shouts the question in a desperate voice. Everyone jumps, then laughs. "Try leading into it," he suggests. "Say you've been hanging out all evening, and now the two of you are back at your room, sitting on the couch. You might say, 'I have had such a great time with you tonight. I really like you. Can I kiss you?'" Trainor's tone completely changes. It's sincere and intimate. It's sexy without being aggressive. People in the audience applaud.

"Which one of you wants to give it a try?" Trainor has turned to them. The applause changes to laughter and whistles. Richard looks at Haley. Her hand shoots up. Matt Trainor smiles at her encouragingly, then steps away from the couch. The room quiets.

Haley's head is bowed, as if she's staring at something in her lap. "Oh my god!" she exclaims. She looks up at Richard with an amazed expression. "You did my problem sets for me!" She leaps from the couch, yells, "Yes!" and pumps her fist. She plops back next to him. "Can I kiss you?" she gleefully asks.

The crowd roars. Matt Trainor laughs as well. A little less enthusiastically.

"That's cute," he concedes, "but may I point out that sexual intimacy should never be given in exchange for something." Richard hears a few groans from the audience. "Richard, want to give it a try?"

What to do? He's not good at being funny on command. His mind races, trying to think of something.

Then his glance falls on Carrie in the second row. Arms folded across her chest, lip curled. Like she's just wishing she had a crossbow right now.

It's all the inspiration he needs.

Richard scootches close to Haley, facing her so their knees touch. He takes both her hands in his and looks sincerely into her eyes.

"You are *so* much nicer than my last girlfriend," he declares earnestly. "Can I kiss *you*?"

More uproarious laughter. And judging from the enthusiastic response from the bros in the front row, more people knew he'd dated Carrie than he realized.

Matt Trainor doesn't even pretend to smile at this point. He looks out toward the audience. He's going to pick other volunteers.

"Can I try again?" Haley asks him. "Seriously?"

Trainor's clearly reluctant, but he nods.

Haley takes one of Richard's hands in both of hers. As the audience settles down, she laces her fingers through his.

"I really like your hands," she tells him. People are saying, "Shush, we can't hear her." She waits for the room to quiet, massaging his hand the whole time. It's strangely intimate. Sexy, even.

"Is that weird to say?" she finally continues. "But it's the first thing I noticed about you. You were helping me with my math homework, and I thought, 'He's got gorgeous hands.'" The room has gone completely silent at this point. Now her hands still. They hold his. Tight.

"I like you. A lot," she says quietly. The microphone barely picks up her voice. "And I'm a little embarrassed to say this, but . . . I've never had a boyfriend." She looks directly into Richard's eyes when she says this.

"I know you have," she continues. "Had girlfriends, that is. But for now, for us? For starters? Can we just . . . kiss?"

Every person in the place stops breathing. At least, that's how it feels to Richard. He knows he's holding his breath.

"Absolutely," he finally says. And then he is. They are. Kissing. On the theater department prop couch, on the stage, in front of half the college. To shouts of "Yes!" from the bros and applause as the kiss continues, and at some point, a standing ovation.

Meanwhile, Matt Trainor wears a delighted grin.

"Now *that*," he says to the audience, "is consent."

. . .

Jordan laughs.

"Swirly?" he says.

"Like everything is swirling around," Jenny hears herself say.

He laughs again.

She feels him touch the top of her head. Kiss the top of her head.

"You are so sweet," he tells her.

She stumbles. She feels him catch her, hold her up.

"Do you want to sit down?" he asks. "I live right here."

. . .

35

Haley

Haley offers to make it up to Richard with lunch at the Forge, her treat. It's a go-to place, an old blacksmith's shop turned bistro on the river with great food.

It's the least she can do for hauling him up on that stage.

He accepts without hesitation; the dining hall will be a zoo. Simply escaping the auditorium post-Trainor took thirty minutes. Their new celebrity couple status means everyone "needs" to talk to them. MacCallum's President Smith, for example: "You were wonderful. Thank you for that!" she enthused while the college photographer clicked away. (*Great,* Haley had thought, *now we're going to end up on the website. Is that the same as "Facebook-official"?*) Her team mobbed her ("You do realize you've basically just announced to the entire campus that you're a virgin," Madison murmured in her ear). Even Mona joined the paparazzi. Haley and Richard were almost at the exit when *poof!* She materialized. Blocking them, hands on hips.

"Uh-oh," Richard said under his breath.

"Hey, Mona," Haley said.

Mona regarded them, squinting. She seemed to be trying to make up her mind about something.

"This is that oops-too-late moment when you wish everyone had had to pass through a metal detector before coming in," Richard said.

Mona burst out laughing. "You read my mind!" She stepped in close. She wrapped Haley in a big bear hug. "Nice job up there. You're braver than you look," she said, releasing her. She turned to Richard and pressed one finger into his shoulder. "I'm still not convinced."

He didn't respond. Wise man.

"Haley's my girl," she continued. "Be good to her. Because I'm watching you, ass-wipe." She gave Haley a little salute and began to walk away.

"I love you, too, Mona," Richard called after her.

She turned. "That's Hippie Witch. To you."

"I think that means we're friends now," he said to Haley as they watched Mona leave.

The Forge is crowded for lunch on a Friday, but they manage to land a quiet table for two near the back. Only one side of the building has windows; the other side is an old flat stone blacksmith's hearth, still streaked with black smudges from coal fires. It's scattered with dozens of flickering tea candles, which account for most of the light in the dim room.

As the hostess leads them to their table, Haley feels the badassedness that fueled her performance at the assembly evaporate. Easy enough to put on a show in front of cheering fans or under stage lights, but in here? One-on-one? Where it counts?

A whole different game. When they're handed menus, she's grateful for something to do. With her eyes. Her hands. She glances at him while he reads.

Richard's hair is a little long and he keeps running his fingers through it, lifting it off his forehead. What color is it? Too light to be brown, not quite blond. She has this crazy impulse to touch it. To reach across the table, right now, and brush it back from his face.

If they were dating, that would be all right. Right? Is he her boyfriend? What the hell *is* this? Haley reminds herself to not look at his hands; she might do something stupid. She wills her eyes back to the menu.

She's tired of wondering. About a lot of things.

"What are you thinking?" Richard asks.

She startles. "I'm sorry?"

"I'm thinking the roast chicken. But the fettuccine alfredo is supposed to be really good."

"Thing about that is three bites into it, you're done," she says. "So rich."

"Chicken," he agrees, pushing his menu to the end of the table.

She places hers there as well. "Mushroom risotto."

"Good choice," he says. He sits back and just . . . looks at her. Smiles. Her stomach is doing flip-flops, but he seems very comfortable. The waitress returns, then takes their orders. He raises his water glass when she leaves.

"Since we're only drinking water, we have to look into each other's eyes as we toast," Richard says. "Otherwise it's bad luck."

Haley picks up her glass. "I've never heard of that," she

says, "but okay." They clink, then sip. Blue-green, his eyes. Not pure blue. He lays one hand, palm open, on the table before her. She places hers on top, and he wraps his fingers around. *God, those hands . . .*

"I feel like we have a lot to talk about," she manages to say.

"You start."

"Well . . . the thing we were fighting about."

The half smile he's worn since they walked into the restaurant fades. "You mean Jordan-and-Jenny stuff?"

"Not exactly. More like your attitude about things."

He takes another drink. "Sure you don't want to talk about what just happened on the stage? Might be more interesting."

"Definitely more interesting," she agrees. "But it's the *second* thing."

Richard sighs, resigned. Not for the first time that day. "To say you surprised me would be an understatement."

"I sort of surprised myself."

"Sort of?"

"Yeah," she admits. "I tend to go for it when I see an opening. That look on Carrie's face motivated me."

"I didn't know that about you," Richard says. "It's cool. A little intimidating, but cool."

Neither of them speaks for a few moments. She waits for him to return to the first thing.

"Listen, Haley, it's no secret I'm not politically correct," he finally begins.

"I'm worried it goes deeper than that."

He drums his fingers on the table with his free hand. "Can I ask you something? What are you doing here with me if you have concerns about my character?"

"I don't."

"Yeah, you do. You're wondering why women you respect, like Gail and Mona and Carrie, can't stand me."

Haley laughs. "I respect Carrie?"

"I do. I don't *like* her and I definitely don't agree with everything she says, but damn, she's got convictions. And she stands by them. And she tries to help people. I think it blinds her in certain ways, but when I'm picking teams? I'll choose her over the Brandon Exleys and Jordan Bockuses of this world every time."

Haley leans forward, her elbows on the table. "Are you over her? Tell me the truth."

"Completely. She scares me."

They both laugh.

"I don't get it." Haley meets his eyes. "I don't get how a guy like you goes from a Carrie to a . . . me."

"You obviously don't see yourself clearly."

"Freckly jock," she tells him. "Poor dresser. Inexperienced. And *don't* tell me that doesn't matter to you."

"That doesn't matter to me."

"Liar."

"The fact that you think that matters to me proves you *don't* know much about guys."

The crimson begins its slow creep across her cheeks. "Okay. So educate me."

Now it's his turn to look uncomfortable. "What, you want Intro to Guys?"

"I want Richard 101. The SparkNotes version."

He turns her hand over in both of his. His thumbs trace deliberate, slow circles that she feels all the way to the soles of her feet.

"I'm . . . imperfect. But loyal. I make mistakes, but hopefully not the same mistake twice. It helps to have someone you trust tell you when you've messed up. My sister is like that. Totally has my back but lets me know when I get it wrong." Haley feels herself smile. It's cute the way he talks about his little sister. "I told her about you."

"Really?" Haley's mind races, trying to imagine that conversation.

Richard smiles. "She said you sound way too cool for me and I'd better not mess this up." He squeezes her fingers.

She feels the heat spreading across her cheeks. But she squeezes back. "You keep slipping into the second thing," she says quietly. "We weren't quite done with the first."

He looks thoughtful. "You and I went off the rails that day at the orchard."

"You seemed to think that rape is another term for morning-after regret," she says.

"I don't," he says firmly. "I think they are two very different things. But both are real. And both have endless . . . permutations. One's a crime. One's a whoops. The problem is, sometimes we disagree on how to tell them apart. And I know damn well there are people out there who would burn me at the stake for saying that, but that's what I think."

She reaches for her glass with her free hand. Takes a sip before responding. "I think it's your vocab choices that piss people off. For example: 'whoops'?"

"I'll spell it out," he says. "Two people at a party. Both have a lot to drink. They start grinding on the dance floor. They end up spending the night together. They realize in the

310

morning that had they been sober they never, ever, would have hooked up. Whoops."

She glances away. At the paintings on the walls. The other diners. "Sounds like you speak from experience."

"I do. I'm sorry if that upsets you. I'm not particularly proud of it, but it's the truth."

It does. Upset her. Maybe not for the reasons it should. The fact is she's just plain old jealous. It bothered her to think of him with Carrie. Now her imagination has a closet-load of other hot women to contend with.

"Richard, what happened to Jenny? That wasn't a 'whoops.' That was rape. She was passed out drunk."

"You can't consent if you're passed out drunk. I get that, Haley. So what about if you're sort of drunk? Is 'very drunk' rape and 'a little drunk' a hookup?"

"You're asking the wrong person to split those hairs," she remarks drily.

He breathes out impatiently. "Frankly, it's over my head, too," he tells her. "It's complicated. You say Jenny was raped, and I say I have no clue what happened. Jordan said it was consensual. Is he lying to me? Or to himself? Or is that the truth? That's why there's an investigation. These things are hard to sort out, and it doesn't make me a bad guy to say that."

"You're not a bad guy," she tells him. "You're just a little . . . what's Gail's word? . . . unevolved."

He laughs. "I like that. Beats ass-wipe."

She returns his smile. Neither of them has released the other's hand.

"Haley." Serious tone in his voice. "I'd like for you to trust me. But if you don't, that would be good to know. Now."

She considers this. Trust. Such a huge word. Such a massive concept, really. There's been a trust deficit in so many of her relationships. Her mother. Coach. Jenny. Carrie. Does she trust Richard?

He annoys her. Excites her. Makes her furious. Makes her laugh. Makes her think. And she knows, without a doubt, that he would never intentionally hurt her. And she can tell him just about anything. Which she tends to do. Sometimes, unfortunately, in front of lots of people.

"Yeah, I do," she says. "Completely."

Their waitress chooses this moment to bring their meals. They disengage their locked fingers so she can place the plates on the table.

When the waitress leaves, Richard looks over at Haley. "I'm glad."

Haley smiles at him. Picks up her fork. She knows she should say something, anything, deep and profound about *them*, but in fact she's thinking his chicken looks way better than the gluey glop, flecked with brown bits, on her plate.

And like that, she knows what to do.

She scoops a big forkful of steaming risotto, then blows gently to cool it. She carefully extends it across the table toward Richard.

His eyes widen. "Soccer Girl. Sharing?"

She doesn't reply, just holds the fork steady. Richard leans forward and allows her to feed him a bite of her meal. He nods his head in approval as he chews. When he's done, he cuts a piece of chicken from his plate and holds it out to her. She places one hand on his, guiding the fork to her mouth.

It's delicious.

Richard waits for Haley to finish before he asks, "So. You're good with this?"

"I am *so* good with this."

. . .

They walk into his room. There is a bed, a desk. Shelves and a chair. Jenny sits on the bed. Her feet hurt. She kicks off the painful shoes.

He sits next to her. She realizes something. Important.

"I don't know your name," she says.

He laughs again. "Yes, you do. I told you. Jordan."

"Jordan," she repeats. "Like the river."

"That's right, Jenny," he says. He touches her mouth with one finger. "Or should I call you Swirly?" He laughs.

She doesn't. She wants to tell him it's not funny, the swirling, but she feels quieter and quieter. Maybe if she just sits here a minute.

His finger traces her cheek. His lips move to hers. Press, a little at first, then harder.

This is kissing, she thinks. Her hand moves to his hair. It's soft. She kisses him back. It's nice.

"You're so pretty," he says.

. . .

36

RICHARD

The word is that the inquisition has ended. Dean Hunt has stopped interviewing witnesses.

Only then does he finally get back to Richard.

It's been, what? A week since Eric pointed out Exley? Richard hadn't wasted any time. He'd walked right from the dining hall that day to the dean's office. Asked the receptionist if he could see him.

One week later, Richard has an appointment. He is not shy about sharing his frustration over this.

Dean Hunt seems unconcerned.

Worse yet, he seems unimpressed. As Richard unpacks his theory that Exley is not only the Dr. Feelgood of The Board but is very likely the person who wrote on Jenny's door, the dean betrays no hint of emotion.

"So, that's it?" he asks when Richard finishes. "His friends call him 'Doctor' and some kid saw him wandering around the freshman dorms?"

Plus he's a douche, Richard doesn't add.

Dean Hunt glances at his watch. "Richard, I appreciate your wanting to help, but I need more than that. Did you actually see Brandon Exley post as Dr. Feelgood on The Board?"

"No," Richard says. "But like I said, I saw him and Jordan doing something on his phone right when it all started. Can't you bring him in and check his phone?"

Dean Hunt laughs quietly. "I have questioned and checked the phones of virtually every witness. Including Mr. Exley. And like Mr. Bockus, he doesn't have that application. No one does. Not a single person. And they all handed over their devices when I asked. One fellow, not very savvy I may add, volunteered his phone before I even asked the question. What do you make of that?"

Richard is dumbfounded. Especially because Joe *told* him he had The Board app. "I don't know."

"Don't you?" Dean Hunt continues, one eyebrow raised as he regards Richard. "I do. Each student deleted the app before he or she came in. After our interview, they could easily reinstall it. They banked on the chances that the college wouldn't go through the trouble and expense of subpoenaing the company and getting the names of everyone at MacCallum who uses The Board. I'm not even sure it's possible. At any rate, it's a distraction. It sheds no light on the case I'm investigating against Mr. Bockus."

"But I thought he was also charged with bullying Jenny," Richard says.

"It's not on his phone, and no one testifies they saw him do it. Even you, Richard; what did you *see*? Nothing, I'm afraid. Unfortunately, a hunch isn't enough."

Something rises in Richard's throat. Outrage, like some toxic gall. He knows in his gut that it's Exley. It's screaming at him. Why can't this guy see it?

Why won't he do something?

"This is just wrong," Richard can't help saying.

A sharp laugh escapes from Dean Hunt. "Which part?" he asks. "The fact that whoever has been bullying Jenny will get away with it, or the fact that your peers' first instinct is to protect themselves?"

"All of it," Richard says. "It sucks. The whole thing."

Dean Hunt tilts back in his chair. His hands form this little triangle, the fingertips pressed together, as he regards Richard. "You know, I'm new to investigating sexual misconduct cases," he begins. "For years I was handling honor code violations. Mostly cheating and plagiarism.

"Lately, I've been reminded of a plagiarism case against a young man. This was before your time; he's long gone from MacCallum. A professor accused him of copying eight paragraphs from a well-known history textbook and including them, without attribution, in a term paper. The charge was solid: he had lifted them, like they were segments of pie, and distributed them throughout his paper. And thought no one would notice." Dean Hunt's eyes trail to the empty seat next to Richard. As if the young man in question were sitting there still.

"I'll never forget what he said when he came in here.

He was quite pleasant. While conceding that 'mistakes were made,' he insisted the professor was wrong. That it wasn't plagiarism. 'No?' I said. 'Then what is it?'

"'It's exhaustion,' he explained. You see, when he used online sources, he created a document filled with notes, copied and pasted from various texts, which he could easily refer to later. He claimed he got so tired, he couldn't keep straight which were the paragraphs *he* wrote, which were simply notes, and which required footnotes.

"'Remind me next time,' he joked, 'to stay the hell away from the Adderall.'"

"Oh no. He didn't," Richard says.

"Oh yes. He did. Then he generously offered to accept a lower grade in exchange for 'redoing' the citations on his paper. You should have seen the look on his face when I told him MacCallum did not offer grades lower than F, and that 'redoing' implied something had been done in the first place. Which, I assured him, it had not."

Dean Hunt takes off his little wire-framed glasses and carefully wipes the lenses with a cloth he produces from a desk drawer.

"Culpability was not part of this young man's worldview. It never occurred to him that he did anything wrong. Or that he was even capable of doing something wrong. And when I got it through his head that he had most definitely screwed up, he was flabbergasted that there was no going back and fixing it. Stunned that there was no getting around the repercussions of his actions."

"What happened to him?" Richard asks.

"He was suspended for a semester, but then decided to transfer," Dean Hunt says. "He ultimately graduated from his father's alma mater."

They sit in silence for a few minutes. Richard doesn't know if he's expected to say anything. He's not sure he gets the point of this story.

"I haven't thought of that young man for a while," Dean Hunt finally continues. "But the underlying problem in both cases is the same." He looks at Richard, as if waiting to see how he'll react. When Richard doesn't comment, the dean sighs.

"I thank you, Richard, for coming in today. But you haven't given me anything I can use."

"Jordan had sex with Jenny," he blurts out, surprising himself. He hadn't planned to reveal this.

Dean Hunt's eyes widen. "Excuse me?"

"He told me," Richard admits. "A few days after it happened. We were having beers and he was bragging about hooking up with some freshman at the Conundrum party."

"Did anyone else hear this?"

"We were alone. But I think he also told Exley. His uncle said Jordan had blabbed to two people."

Dean Hunt rises from his chair and walks over to the window. He stares out for a long minute, not speaking. When he turns, deep lines furrow his forehead. He doesn't look happy.

"His uncle. You mean the lawyer who's been accompanying him since you 'resigned' as his advisor?"

Richard is surprised again. He wasn't aware that Uncle Bruce was still skulking around.

"Bruce Bockus is his uncle. Is that who you're talking about?"

He hears Dean Hunt breathe heavily. "Why didn't you say something earlier?"

"You didn't ask," Richard replies. He can hear how lame this sounds.

But instead of looking angry, Dean Hunt seems taken aback.

"You're right," he concedes. "I didn't." He returns to his window, arms wrapped tightly across his chest. "Shame on me," he says to the glass.

A long silence follows.

"What other details did Mr. Bockus share with you?" he finally says. His back is turned to Richard as he speaks.

"Pretty much nothing," Richard says. "I didn't even know her name until she charged him. He just said he'd hooked up with a freshman."

"Besides Mr. Exley, did he tell anyone else?"

"I don't think so."

Dean Hunt wheels around. "Did anyone mention that they saw Jordan and Jenny together at that party?"

"Together?"

"Yes. Interacting with each other. Talking, dancing, drinking . . . *with each other*. Leaving the party *with each other*." He emphasizes the last three words almost angrily.

Richard combs his memory, trying to recall anything. He draws a blank. "I don't think so," he repeats.

Dean Hunt returns to his chair. "Okay," he says. More to himself than to Richard.

They sit, not speaking, for what feels to Richard like a long time.

When Dean Hunt finally breaks the silence, his tone has

changed. It's as if he's made up his mind about something. He stands. "Thanks for coming in today," he says, extending his hand. His expression is unreadable.

Richard rises slowly to his feet. They shake. "That's it?"

Dean Hunt purses his lips in a tight line. "That's it."

There's nothing to do except leave. *What the hell?* Richard wonders as he heads for the door. His hand is on the knob when the dean speaks one last time.

"Richard."

He turns.

"Let go of this now," Dean Hunt says. "Trust me."

. . .

They aren't sitting anymore. They lie side by side on the bed, kissing.

Jordan kisses Jenny's neck, the space at the bottom of her throat. He kisses the place behind her ears, where her hair starts. His lips move down her chest, to the V of her dress. He kisses her there as his hand cups her breast.

She breathes in sharply. He looks at her. Her eyes are wide, surprised. Jordan presses his lips against hers. Hard this time, parting her lips, his tongue in her mouth. His hand moves from her breast to her thigh, slips beneath the scarcely-a-dress. His hand is on her hip. His hand is on her crotch, holding her crotch, while his tongue, in her mouth, rotates.

She pushes away, her hand on his chest. She gasps, a little intake of air as his mouth detaches from hers. She grasps his wrist from between her legs, pulls it away.

"Jordan," she says. "I haven't . . ." Her heart pounds.

He smiles. He strokes her hair.

"We can slow down," he whispers.

Relief, like a warm wave. She closes her eyes. Snuggles warmly against him.

"I'm so tired," she tells him. She buries her face in his neck. She feels shadows, like giant wings, pass over them. "I'm so tired," she repeats.

. . .

37

Haley

The look on Madison's face when Haley tells her is somewhere between aghast and amused.

"The dawn run?" she exclaims. "You're nuts!"

It's the countdown before Thanksgiving break, and the level of postmidterm angst and prevacation excitement in Main dining hall is deafening. She and Madison have finished lunch. Both nurse cups of something hot and caffeinated in white, institutional mugs. Their season has officially ended—for Madison, an eight-month hiatus; for Haley, forever.

Madison, in a rare moment of emotional sensitivity, has asked her how she feels about that.

Haley's been surprised by what she'll miss most. Teammates, for sure, but she's still friends with a few of them. Admittedly, the competition. The game itself, because soccer is great.

But what she'll really miss is the dawn run.

The whole team, early misty mornings, the campus still asleep, passing townies emerging from the bakery clutching brown bags and steaming cups as they clop-clopped past, half dreaming.

She thought she hated it. Hated that alarm going off in the near-dark, hated the acid in her still-sleeping stomach, the rubber-band stretch of tight muscles. Hated the calf burn and ankle ache, someone's phlegmy cough when they set off at a slow trot. Lung sear, eye tear when the leaders picked up the pace. She even thought she hated her teammates. Especially the one who always commented on the gorgeous view.

Then the burn would settle into warmth, the footbeats a steady rhythm. The thudding in her chest would feel less like pain and more like excitement when they climbed a familiar hill and had energy to spare at the top. She'd switch from struggling to autopilot, and while her legs still worked and the bellows in her chest continued to blow air in and out, she felt less trapped in the cage of her body and more just along for the ride. So when the telephone pole signaling the end loomed and the captains called for the kick and she put on a burst, pouring everything into those last hundred yards, she couldn't help but feel amazed by what her body could do. Grateful to be part of those mornings.

It was never, she realizes, about the uniform.

"What about Mr. Hottie?" Madison presses. "Didn't you tell me he runs?"

Since the Matt Trainor event, Madison and the rest of the team have dubbed Richard "Mr. Hottie."

"That would end us," Haley tells her, not bothering to explain that it's the runners and not the running she'll miss. "He's definitely not an early-morning person."

"More the late-night type?" Madison says suggestively.

Haley smiles but doesn't elaborate. They return to wondering aloud what it will be like to see old high school friends after their first semester at college.

"You're going back a NARP," Madison teases, then looks instantly sorry.

Haley shrugs it off. "I suspect that'll be harder on my mother than on me."

She'd considered not going home at all for Thanksgiving. Their blowout, when she finally confronted Mom about calling Jenny's mother, was epic. But once the dust cleared and they realized the battery of hard words had not left anyone mortally wounded, they agreed to limp through the holiday together for her dad's sake. He deserved to have his daughter home.

"Speaking of hotties," Haley says now, glancing behind Madison, "Kyle alert."

Madison doesn't turn. As he passes their table, carrying his plate, she wears a pained expression. "So gorgeous," Madison moans. "Let's hope next time I fall for a hipster, he's straight."

"Now he's a hipster? I thought you said he's a lumbersexual?"

"Slight difference. Think more artsy, less outdoorsy. More Freeport Signature, less North Face. At any rate, it's depressing. Have you noticed that the best-looking guys around here are dating each other?"

"Or me," Haley says.

Madison kicks her under the table. "I still haven't forgiven you for not warning me in time. I show up at Out House one night, all set to flirt outrageously, and there he was, all cozy on the couch with his equally gorgeous boyfriend," she says. "At least Jenny seemed happy to see me."

"How was she?"

"Good, considering. Everyone there seems to really like her. And for the record, can I just say I think it's super stupid that you two aren't speaking?"

"We speak," Haley corrects her, "when we see each other. We just don't cross paths is all."

Neither of them says anything for a minute.

Madison seems focused on her tea bag, repeatedly dunking it in her full mug. "So, where's that whole thing at, if I may ask? Or are you still not allowed to talk about it?"

"The process is no secret. Mona told me that it's at some review stage. The investigator put together this packet with all the witness statements, including what Jenny and the guy she's accused said, and both of them have a week to read it and decide if they want to add anything. It's a total pain; they can only read the report at the office where it's kept. They can't make copies, can't check it out. It's this bizarre, ultrasecret thing. Anyway, once they're done reading and amending, the investigator files a final report and a committee decides what happens."

"How long will that take?"

"I don't know. Probably the end of the semester."

Madison doesn't comment right away. She seems very interested in her tea bag. "You know, Tamra and Marliese, they talk about what happened that night."

"Well, they shouldn't," Haley snaps. "Tell them to shut up."

That's Madison's cue to change the subject. But she doesn't.

"They said the guy? Jordan Somebody? They said he got shut out of that party. Marliese and the other girls saw it. He walked out and couldn't get back in. Dude was furious. And Jenny? They said she was talking to a different guy most of the night."

Haley stares at her. She knows she should tell Madison to stop speaking right now. But she's practically paralyzed by her own surprise.

"Tamra says hardly anyone noticed Jenny at the party, and the ones who did? They never saw her with Jordan."

"Oh, so the all-knowing T has checked in with every witness? Tamra and Marliese, who deserted Jenny at that place and now need to cover their guilty asses?" Haley finally manages. "Give me a break. Hundreds of people were in and out of there that night."

"I don't know, Haley. The whole thing sounds sketch. And Tamra—"

"You know what? We've crossed into the not-supposed-to-be-talking-about-it stuff," Haley interrupts.

Madison looks insulted. Which annoys Haley even more. Why does it take hitting this person over the head with a two-by-four to get through to her?

"How about you chill, okay?" Madison says. "It's not like what you and I say is going to make any difference." She abandons the sodden tea bag in the cup and begins gathering her things.

Just as well, Haley thinks. *Before one of us says something we'll both regret.* She begins clearing her tray when her phone chimes. Text.

It's from Mona.

Have u heard about J's case?

Haley texts back: *??*

"I'll see you later," she hears Madison say.

"Wait . . . M," Haley begins, but Madison heads toward the exit. The phone chimes again.

College dropped it. J freaking out

Haley stares at the screen. What does she mean "dropped"? She return-texts: *???????????*

She stares at the screen, waiting impatiently for Mona's answer. Meanwhile, the dining hall around her is clearing out as students depart for the first round of afternoon classes.

Text chime.

Out House now. meet us

She doesn't bother reminding Mona that she and Jen haven't been speaking. She shoves the phone in her pack, grabs her dishes, and tosses them on the conveyor belt without bothering to separate her trash into the various containers.

So much for class, she thinks as she exits the building and runs toward Out House.

. . .

She wakes to a kiss.

His mouth on hers, insistent. Her lips part of their own accord, and then his tongue again. She makes a sound. "Ummmm." They were just talking. Were they just talking? He was. His voice, in her ear, as he touched her body.

His hand, again, is between her legs. Slips inside her underwear. His fingers probe. She feels his hips press against the side of her leg. He rocks. He breathes hard. She pulls her face away from his.

"Jordan." Her voice comes out like a whisper even though in her head she shouts. She tries to push his hand away, but her bones are gone. She thinks of a rag doll. Floppy head, limp arms.

He takes her hand. He presses her palm against him, the place between his hips. He massages the bulge between his legs with her open hand. "Yeah," he breathes into her ear.

"What?" she manages. "What?" She sounds far away. She feels far away from her voice. Feels far away from her own body.

He shifts, drops her hand. She hears sounds. Rustling. Zipping. She thinks about sitting up. Can she get up? Can she walk without bones?

Then suddenly his face looms. His eyes are wide, but they don't look into hers. He stares at something not-her, intent on something only he sees. She feels him reach, slide, beneath the dress, and pull her underwear down. She gasps.

His knees push her legs apart, and what is happening, about to happen, envelopes her. Like something spilled, a glass tipped, spreading, unchecked, while she—frozen—watches.

She tries to kick, to use her heels, but she moves in slow motion while he moves fast. He presses on her chest, his hair and the top of his head in her nose. She smells his skin, his scalp.

The shock, when he pushes inside her, is knife-sharp. She reels, her mind frenzied, her body unresponsive. She tries to scream, to speak, to move. I am paralyzed goes through her head. How did I get paralyzed?

She wills her hands to his shoulders and pushes, but he is boulder weight. He says her name. Faster, her name, over and over, and the pain is so bad, searing, screaming pain, and then he yells, angry, in her ear, and cries out, this animal noise. Then stops. Collapses on her, his full weight on her chest, and she knows, right then, that she will die. Because she can't breathe. He is crushing her, her hands helpless to move him away.

Then he rolls away. Off her, out of her, one last swipe of pain. He breathes heavily into her ear. She feels it damply on her neck.

"You are so sweet," she hears him say.

. . .

38

RICHARD

The Audi and another car, an SUV with Jersey plates, are parked in front of Taylor House. The hatch of the SUV is open and the guts of a dorm room threaten to spill out: stray shoes, stacks of shirts still on hangers, a floor lamp. A dirty rug is rolled up and wedged in between a mini-fridge and a carton of books.

Jordan's packing up.

Richard wanders into the common room. A few of the guys occupy the couches in front of the fireplace. Rob and Justin. They end their conversation when he enters.

"Somebody want to tell me what's going on?" Richard asks.

"You haven't heard?" Rob says. "Bockus is out of here."

"The Doctor, too," Justin adds.

Richard isn't sure he's heard them correctly. "What do you mean 'out of here'?" He notices Rob glance at Justin and roll his eyes. As if Richard's stupid.

Or is it more like, *Can you believe this guy?*

"Meaning leaving MacCallum," Justin answers. "They've dropped out."

"Thrown out, more like," Rob comments.

"Dude: no," Justin says. "Jordan said 'withdrawn.' Nobody's kicking him out. Get your facts straight."

Richard sits on one of the couch arms. "Why?"

Rob snorts. "You tell us. Haven't you been going to all this trial stuff with him?"

"No, not anymore," Richard says. "Wait, this has to do with the investigation? They've made a decision?" Haley had told him it was weeks away from anything final.

Rob seems clueless. "Jordan won't give anybody a straight answer. Except to say he hasn't been found guilty of anything, but his family decided he'd be better off getting the hell out of MacCallum and starting over somewhere else."

"So why's Exley leaving?" Richard asks.

"No idea, man. At any rate, he's already gone. Took him two hours to cram all his stuff in his car and disappear."

Richard doesn't know what to say. Before he can think of another question to ask, he sees the guys' eyes shift to the entryway. Richard turns.

Uncle Bruce. In jeans and a T-shirt. He looks sweaty. Like he's been carrying heavy items.

"Just the man I was hoping might turn up," he remarks casually. "Do you have a minute, Richard?"

Richard practically feels the other guys' stares lasering into his back as he leaves the room with Uncle Bruce. The older man heads out of the building.

"Walk with me?" he suggests. Pleasantly enough.

Richard's curiosity outweighs his instinct for self-preservation at this moment. He doesn't particularly like the idea of being alone with Uncle Hard-ass. But he really wants to know what the hell is going on.

Once they're a few hundred feet from Taylor, Uncle Bruce begins talking. "I suppose I don't need to tell you what's happened."

"Actually, I'm completely in the dark," Richard says. "The guys just told me Jordan's leaving?"

Uncle Bruce glances at him, eyebrows raised. Assessing. He seems genuinely surprised by Richard's surprise. "Yes," he says. "That was my advice, and for once, he took it."

Richard stops walking. "The investigation—"

"Was dropped," he says abruptly. "You can't investigate someone who is not a student. Jordan has withdrawn from MacCallum, so the claim against him no longer exists."

"I don't get it," Richard says. "Why?"

The expression on Uncle Bruce's face puzzles him. A mixture of anger and amusement. He begins walking again.

"The investigator met with Jordan yesterday. Seems some new information was brought to his attention. Something that didn't make it into the witness statements released to Jordan and Jenny earlier this week."

Richard feels the man's glance as they walk, as if he's gauging his reaction to these words. Richard concentrates on the sidewalk ahead. Wills his expression to remain neutral.

"Someone came forward and testified that they knew for a fact that Jordan had had sexual intercourse with Jenny. Since the investigator didn't learn of this until after he presented the witness statements to Jordan and Jenny, he thought he'd do Jordan the . . . courtesy of telling him directly. Especially because this information represented a shift from everything that came before. See, until this particular witness spoke up, Dean Hunt had not been able to find a single person who had seen Jordan and Jenny together that night. Dozens of witnesses, and not one person saw Jordan so much as brush shoulders with that girl."

Uncle Bruce bends. The sidewalk is plastered with wet leaves, like splashes of red, gold, and brown paint. He picks up a brightly colored maple leaf. As he stands there talking to Richard, he methodically separates the lamina from the veins.

"Dean Hunt was planning, he told us, to recommend a finding of 'no sanction' to the committee. Because he couldn't corroborate a single thing Jenny had said. What's more, her statement was inconsistent. She had trouble remembering where she'd been, who she was with, and how she got home. It was going to be quite a reach, he said, for a committee to find in her favor with so many holes in her story. Until now. Until this witness. Now, Dean Hunt said, he was planning to go the other way. He would recommend expulsion for Jordan."

Uncle Bruce holds the maple leaf by its stem. It reminds Richard of an exposed skeleton. The man twirls it between his fingers, then drops it. He looks at Richard.

"It was a courtesy, you see," he explains. "Giving Jordan the heads-up. Letting him know which way the wind was blowing so he could, while he had the chance, withdraw from MacCallum with his record clean. Before the committee expelled him for sexual misconduct and ruined his chances of getting an education, or a job for that matter, elsewhere. You know, I'm not much of a poker player. What about you?"

The question is sudden and takes Richard aback.

"Uh . . . a little Texas Hold'em. I'm not very good."

Uncle Bruce nods. "I suspect," he says, "that Dean Hunt is very good. Or at the very least, better than me. Because I could not tell if he was bluffing. And I wasn't willing to bet my nephew's future that he wasn't. I recommended we fold, and for once in his life, Jordan listened to reason." Uncle Bruce glances at his watch. "So we are driving out of here very soon, and you, young man, will probably never see us again."

Richard hopes that the relief he feels is not overly apparent. "Tell Jordan I said good luck."

Uncle Bruce doesn't comment on whether he plans to relay that message. "Aren't you going to ask me about Brandon Exley?" The silk in his voice has disappeared.

"What about Exley?"

"Oh, he's the key to all of this!" Uncle Bruce says with a cutting laugh. "You see, the mystery witness? This person apparently also told Dean Hunt that Jordan was involved with bullying Jenny. Writing on her door, starting the online thread, everything. Well, Jordan heard that and he just popped. Before I could clap a hand over his mouth and drag him from the room, he told the dean that it was all Exley, from the beginning. Dr. Feelgood, I think he called him."

Richard tries to imagine this scene. Dean Hunt playing Jordan like a cat teasing a dog on a leash. The animal lunging, choking, wondering stupidly why it can't breathe.

"My nephew never suspected *you*," Uncle Bruce continues. "You didn't know anything about The Board. But Exley did. So Jordan made that leap. Put two and two together and got . . . Well, you know. You're good at math."

Richard doesn't respond. His gut warns him that there is nothing to be gained by revealing anything to Uncle Hard-ass.

"But as smart as you are, Richard, I have to say, top prize goes to Dean Elliot Hunt, who outsmarted us all. Because you know what I learned? He met with Exley and generously suggested he withdraw . . . *after* he spoke to Jordan. I won't bore you with how I know that."

At first Richard doesn't understand the significance of what Jordan's uncle is saying. But as it sinks in, there's no hiding the flush that spreads across his cheeks.

"Yeah, that's pretty much what I figured," the older man says, watching Richard's expression. "And just in case you were wondering, it's called the Reid Technique. It's a classic police interrogation strategy where you pit one suspect against the other and they rat each other out."

They hear marimba music. It's Uncle Bruce's phone. He pulls it out, checks the screen, takes the call. "Yeah," he says. Richard hears a woman's voice.

A cold breeze rattles the scrabble of leaves still clinging to branches. It smells like mold, wood smoke. Snow in the air. Possibly tonight.

"I'm heading back now. Give me five minutes," Uncle Bruce says. He ends the call. "That was Jordan's mom. They're leaving."

336

Richard doesn't say anything. This guy can't leave fast enough to suit him.

"Just so you know," Uncle Bruce says, "I didn't tell Jordan it was you. I think enough people have gotten screwed over at this place. I don't want to be responsible for one more."

Bruce Bockus turns and walks away; no handshake, no good-bye. Richard watches until he disappears into the winding wooded paths leading back to Taylor and Conundrum.

. . .

She lies there, motionless. She's not sure for how long.

He has moved away from her ear, her neck. They lie side by side on the long single bed, their arms, shoulders, the length of their legs pressed against each other. She hears him breathe.

She scarcely breathes. She feels numb.

"Do you want anything?" she hears him say. "I'm going to the kitchen for a water."

"No," she whispers.

"You're sure? Sometimes there's juice. Or I can get you a beer, even?"

"No," she repeats.

He gets up. She doesn't turn. Doesn't want to see him, any part of him. She hears the rustle of his pants, a zip. He leaves the room.

The moment the latch clicks, Jenny sits up. Her underwear is around one ankle; she pulls it up. She stands, searches for the shoes. They are under the desk chair, and she slips them on. She opens the door, just a crack. Fluorescent light from the hallway pours in.

She sticks her head out the door. She sees no one.

Jenny runs.

. . .

39

Haley

Haley hears low voices behind the closed door. She knocks as she walks in.

They are all on Carrie's double bed: Jenny, Mona, Gail, Carrie. Jenny has her back pressed to the wall, legs tucked beneath her, box of tissues in her lap. Her eyes are swollen and red.

"Hey," Haley says. She has no idea what sort of reception awaits. It feels like a long time since she's been in the same room as Carrie and Jenny. "Mona just texted me."

Carrie looks at Jenny. Places a questioning hand on her knee. Jenny shrugs.

"C'mon, girl," Mona says, shifting closer to the huddle. "There's plenty of room." She pats the empty space on the comforter. Gail winks at her. "Jen was just telling us," Mona says as Haley settles down, "about her meeting with Carole Patterson." They all turn back to Jenny, who wipes her nose.

"If you could call it a meeting," she says. "It was more like an announcement. Followed by a dismissal. Check that box."

"The woman needs a heart transplant," Mona murmurs. "No compassion." Gail nods in agreement.

"Would she tell you *why* he withdrew?" Carrie asks.

"Nope. She said for reasons of privacy she couldn't. So I said, 'But if it has to do with my case, don't I have the right to know?' and she said his withdrawal was a private action. She said it was not a sanction resulting from the investigation."

"Complete horseshit," Gail bursts out. "Why else would he suddenly leave?"

"But technically that might be true," Mona says. "He's left before it's over. It's not even at the committee stage yet. Right, Jen?"

"It's not at any stage anymore," Jenny says. "Carole says they only investigate claims against students. Since he's not a student here anymore, the claim is dropped."

Her tone jolts Haley. She sounds devastated. Looks devastated. She's acting as if they found him innocent. But he's gone. Out of her life, probably forever.

Why isn't she relieved?

If Jenny looks wrecked, then Carrie looks furious.

"There must be some way to find out what's going on," Carrie says.

Mona chimes in. "No way. FERPA." Everyone looks at her like she's lost her mind. "Wait. You guys don't know about FERPA?"

"Translate, Ms. Pre-law," Gail says.

Delight on Mona's face. "I actually know something Carrie doesn't. Wait. Just . . . let me revel in this for a second."

Carrie rolls her eyes.

"So FERPA," Mona explains, "is the Family Education Rights and Privacy Act. It protects everything from disciplinary hearings to academic records. It's why your parents can't access your grades unless you give them your password. It's why the results of judicial proceedings on campus aren't publicized. Carole couldn't tell Jenny what's going on even if she wanted to."

"Kind of just one big 'FERP you,'" Haley says. Instantly horrified by her own joke. Everyone stares; then, to her relief, they laugh. A little.

"The thing is," Jenny continues when they stop laughing, "I'm really, really . . . mad." Her face crumples when she says this. Tears slip down her cheeks. One fist rhythmically pounds the pillow alongside her. "I mean, all this, for what? Nothing? He gets off, with nothing?"

No one speaks at first.

"It would appear that way," Carrie finally says. Her words short, clipped.

Haley can't help herself. "No, not nothing! He's gone. For whatever reason. You can walk around here feeling safe again. Wasn't that the point? I mean, the most the college was ever going to do was throw him out."

"She just. Doesn't. Get it." Carrie says this to the window, her voice dripping with contempt.

"Well, why don't you educate me?" Haley demands. "Since you seem to know so much."

"You know, I don't think this is what Jenny needs right now," Gail says, jumping in.

But it's too late. Carrie whips her head around and stares at Haley. "One," she says, holding up a finger, "there's no closure. Not for Jenny or anyone on this campus. It's like smoke: just drifts off and disappears. And eventually it will be forgotten. Until it happens to another woman. Two: no consequences for him. He rides off into the sunset like some happy transfer student. Three: he's free to do it again because there's nothing on his record and the next college that takes him will be clueless. Four . . . do you really want me to keep going?"

"Okay, how about this," Haley says. "One: he looks guilty because he's dropping out. Two: it won't be forgotten! We just did this big education thing on campus. Everybody knows tons more about this issue. Three: he's gone! The point was to get him out of here, right?"

Carrie looks at Gail and throws up her hands. *Help me out here*, her expression seems to say.

"Actually, Haley," Gail says quietly, "the point was accountability. The point was for Jordan to face up to what he did. For Jenny to have made that happen."

"Which would only have happened if the committee decided he was guilty," Mona adds. "Sorry, but I'm going to get all pre-law on you again. Yeah, getting him out of here, making him accountable, having him suffer consequences, all of it was 'the point.' But none of it would have happened if the committee

342

let him off. And Jen?" She turns and looks directly at Jenny when she says this. "It wasn't looking so good. Was it?"

Jenny stares at Mona, her face blank. She seems to be thinking, hard. Eventually, though, her expression changes. Relaxes. As if she's come to some realization.

"The last few days," Jenny says, "I've been reading the witness statements. It wasn't like getting raped all over again. But it came close."

Carrie puts her hand on Jen's arm, briefly, and squeezes.

Jenny looks directly at Haley. "No one stood up for me," she says. "T and the girls? They wouldn't admit they left; they said I 'disappeared.' No one saw me with Jordan. Brandon Exley said I was having fun dancing. Hardly anyone saw me drink. You'd think I was invisible. Or making the whole thing up. Even the investigator. You were there. He thought I was crazy, didn't he?"

Haley knows this isn't the time to argue with Jenny, but she can't let this go. "I know that's how you felt, but I don't think he thought you were crazy. He thought you were drunk. And he asked hard questions because he was trying to sort it out. No one thinks you're crazy." ·

"Everyone thinks I'm a liar," Jenny says. Her voice is flat. "I've been called a slut. An attention-seeker. A lying bitch. A few more horrible things I can't even make myself say. On the Internet and on my *door*. Where I *live*. I walk into the dining hall and everyone stares. Like I've got 'The Raped Girl' stamped on my forehead. No, not even that, because he was never found guilty. It's 'The Girl Who Cried Rape.' And the whole time I'm making a sandwich or pouring milk or walking to class, I look around and wonder which of them posted those things about me. Who believes me? Who pities me? Who hates me?"

As she speaks, the emotion creeps back into her expression, her voice, again. Her eyes fill. Haley's do, too. She glances around the circle. Even Carrie wipes her eyes.

"I know you think the point was to get him out of here, Haley," Jenny says. "But the fact is he's free and I'm left with all this crap. And it's wrong."

. . .

The corridor sways.

"Whoa," Jordan mutters, leaning against the wall. He pauses, waits for his feet to steady. One hand holds a bottle of water, the other a cranapple juice. She might have changed her mind.

Plus, it masks the real reason for his departure: he wanted a couple more condoms from the bathroom dispenser. He only had the one he'd been carrying in his pocket.

When the fun-house motion of the hallway slows, he continues his walk back to the room. He swings the door open.

She's not there.

"Jenny?" he says. As if she's playing a game. Hiding in the closet or under the bed. He knows she's not in the bathroom since he was just there.

He hears voices down the hall. People returning from the party. The house had been silent up to now. He briefly considers asking if they passed her, saw her, but decides against it. Decides against announcing that whatever girl he brought back to his room tonight has slipped out without telling him.

Jordan tosses the bottles on the floor, strips off his clothes, and climbs into bed. He's asleep within minutes. A deep sleep, untroubled by the loud laughter and door-slamming of still-staggering housemates.

Dreamless sleep.

. . .

40

RICHARD

Against his better judgment, Richard agrees to meet her. He has trouble saying no to Haley.

"What's the politically correct therapy-speak term? Oh, I know: 'I don't feel safe.' But in this case, I mean literally," he'd said. "Mona and the rest of her coven will be waiting for me right outside the door with a hanging noose."

Haley didn't laugh, which wasn't reassuring. Made him think this had occurred to her as well.

"Just tell her what you told me," she pleaded. "I think it would be good for her to hear."

"Why would she ever want to speak with me?" he continued. "I'm the enemy."

"Once she hears what you did, she'll know you're not."

"Why can't you tell her?"

"Because I think it would be good for you, too," she said. "It'll give you some closure."

Closure. More therapy-speak. He feels like the entire campus is engulfed in it following the assembly. Not that it's a bad thing, but with his tendency to accidentally stamp through the carefully laid minefields of politically correct language, it's nerve-racking. He keeps expecting something to blow.

He's nervous now, sitting in the Hard Math Café, waiting for Haley and Jenny. Gail told them this would be a good time, and she was right; the place is deserted. Partly because half the campus has already cleared out for Thanksgiving, partly because at two o'clock people are still running off fumes from the lunchtime caffeine.

As he waits, he gets a text. It's a guy from the house, Colin. Wants to know how many, if any, people are staying through the break.

"Damned if I know," Richard mutters to himself as he shoots Colin a response. But maybe, he thinks, given his new role, he's supposed to know.

Exley had scarcely left campus before guys from Taylor approached Richard. They wanted him to take Exley's spot as the house social chair.

He couldn't have been more surprised.

"I'm not really the person to fill the Doctor's shoes," he said. "I can't remember the last time I was at Wednesday night pool shots."

"We're thinking a new direction might be good," Colin said. "Like maybe some coed events that aren't ragers? Might be your thing. Now that you've gotten all domesticated, with a girlfriend and everything."

"Right, we'll do chick flick night and serve chardonnay and brie. I'm not that guy, either," he said, laughing. But he said yes. What the hell. Maybe the college would lift the sanction on Taylor House if they could prove ten or more of them could congregate without getting hammered.

He sees Haley and Jenny enter. The first thing that goes through his mind is: *mouse*. She is little and brown-haired, like Haley described. Her thin frame seems almost childlike next to Haley's athlete's body.

She's the girl guys tend to overlook. Who dresses in forgettable clothes. Listens instead of inserting herself. The chorus, the wallpaper, the background-music girl.

He can't help it: in this moment, Jordan comes to mind. Their conversation over those pilfered Blue Moons. And Exley. Telling Jenny to bring friends to the party. This girl? Seriously? It makes him angry.

As they draw close, though, he notices her eyes. Pale gray and clear. Metallic. They meet his, unblinking. Richard stands.

"Hope you haven't been waiting long," Haley begins.

Richard leans toward her and brushes her cheek with his lips. "Not long," he murmurs. He extends his hand toward Jenny. "Hi. I'm Richard."

Her grip is firm. She holds on just long enough. "Jenny," she answers.

They sit.

Haley begins to speak; she obviously feels responsible for this conversation. But Richard puts one hand over hers, stopping her. He knows how this needs to start.

"I want you to know," he says to Jenny, "how sorry I am about everything that's happened to you." He doesn't elaborate. He doesn't want to, and he's not sure he can. "I don't pretend to fully know what that is. But Haley says it's been awful for you, and I'm sorry about that."

Jenny looks at him for what feels like a long time, but is probably only a few seconds.

"I didn't really want to do this," she finally says. "Sit here, across a table from one of Jordan's friends. I'm not sure I get your motivation."

Her directness startles him.

"Me neither," he flash-answers. "Meet with you, that is. I'm here because Haley asked me to. No motivation beyond that."

Jenny raises one eyebrow. Her mouth forms a closed, slight smile. "Really? Not trying to relieve a guilty conscience? Because if that's what you're after, I'm going to have to disappoint you."

Richard returns her stare. "I don't feel guilty." *What the hell?* He glances at Haley. Who looks very uncomfortable.

"Jen," Haley says. "Richard has an idea about why Jordan and Brandon Exley withdrew. Just hear him out, okay?"

Jenny shifts in her seat. For a moment, it looks like she might get up and leave.

"Okay," she finally says.

He keeps it short and sweet and doesn't spare himself. He recounts each conversation and shares his theory: Dean Hunt bluffed. He brought the guys individually into his office, told them he had enough to hang them with. Told them he'd do them a favor and give them a chance to escape with their records intact. Both went for it, believing the other had been the source of the damning information. Once they had officially withdrawn, the college had to drop the case.

Jenny is quiet after Richard finishes. She stares intently at the salt and pepper shakers on the table before she speaks.

"Why would Dean Hunt do that?" she finally asks.

"He thought they were scum and couldn't figure out another way to get them out of here," Richard says.

For the first time since they'd all sat, Jenny looks upset. "But if he believed me, why not take it to the committee? Throw them out that way. Get it on their records. Instead, they got off with nothing."

"Maybe because he didn't think the committee *would* throw them out," Richard says, as gently as he can. He's a little surprised he needs to spell this out for her.

"Because *they* wouldn't believe me?" she says, the hard edge returning to her voice.

"He wanted a guarantee," Richard says. He has no interest in debating who believes her and who doesn't. "He wanted a win. Look, from the college's point of view, this is the best possible outcome. You're safe and the bad guys are gone . . . but with nothing for their alumni parents to complain about and no rape stat on MacCallum's record."

"But what about my point of view?" Jenny challenges.

"Honestly," he says, "I get how this is disappointing for you, because you wanted to see justice done. But I also get that this probably saved you from the devastation of a 'no sanction' decision. I mean, wouldn't it suck more if the committee found in Jordan's favor and he and Exley were still prancing around here?"

To his left he sees Haley wince slightly. What? More offensive vocab? His choice of 'prancing'? Or something else he completely doesn't get?

Jenny doesn't look particularly pleased, either. "So you're telling me I'm supposed to be happy that Dean Hunt fixed everything?"

"I'm not telling you how to feel," he answers without hesitation. "And I don't for one minute think he fixed anything. I think this was broken beyond repair. But here's what I do know." He leans forward, his elbows on the table. "Dean Hunt believed you. I hope it helps. Knowing that."

Jenny looks at Richard carefully. Whether she's trying to decide whether to believe him or she's gauging her own reaction, he can't tell. Maybe she's waiting for him to say more. Finally, when she realizes he's done, she takes a deep breath and stands.

"It does. Help, that is. It's not nearly enough, but it helps to think he believed me." Jenny turns to Haley. "Thanks. You were right. This was . . . okay." Her eyes rest briefly on Richard. "Thank you." She shoulders her backpack—he's startled by its size compared to her—and leaves the café.

Haley waits until the door closes behind Jenny to speak. "Not really impressed by the warmth of that exchange."

Richard doesn't respond right away. He feels wrung out.

"It was never going to end with a group hug," he finally says. Haley punches him softly on the arm. "So I have to ask: what's she going to do?"

"Do?"

"Will she stay at MacCallum?"

"That's the most surprising part of this whole thing," Haley says. "She *refuses* to go. Her parents think she should transfer. Her dad even threatened to pull her tuition, but she told him she'd get herself financially emancipated and take out massive loans if he tried it, so he backed off. At any rate, she's staying. Res Life is making her a permanent Out-Houser, and her profs say she can get any extensions she needs for this semester."

"That's pretty cool," Richard says.

"Yeah," Haley agrees. She looks across the table at him, an expression he can't quite read on her face. "Here's what's cool: you. Thanks for talking to her."

She thinks I'm better than I am. It's worrisome. The opportunities for disappointing her are vast.

Then again, it beats Carrie's relentless underestimation of him. Hands down.

"So, am I to believe you now have a *permanent* single?" Richard grins at Haley. He watches as the blush makes its slow journey across her cheeks.

．．．

No.

She's broken a heel clean off. At first she doesn't understand her own steps, the lurching stumble of her own feet over cracked, winding sidewalks through the woods. When she does realize, she stops, looks. These aren't her shoes.

"Oh no," she breathes out loud. She doesn't see the heel. She can't find the heel. Tamra? Marliese? Whose shoes are these? Someone is going to be angry with her.

These aren't her clothes.

She isn't this girl.

This didn't happen. Tonight. This night didn't happen. This couldn't happen.

No.

Somehow the woods end. She recognizes things. The bell tower in the distance. She points herself at what she knows. Her legs obey. She wants nothing more than her own room. Her bed. This night to end.

These are not her clothes, and she isn't this girl. No. Not her. She begins to run. Jenny runs as fast as she can in someone's broken shoes. She imagines she can run from this night. Outrun this night.

No.

．．．

41

Haley

As Haley and Richard leave the Hard Math Café shortly after Jenny, Haley finds herself checking behind the swinging doors for Carrie and Co., Richard's crack from before in mind.

"All clear?" he jokes, watching her.

"Get out of my head," she says with a laugh. "How did you know?"

"Because it's what I was thinking."

They step outside into a blast of raw November air. Leaves scudder along the sidewalk. It's only midafternoon, but already the promise of a four-thirty sunset creeps over the horizon. She instinctively moves closer to him. He wraps one arm around her shoulders. They head toward her dorm.

Her ride leaves in about an hour. Then it's a four-hour

drive home and a four-day Thanksgiving break. She's not looking forward to seeing her mom, but luckily the house will be packed with relatives. Cute little cousins. Aunts in the kitchen making pies. Her uncle's sausage stuffing. She can do this. They'll make it work.

And when she gets back, there's this Richard person waiting for her.

"So what's your favorite Thanksgiving side dish?" she asks.

"Totally, without question, gloppy green bean casserole with the fried onion rings on top," he says.

She stops despite the cold and pulls away from him. "That's just so wrong. Next you'll tell me you like the cranberry sauce out of the can."

"And served intact on a plate, so you can still see the rings."

Haley moans in mock-horror. "I don't know if I can date someone with such lowbrow taste."

He smiles, steps in close, and pulls her toward him. "Sure you can," he breathes into her ear. "Because you eat Fritos."

She bursts out laughing. *Yes,* she thinks, *I do.* And yes, it's one of those dumb embarrassing things he knows about her and finds endearing. And one of their first inside jokes. The first of many inside jokes to come.

Richard hugs her against the wind. She hugs back. Maybe she's a hugger, after all? At least this way. With him. Yes, she is. This huggie girl. Woman. All of the above.

"I'm freezing," he says.

"Want to go inside?"

He nods. *Yes.*

The dorm is emptying out. A few students push past them in the hall lugging huge duffels. You'd think they were leaving for a month.

"Have a great break, Haley!"

"See ya."

"Later, guys."

They enter her room. It still looks bare without Jenny's things. Richard slips out of his jacket.

"When are you heading out?" he asks.

"I have to be outside the union in an hour." Haley's coat comes off as well.

Richard steps in close to her. "That gives us a little time."

"Time for what?" She moves her face close to his so he doesn't see the warmth spread on her cheeks. She's like a human thermometer—so embarrassing.

He lifts one hand to her brow, weaves his fingers through her hair. He combs her hair back from her face. His eyes are inches from hers.

"I think this is the part when we kiss," he says.

He says this so quietly, she's not sure what she's heard. But then his lips are on hers, gently at first, then pressing, warm, and his meaning is clear. His face feels scratchy, like fine sandpaper. He smells like soap. Like cold wind. Like damp earth and dry leaves.

When the kiss ends, Richard draws back, slightly, and looks at her.

"Is this okay?"

Haley's mouth opens slightly as she leans forward, her

breath mingling with his. *Yes.* She hears a foot scrape as he shifts closer. His lips part as they move against hers, and . . . yes. Like a sigh. Like a secret. Like warm melt.

Yes.

"Yes."

A Reader's Guide to

WRECKED

1. What does the "fishing" metaphor on pages 41 and 42 tell us about Jordan's attitude toward sex and women? What does the metaphor about college as a "buffet" mean?

2. Once Jenny reports the rape, to what extent is she free to make her own choices about everything that follows? Who respects her boundaries? Who pushes them?

3. On page 146, Richard expresses the idea that sometimes "yes the night before turns into no the morning after." What is the difference between this perception and what happened to Jenny?

4. On page 48, Jenny wonders, "How come I didn't fight him off?" We later learn why: her body froze in panic. This is a common physiological stress response among sexual assault survivors—not "fight or flight," but "freeze." How does Jenny's behavior during the assault—saying "I'm so tired," passing

out, and being paralyzed—compare with the behavior of a person who is enthusiastically consenting to sex? If a person's consent is not verbal, are there any other ways they might communicate "yes"?

5. On page 170, Haley notes that "Jenny was complicated." What does Jenny say or do that leads Haley to that conclusion? How does what happens to Jenny influence how others around her interact with her and/or perceive her?

6. If you were named as a witness by either side in this case and had to speak with the dean, would that be an easy conversation? What might you be worried about? What do you think of Dean Hunt's comment that witnesses seemed more concerned with protecting themselves than with the truth?

7. What is the "underlying problem" Dean Hunt refers to on page 319, when he compares the sexual assault case to the plagiarism case?

8. What do you think of Dean Hunt's efforts to have the accused students withdraw? Would it surprise you to learn that in reality, only about 10–30 percent of college students who are found responsible for sexual misconduct are expelled?

9. What is "wrecked" in the story? What does Richard mean when he says, "I think this was broken beyond repair" (page 351)?

10. What does Richard think about the idea of asking "Can I kiss you?" before Matt Trainor's consent presentation? What does he think about it afterward?

11. Imagine that Jordan saw Matt Trainor's consent talk. What would he think or say about the idea of asking (page 300) "Can I kiss you?"

12. Imagine a college conduct system in which the evidence available would have been enough to find Jordan responsible for violating the code of conduct. How would the story have been different?

For more information about sexual assault, visit:

- American Association of University Women: aauw.org
- Campus Action Network: now.org/getinvolved/campus -action-network
- End Rape on Campus: endrapeoncampus.org
- RAINN (Rape, Abuse & Incest National Network): rainn.org
- Safer: safercampus.org
- Take Back the Night: takebackthenight.org